From the Sex Diary of Suzie Berring . . .

Weekend in Greenwich. Dear Mother (or should I say Mother Dear?) looks me over like I'm a tainted fish. Her nostrils quiver. She smells naughtiness, decay. Not my bod, I know—my epidermis is immaculate. I use feminine hygiene spray, keep my underarms pristine, rinse out my mouth with pucker-power. No—what she smells is deep inside—my unhappy putrefying soul. But when I check myself out in the mirror, I can't imagine how she knows. I'm gorgeous, stunning.

Daddy-O, on the other hand, reveals nothing. . . . I'm sure he has a mistress, some dusky lady stashed away in town someplace, in a little tax deduction of a penthouse he rents for her on the sly, a pied-à-terre near Sutton Place filled with shiny plants, sexy jungle plants with oily leaves. He pinions her hands above her head, lowers himself slowly, taunting her, making her strain upward . . .

Punish Me With Kisses

William Bayer

PUBLISHED BY POCKET BOOKS NEW YORK

POCKET BOOKS, a Simon & Schuster division of
GULF & WESTERN CORPORATION
1230 Avenue of the Americas, New York, N.Y. 10020

Published by arrangement with Congdon & Lattès, Inc.
Library of Congress Catalog Card Number: 80-66700

ISBN: 0-671-41991-9

First Pocket Books printing August, 1981

10 9 8 7 6 5 4 3 2 1

POCKET and colophon are trademarks of Simon & Schuster.

Printed in the U.S.A.

I

Plans for the summer: Get a tan that'll really last—through Thanksgiving at least. Work on backhand and serve. Be outrageous. Screw every stud on the Godforsaken island. Feast upon the flesh. . . .

THERE HAD been a strange quality to her memories of that summer, Penny realized later on, that had reduced those months before the crime to jagged moments indelibly engraved. They were vivid, dreamlike, too, clouded by distortion, as if her angle of vision had been cockeyed.

She'd seen but she hadn't seen—it was something like that, she thought. She'd watched, observed, figured things out a certain way, but in the end had gotten everything wrong.

Bar Harbor had been filled with college kids. There were parties day and night—pot parties, sex parties, sailing parties, parties on the beach, so many they all blurred into one. And the boys who followed after Suzie, those tits-and-ass men from Princeton and Yale, they blurred, too, she thought, into a savage pack. It was as if Suzie gave off a perfume and the boys were dogs who'd caught her scent. They pranced and strut-

3

ted, were chosen and used; then, discarded, they limped away. It was, Penny thought, a massacre: young men broken one by one upon a battlefield of lust.

She had watched nights from the rocking chair by the open window of her room, making the rockers creak back and forth against the old wooden floor of the Victorian house. The window looked out on the garden and the little cottage by the pool where Suzie played and slept. All summer Penny studied her sister, wondered about her, tried to understand what she was doing down there and why.

It was love that forced her to watch, love for Suzie, deep concern and fear—fear that something was terribly wrong and that there was another story containing a deeper truth hiding in the shadows around the poolhouse at night.

All summer she had read, devoured novels. She flew through Jane Austen, George Eliot, Dickens, Thackeray, the Brontës, flew through the pages, became heady on the words. She hated Bar Harbor and promised herself she'd never spend another summer there again.

On the Fourth of July she watched Suzie move into the poolhouse. Several of her boyfriends helped, former and would-be lovers, stupid Yalies, Princeton jocks. They carried Suzie's clothes and her stereo and her furniture and her waterbed which first, under her supervision, they emptied out the window through a hose. The gardener was annoyed. Penny could tell because of the fierce way he snapped his trimming shears. The contents of the waterbed, poured out the window, turned his flowerbeds into lakes. Her mother watched, too, standing on the terrace, a long frosted goblet in her hand. She didn't say anything, just stood very still—thin, withered, pale—watching Suzie move.

Suzie's explanations: her bedroom was too hot; in

4

the cottage she'd sleep better; she wanted to play her stereo at night without worrying about disturbing other members of the family. Her real reason, Penny knew, was that she wanted to make love to her army of boy-friends without trooping them through the house.

After they helped her the boys got their rewards. Suzie pushed all three of them into the pool and then stood on the edge, hands on her hips, roaring with laughter while they thrashed about. Suzie's best friend, Cynthia French, stood beside her and laughed, too. They wore matching Sarah Lawrence T-shirts and running shorts with racing stripes.

Later, one of the boys, trying to redeem himself, prepared to make a flashy dive. Penny saw Suzie watch him with contempt, then turn away just before his plunge.

"Mother—I'm sick and tired of having sunmarks on my back. *All right?*"

"Still, dear—"

"Nobody gives a *shit,* mother. In Europe *everyone* goes bare-chested on the beach."

"But the gardener, dear."

"Let him gape if it turns him on. For God's *sake,* mother, who *cares* what Tucker thinks?"

Mrs. Berring took another sip of gin. "We'll wait and see what your father says."

"He won't say anything I bet."

Suzie was right. When their father came up to Maine that weekend, he didn't say a word. He always favored Suzie, gave her everything she wanted, and when he told stories of his business dealings it was she who listened and understood. They played a game together, chanted aphorisms in unison, little truths about the business world. "Break them or they'll break you." "The shark'll come if you begin to bleed." Suzie's eyes would gleam as she chanted away. They'd nod together to the rhythm. They were two of a kind, and if Suzie wanted to be outrageous, go around half-naked showing off her boobs, she had his unspoken permission to do that, too.

By her topless swimming and sunbathing she effectively blocked Penny from the pool. This wasn't intentional; Suzie was always nice to her, always encouraging and kind. It was just that even in a bikini (and Penny didn't think she looked good in one) she felt ridiculous beside Suzie—modest, prissy, out-of-place.

Cynthia French went topless, too, and between the two of them they drove everybody mad. Penny, from her rocking chair, spied upon the show: all sorts of unknown boys turning up at odd times to gape and swim; her mother wandering drunk through the garden; boys being pushed in; Suzie and Cynthia leering, roaring; Tucker snapping his shears ever more ferociously.

Penny, standing nude in her bedroom, studied herself before a full-length mirror. She knew she bore a resemblance to Suzie, and she also knew she didn't look like her at all. They had the same gray eyes, but Suzie's danced and shined, the same light brown hair, but Suzie's was glossy, coppery and full. Her own body was too narrow, her flesh too pale, her chest a bit too flat. It wasn't that she was ugly—everything was all right as far as it went. That was the trouble—everything was just "all right." Maybe if she didn't stand so straight. Maybe if she stuck out her rear a little, and bent one knee to lower a hip. That was better, but there was still the problem of her face. It was irregular, uneven, "off." Her profiles didn't match, and she didn't know which side was better. There was something mousy about her, something unsensual, tentative and dull. Suzie had advised her to show more confidence. "Think *sexy*, Child," she'd said. "Believe me, you'll *be* sexy then. *OK?*"

Suzie always called her "Child." She was two and a half years older than Penny, who was nineteen and still in college. Suzie had dropped out of Sarah Lawrence in January, let an apartment and taken a job as assistant to a fashion photographer in New York. She'd quit on him to spend the summer in Maine. Penny overheard her talking to him on the phone: "Well, all right Jamie—I *did* walk out. I left you stranded. I'm a bitch. *OK?* If it makes you feel any better, then just think of me as a bitch. *OK? All right? Feel better now?* And I'll just think of you as one, too. *OK?*"

Sometimes when she was reading Penny would feel compelled to put down her book and look across the lawn. There was something, she sensed, about to happen, some drama about to be played. She'd try to fight the desire, try to lose herself again in the words of the novel, but sounds would intrude, the whirring of the sprinkler set out to water the lawn, a male bellow from the poolhouse, Tucker's shears, a high-pitched laugh, noise created by Suzie and her friends. Then it was impossible—she would have to raise her eyes.

Sometimes, just to get away, she'd mount her bicycle and ride. She'd have no particular destination in mind; she would simply wander along the network of paths that crisscrossed Mount Desert. Sometimes she'd ride into the forest, find a quiet place, lean her bike against a tree, and lie on the pine-bed staring at the sky. Other times she'd ride along the coast stopping every so often to listen to the surf. She avoided the towns, Bar Harbor and Seal Harbor. There were too many tourists, the yachts outnumbered the fishing boats, and the beautiful weathered gray shingled buildings were festooned with junk for sale.

Suzie sunbathing with Cynthia French, the two of

them lying on their stomachs, Suzie's copper hair cascading down her back:

"Sorry, Suze. Thought he'd be OK."

"Yeah."

"Nice arms. Cute ass. You know—"

"Well, he sure wasn't that great a fuck, I can tell you. D, D minus, something like that."

"Wow—I'm sorry. You're really hard to please these days."

"Uh-huh."

"Anyway I don't see what difference it makes."

Suzie laughed, then turned herself over to tan her front. "Well, I know how you feel, Cin, but it makes a big difference to me." She gave Cynthia a kick. *"All right?"*

Suzie playing tennis: Penny looked out at the court just in time to see her sister smash down a volley at a lovestruck opponent's feet. She had a special way of showing she was pleased when she made a shot like that. While Cynthia applauded from the sidelines and some other boy who was in love with her (Dartmouth soccer player, Amherst track star—who could tell? They all looked alike anyway) gasped at what she'd done, Suzie stood there with her racket over one shoulder, her other hand resting lightly on her hip, smiling as she watched the ball skid away.

How did she get away with it, savoring her little victories like that? The boys she was always beating at tennis, and shoving off balance and into the pool, seemed to adore her all the more for her abuse. They panted all the harder for her attention and felt all the more fortunate when she finally invited them to join her in the poolhouse for a night. A night was all they usually got, unless they were especially amusing and adept, in which case they were asked back. In the end, though, there would come a morning when they'd be sent away. Then Penny would see them stumbling across the garden, confused, wondering what they'd done to earn Suzie's displeasure, why her passion had turned so quickly to indifference once they'd held her in their arms.

Her mother drank so much she looked mummified by the afternoon, pale and pickled, Penny thought, stumbling about, trying to keep her dignity intact. She'd speak slowly, try too hard to be accurate with her pronunciation, and when she walked in the garden she took slow deliberate steps. Sometimes she just stood in the living room frozen like a statue, looking out through the French doors toward the pool. Once Penny had come upon her like that and, herself unseen, watched with fascination: her mother wasn't still but was trembling, shaking, fists clenched at her sides.

When her father flew in for weekends he seemed to Penny the very essence of success—pressed, cool, boyish, every hair in place, voice soothing, sincere, concealing raw energy and power. Even in his Maine lumberjack's shirt he was the square-jawed boy-wonder entrepreneur. Penny had read an article about him in a business magazine. His holdings in Chapman International were estimated at between seven and eleven million dollars. He had enemies. An unnamed rival called him "sanctimonious." A worshipful subordinate said he was "brilliant," admired his "daring strokes" and "ruthless cuts."

The Berrings slept in adjoining bedrooms. They quarreled in penetrating whispers muffled by the walls. Her mother looked fifteen years older than her father. Sometimes Penny could hear her weep and shriek; her father's voice was always hushed. Their lights were usually off by ten, which was the time Suzie's parties usually began.

Penny didn't find her sister's little dramas of love

9

and torment particularly painful at first. She was a spy, clinically detached, fascinated by the little flashes she saw, the bits of sound she overheard.

Music: that was always the beginning, old mournful out-of-date Bob Dylan tunes, "Just Like a Woman" and "Sad-Eyed Lady of the Lowlands" played on Suzie's stereo over and over again. There'd be dancing—she'd see the movements through the window, and later, when her parents were asleep, the inevitable nude swim, which Penny could make out clearly or vaguely depending upon the moonlight and the fog. There would be giggling, then, as they wrestled in the water and kissed, and as they moved back to the cottage, naked silhouettes against the shimmering surface of the pool, low murmurs broken by an occasional raucous laugh. They'd be smoking joints, she knew, getting high.

There was evidence, sometimes, to be examined in the dawn: a piece of discarded male underwear half-sinking in the pool, a damp towel or two, reefer butts crushed out against the tiles. Sometimes, very cautiously, Penny would approach the door of the cottage and gaze inside, at Suzie and her lover lying tangled on the waterbed, the sheets pushed away to the sides, the bed undulating slightly as their bodies trembled in sleep. She'd peer in at Suzie's face, blank and passionless. Inhaling deeply she'd catch a whiff of mingled odors: sweat and sex, the stale smoke of pot, and the rich dark aroma of Suzie's perfume, Amazone. Once she saw Cynthia French tangled with them, which meant there'd been an orgy and the nameless boy in the center had been used to satisfy them both.

She'd wonder about the boys as she'd walk softly back to the house to feed the dogs, her bare feet slipping in the grass, cool and moist with morning dew. Those poor beautiful sun-tanned boys dreaming proud dreams of having possessed the most desired girl at the resort. What did Suzie do to them? What scars did she leave? When they grew up, became lawyers and brokers and businessmen, would they look back upon their night or two with her and still feel some residue of pain?

Sometimes Penny could hear the dismissals, Suzie's words so sharp they sliced through the morning fog:

"Bye-bye."

"You're kidding."

"Uh-uh. It's bye-bye time."

"What's bugging you?"

"Please just go *away*."

"Come on, Suze—"

"Bug off—*OK?* I really want to be alone. Can't you get that through your skull?"

"Look, if I *did* something—"

"*Jes-sus!*"

"Okay, if that's the way you want it. You're really being a shit."

"So I'm a shit. *So what?* I know that—OK? And you're not so great yourself this morning either. You're really not. *All right?*"

Penny wondered what drove Suzie to perform these nightly rituals of seduction and dismissal. What did she gain by them? *Why?* Then Penny would think about herself, the outsider watching, imagining the intimate things her sister did. Thinking of herself peering out her window and gazing through the poolhouse door, she felt appalled. Would her own life always be like this? Would the melancholy longing she felt to participate, to put down her books and to live—would that and her painful solitude turn to bitterness until she ended up one of those terse, bony-faced ladies who run needlecraft shops in little towns?

She envied Suzie for doing what she pleased, moving out to the poolhouse, going topless, taking lovers, not caring who watched or what they thought. Better to

be an actor, she thought, than to sit in the audience.
Better to suffer and cause suffering than to feel nothing
but the safe smug superiority of the voyeur, hidden,
envious, alone.

Later, looking back upon that summer, asking herself if there'd been an omen of its end, Penny remembered the angry cadence of Tucker's shears.

She met Jared Evans the second week of August.
She was bicycling along the cliffs above the sea looking
for a place to spread her blanket, lie down out of the
wind and read. Then she heard him, shouting, or so
she thought until she realized that his words were
rhythmic and that he was declaiming against the surf.

It took her a little while to find him—the wind confused her, blew his words about. Finally she spotted
a motorcycle, and then she saw him sitting on a rock
precipice below the path where the waves were breaking and spewing spray. He was shirtless, his arms
wrapped around his jean-clad knees, fighting the sea-
roar with a poem:

> ". . . caught this morning morning's . . .
> kingdom of daylight's dauphin, dapple-
> dawn-drawn Falcon . . ."

She recognized "The Windhover" at once, she had
memorized it her freshman year at Wellesley and had
whispered it to herself certain winter nights huddled
beneath her blankets in her dormitory room. She
moved forward until she found a place above him
where she could sit and look directly down upon his
dark curly hair and listen.

> ". . . air, pride, plume . . .
> . . . the fire that breaks from thee . . . a
> billion

Times told lovelier, more dangerous . . ."

Even when his words were lost to her she was able to fill them in from memory. The poem still moved her, which amazed her nearly as much as stumbling upon this boy, sitting on the rocks, his voice sharp, fierce, flinging poetry against the wind and spray.

She was inspecting him with extreme curiosity, wondering just who he was and what he was doing and how he'd gotten himself down upon those boulders, when, seeming to sense her presence, he suddenly turned around. "Hi!"

She wanted to run away. It was awful to be caught like that, staring down like a spy. "Sorry," she said. "I was passing. I heard you and I—"

"Where?"

She didn't understand him. *"What?"*

"Where were you when you heard me?"

She pointed at a spot a hundred feet farther along the ledge. He stood and raised his hand to shield his eyes. "From all the way down there? Wow! I had no idea I was reaching back that far."

He was beautiful—she recognized that at once; like a classic sculpture, she thought, an Athenian, dark, lean, his cheeks sheer, his lips full, lovingly carved. She was marveling at how beautiful he was, how finely made and poised, but when she saw that he was going to climb up to where she stood she began to back away. She thought of fleeing, running back along the cliffs to her bike. Then angry with herself for being afraid, she stood her ground and watched him climb. He moved lightly, with the suppleness of a gymnast. His bare torso, gleaming in the sun, looked all the darker against the pale rocks and foaming surf below. As he twisted and stretched to pull himself up the last few feet, she gasped at the beauty of his back, his straining flesh taut against his spine.

13

"Hi. My name's Jared. I'm with the theater company at Hull's Cove."

Such a beautiful actor he was, she kept thinking, as they shook hands and began to talk. She gazed at his sculpted cheeks while he explained that he'd been practicing throwing his voice; she searched his dark liquid eyes as he spoke of the need he felt to project himself into every crevice in the rocks.

"Like in the theater, I want to reach into all the corners, even underneath the seats." He laughed, and as he did she regarded the perfect whiteness of his teeth. "Kind of old-fashioned, I guess. Everyone else likes to mumble and scratch." He scratched in mimicry of them, scratched at the curly dark hairs on his chest which matched the thick curls around his ears. She found herself becoming extremely conscious of his body, even the little droplets of sweat upon his brow and beneath his lips; quite unaccountably, she wanted to wipe the drops away.

"Seen us?" She shook her head. He shrugged. "Not surprised. We do these warmed-over Broadway comedies, and we don't do them very well. The company's practically bankrupt anyway. The guy who owns the building keeps threatening to throw us out. I doubt we'll last the season. The people who summer up here—people like you, I guess—haven't picked up on our act. Hey—" He studied her face. "Don't be afraid of me. I won't eat you. Relax." He smiled. "You looked good, really good standing up here. I had to climb up to see you close, see if you really looked so good." She didn't say anything. "Well—you *do*." Slowly he raised his arms toward her and put his hands on her shoulders. "Kind of like a Muse, the way you appeared up here. You were listening for quite a while, weren't you? You like poetry. I bet you do."

He was looking directly into her eyes, and she could

feel the strength in his fingers as he put pressure on the back of her neck to gently coax out her reply.

"I know that Hopkins poem," she said, surprised that she could speak at all, very conscious of his touch. "I once memorized it myself."

"What else do you know? Tell me."

Later she would remember the moment well, a turning point she'd think, a moment upon which her life suddenly pivoted. Below the sea smashed upon the rocks. In the distance, on the horizon, a sailboat with an orange spinnaker cut the pale blue summer sky. The smell of Maine was there, too, pine forest and seaweed, and then something of this young man, something coming off his body, an essence that made her dizzy, reel, flush. Yes, it was just then, in an instant she'd fix forever—feeling his hands link behind her neck and draw her slowly toward him, seeing his lips part and his head tilt down, knowing that he was going to kiss her, knowing that in a second her mouth would feel the warmth of his—it was just then that she knew she could let go. She was so happy, thrilled at the discovery, the dry destiny she'd feared for herself dissolving as she closed her eyes. She was crossing the line, she knew, from thinking to feeling, from books to life, and having crossed it she knew she'd never willingly return to the other side.

"Hey. Hey. *Hey.*" His voice, soft, hushed, even softer, more hushed than her father's, encouraged her. "Hey—you're beautiful, babe. Really beautiful. Really good." He'd unbuttoned her shirt after he'd kissed her. Now they were on the ground, she lying on her back, her knees bent, he sitting beside her, lightly tracing his finger upon her breasts. "Feels good, doesn't it? Yeah—I could tell."

"What?"

"You'd like to be touched."

"How?"

"How did I know that?" He laughed. "I *knew*."

There was no clumsiness about him, no desperate grappling. She felt like a treasured harp which he plucked and strummed.

"Oh—"

"You like that."

"—yes."

"I knew you would. I knew."

"Oh, God—"

Seagulls were circling above. A single cloud, full yet lightly spun, hung magically in the sky.

"Sun feels good, doesn't it."

"Uh-huh."

He bent down. She poised herself. She knew he was going to kiss her again. She placed her hands on his cheeks, felt the roughness of them, then probed with outspread fingers into the thickness of his hair. And then she was lost, lost as he whispered to her, encouraged her to open up, to yield. His whispering was like a spell, and all her control weakened, ebbed away as he undressed her, touched her, kissed her, stroked her, and came inside her while she lay back and stared up at the sun.

She'd never felt anything like it before. She was melting, melting away. If she sometimes became heady when she read, now she was intoxicated, giving herself to his dark hard body, gripping, feeling something deep within her erupting in pants and sighs.

"Don't stop—"

She was shaking, moaning and she didn't care. Pinned down by him, writhing beneath him, she felt the power of his sex and a counterforce within herself rising with a fury that made her blind.

"Babe—"

"Oh, *yes*—"

Later, bicycling back to the house, she couldn't quite believe what she'd done. He was a stranger, an utter stranger, they'd barely talked, she had no notion of who he was. And yet she'd given herself to him, with hardly a word spoken, had lain naked beneath the sun while this strange strong dark young man lay upon her. They'd ground themselves against each other, wriggled, cried out, let go. They'd met and parted like wild animals in the forest. There'd been tenderness between them, but also something so lustful, direct, unguarded and shameless she could hardly believe that she herself had been involved.

At home, she inspected herself in the mirror, looking for evidence on her body. She could find nothing, no marks or other hints of what had taken place. Perhaps she'd dreamt it all. That was the sort of thing that happened, she knew, with repressed and lonely girls who lived in worlds of books and dreams. Still there was something faint on her, a trace of something male, a smell perhaps, that same essence that had made her reel and feel weak when he'd linked his hands behind her neck. She wasn't sure. It seemed to come and go. She caught it, sniffed hard, then lost it again. Finally, reluctantly, she bathed.

That night, ensconced in her rocking chair, in her nightgown and her robe, peering down at the poolhouse waiting for Suzie's latest lover to arrive, she didn't feel envious at all. She could be like that, too, now, she knew—stroke skin, taste flesh, requite desire.

She made love with him a second time in the forest and twice on successive rainy afternoons in the little room he shared with another actor in a boarding house in town. The last time they'd smoked pot and everything had been slow and strange. Afterwards they'd collapsed together, spent limp bodies welded with a seal of sweat.

He called her "babe," and she liked that a lot—it made her feel sexy, like a girl in a popular song. So did the rides they took on his motorcycle, zooming along the winding roads of the resort, her arms clasped around him, her head pressed against his back. Vibrations coursed through her as she shut her eyes and squeezed his chest. She thought of herself as the subject of an impassioned ballad sung by a wild-haired rock singer to a huge raucous audience in the night.

He didn't tell her much about himself, only that he'd been in the Marines, that he was twenty-four years old, that he'd appeared in a few TV commercials and acted in what he called "some third-rate independent films." He joined the Bar Harbor summer theater company to get out of New York during the heat. He was ambitious, he told her, to hone his craft and to play important roles.

She didn't care about his past; she preferred him as a stranger, dark and sensitive, who caressed her with powerful hands until she moaned. She'd always dreamed of a lover, someone fierce-looking but gentle, who would come upon her like the lion sniffing at the sleeping shepherd in the painting by Rousseau. Now she'd found this actor who rode a roaring motorcycle and shouted out poems against the sea. He was a gift to her, someone she'd stumbled upon in time to save her from despair.

On the fifth day she invited him to the house to play tennis. That was a mistake.

"Oh, Pen—he's *gorgeous*."

"Eat your heart out, Cin," Suzie said.

"You just found him there, on the rocks?" Cynthia wet her lips. *"God*—I don't believe it. *God*—he just makes you want to *drool*."

Suzie and Cynthia were supposed to be off sailing that afternoon. But they'd been bored by the boys they'd gone with and came back home referring to them contemptuously as "duds."

"Where've you been hiding him?"

"Come on, Cin—leave her alone."

"Let us know when you're finished with him, Pen. Let us know soon as he's up for *grabs*."

Suzie took her aside, told her not to pay any attention to Cynthia. "She couldn't take him away from you if she tried. He *is* gorgeous, though." She touched Penny on the cheek. "Congratulations, Child. Thought I'd scoured this joint. Never thought of that theater crowd myself."

Her father flew up in early August to stay on through Labor Day. There was a local painter who came by in the mornings to work on his portrait, a larger than life-size thing which would adorn the Chapman boardroom in New York. The painting was to show him on his sailboat, waves behind, wind-filled sails, the boat heeling as he tacked, but he posed in his study at a helm that had been transported to the house, standing erect and grave as if he were really wrestling the elements, his hair artfully brushed so that it looked windswept. She paused in the doorway one day and watched the scene, the painter, intent on a successful completion of his commission, dabbing seriously at the canvas. When her father caught her eye, he laughed. "Well, kiddo," he said, "now you know what a fake I am."

One night at dinner her mother sat bored and listless as he described how he was taking over an armor-plate company in Detroit. His plan was intricate, involved an exacting use of pressure, a careful wielding of power. Suzie was excited by the details. Her eyes shined brightly as he explained his manipulation, his squeeze-play, his final offer, the bluff they'd never call. "You sure know how to break balls, Daddy-O," she said at the end. Then she flung down her napkin and strode out of the house.

"She's running wild," her mother announced after they heard the whirl of tires in the drive.

"She'll come around. Just a stage."

19

"I wish she didn't hang around with Cynthia. I don't think Cynthia's very nice."

"Well, who *is* nice?" her father asked. "I'm not nice, nor, in my experience, are very many people in the world. No one's nice around this house except maybe kiddo, here."

"Oh, no," said Penny. "I'm not nice. Not at all."

"Well, there you are," he said and grinned. "No one's *nice*. No one in this family, anyway. So—what else is new?"

Her mother glared down at the remnants of her cheese.

It was never a question, Penny was certain, of her sister trying to steal Jared away. It just didn't happen like that, although later many people would say it had. She knew it had been her fault—not Suzie's, not Jared's, her own. She wasn't sufficiently sexy, she thought, probably just a "D minus" in the sack. She'd been selfish, had been too passive, hadn't asked him enough questions about acting and the theater, who he was and what he dreamed. Then everything had been inevitable. Suzie'd been there, Jared had seen her, and that had been enough. Suzie was so vivid, so striking, so purely physical, she knew that by comparison she must seem pale and flat. Jared was sweet to her as he slipped away, tried hard not to hurt her feelings, but when he turned up at the pool it was clear whom he'd come to see. She watched, angry at first, jealous as he fell under Suzie's spell. Then, feeling helpless, diminished, aching but refusing to blame anyone but herself, she was grateful that at least she'd tasted a little crust of life, and she turned back sadly to her books.

"Come on, Child, down to the pool. He's been waiting now an hour."

"I'm busy."

"Why don't you just put down that book?"

"It's *Ethan Frome*."

"Well, hoopty-doo."

They stared at each other for a while. Then Penny turned the book over on her lap. "He's not here to see me anyway, so what difference does it make?"

"You know, you're really silly, brooding, staying up here all the time, feeling sorry for yourself. Come on down now, OK? You'd really make me happy if you would."

"I don't see the point—"

"Look—do I have to beg? Is that it? *Huh?*"

"Of course not—"

"Then get your ass in gear for shit's sakes. Before Cynthia gets her disgusting mitts on him. *OK?*"

Suzie was staring at her the way she stared at boys when she sized them up. Penny looked up at her again.

"He's not all that interested in me anymore, and I'm not all that interested in him."

"Well, he's sure as hell not going to get *re-interested* if you hide yourself up here in this lousy room."

That made her mad. "You know what I wish, Suzie?"

"Tell me, Child. Tell me what you wish."

"I wish I were a free-spirited totally liberated good-time sexpot bitch just like you, someone who could fuck everyone I wanted, every tits-and-ass man in the whole Ivy League if I felt like it, and never feel a qualm. But since I'm not like that, I'm really not, I wish you'd just leave me alone."

She squeezed her eyes shut to push back her tears while Suzie stood very still, then finally cleared her throat.

"That's pretty tough talk, Child, as I'm sure you know."

"Yes. I know." She met Suzie's eyes head-on.

"OK. I'll see you later then." She paused at the

21

door. Penny prayed she'd go before she saw her cry. "Maybe you'll change your mind and come down a little later on. I hope you do. *OK?*"

That was the closest they ever came to a confrontation. She had spoken harshly, had said things she regretted the moment Suzie left the room. Afterwards there were no opportunities to take them back. Suzie avoided her, and then an almost palpable tension began to build up in the house.

Her mother's hands shook all the time. When she ate, her silverware shivered against the china plates. Her father, closeted mornings with the painter, went off sailing by himself in the afternoons. Suzie, with Cynthia French, continued to entertain callers around the tennis court and pool. Jared was among them now, panting around Suzie like the others, different only in that he was darker and older and not going back to college in the fall.

Penny, starting a new Jane Austen, found it difficult to concentrate. There were too many clashing thoughts, anger and resignation, emotions that didn't cancel out. Sometimes when her confinement became oppressive she'd get on her bicycle and ride toward the sea, then along the same path above the cliffs where she'd discovered Jared the first time. He seemed like a figure in a romantic dream to her—a vague personage who'd appeared out of nowhere, had entered her life for several days, then had gone his own way, leaving little trace except the memory of a scent and a sadness she now savored even as she hurt.

Puzzled, seized with vague premonitions and a sense of doom, she went about her life much as she had before, rising late, reading through the afternoons, watching from her rocking chair at night. Sometimes crossing the path of a member of the family she felt she was living with people trying to avoid contact at almost any cost.

Her mother, drinking steadily now from morning to night, stalked the lower part of the house with a mad smile that seemed painted on her face. Her father ate his meals alone in his study off a tray. Sometimes, passing his door in the evening, she could hear him whispering, dictating a lecture he was to give, about the reconciliations between humanism and business, before a manufacturer's convention in the fall. If her mother hardly left the house, Suzie hardly entered it. She had her meals served to her in the poolhouse. Twice Penny saw Cynthia French carrying polyethylene garbage bags to her car.

Penny watched every evening, expectant, waiting, and then, finally, it happened—she heard Jared's motorcycle coughing in the dark.

She wished that night that she could feel bitter, could hate him for coming, could hate Suzie, too, for luring him in. But she couldn't. As much as she longed to feel hatred, she could not quell a lingering affection for Jared, a sense of gratitude for what he'd been to her, and a fascination with Suzie and her nocturnal rituals, a fascination that she recognized as perverse. That was what was so strange. As painful as it was for her now to watch Jared steal across the fog-shrouded lawn, and approach the poolhouse, knowing as she did that he was going to make love with Suzie, knowing how he would do it, wishing, imagining that he would do it with her, still she felt the cold almost cruel power of the voyeur, seeing yet unseen, surveying the poolhouse from her dark hiding place above, looking down, spying, as thrilled as a tourist in Africa hidden in an observation post high up in a tree watching wild animals congregate, drink, copulate and growl.

He paused in the middle of the lawn, turned and scanned the main house. She rocked back in her chair, braced her feet, held her breath. He couldn't see her; she was sitting in darkness. But still she wondered:

might he have caught a glimmer of movement, have noticed a reflection, some clue to her presence there? Suddenly he was revealed, etched out, his dark hair highlighted by a beam. Then, just as quickly, he was lost again in the gloom. She was startled for a second until she realized what had happened, that there'd been a break in the clouds passing before the moon, a gap just large enough to admit a momentary shaft of light.

That vision of him, short as it was, stayed with her, even as she saw him turn toward the poolhouse again. It was as if the moonlight had frozen him for an instant the way a flashlight beam can catch and freeze a prowling deer, and in those few seconds of illumination she thought she'd seen something on his face—indecision, perhaps, or worry, or something else, something attentive and alert, as if he felt himself in danger, as if he knew he was being watched.

Voices, then—she strained to listen. They were greeting one another. She heard a laugh. The ritual she knew so well began: the old Dylan tunes, vague movements beyond the windows—little flashes of clothing, flesh, the suggestion of a dance. She couldn't see much, the moon was cut off again by the clouds, and the Maine night fog hung like thick black smoke just above the grass. She closed her eyes, imagined the two of them moving, swaying, a vacant smile on Suzie's face, a smoldering, a hunger distending his. They wouldn't touch, though they would come unbearably close. She imagined herself, then, in Suzie's place, synchronizing, matching her movements to his, feeling him, too, his aura, that dizzying essence that came off his body when he was eager, warm and close. He'd raised his hands now—she was sure of that, could feel them as they came down upon her shoulders. She'd reach out with her own hands, place them lightly on his hips. They'd be barely dancing now, just moving back and forth, creating a slow, wonderful, agonizing tempo, rolling in unison, swaying with desire.

Her rocking chair creaked back and forth as she dreamt of all of this, and then of Jared taking her in his arms.

Had she slept? She shook her head, peered out again, tried to penetrate the darkness, the fog. There was no sign of anything, no sounds, though the lights in the poolhouse still were on. Far in the distance she could hear the roar of the sea, then something coming from the trees, the sound of an owl perhaps, then silence.

They were smoking now—she was sure of it; that was the pattern, Suzie and her boyfriends made love, then smoked, then made love again. Were they tangled up with each other, naked limbs entwined, sharing a reefer now from Suzie's stash of dope? Perhaps she should go outside, creep around to one of the windows of the poolhouse and check. But that was crazy. She closed her eyes again and tried to recapture what it had been like, resting beside Jared that final time three weeks before when they'd made love in his room in town.

He'd kissed her many times, and she remembered whispering to him as he did: "Yes, yes, I love you. Yes, I love you. Yes—"

Suzie was right—she really *was* a child. Out of all her reading, her novels, her fantasies she'd spun a fabric of illusions. Thinking back made her flush with shame. She'd tried to turn a rough carnal exchange into a romance. She'd been a fool.

Tears suddenly pulsed up to her eyes. The banality of her predicament—the lonely, neurotic, unsexy sibling who'd lost a boyfriend to her popular extroverted sister—made her want to cry. *It was so stupid, such a stupid, dreary, tedious cliché.* What was she doing now, staring down at the poolhouse, imagining herself with Jared, imagining him holding her, kissing her, then feeling so miserably sorry for herself? He'd been nice but shallow. She'd been nothing to him but an audience before whom he could rehearse his act, the sensitive primitive in need of a muse as he declaimed poetry to the sea. Suzie was right—it was better to use people than to be used. She, too, now would have to start dealing with the world as it was. She would find lovers, and enjoy them, and when she was done with them, when they bored her, when the magic was gone, she would send them away without a pang. She would harden herself, make herself strong and ruthless. Maybe that was the lesson of the summer, something valuable she could extract from all the pain.

She squeezed her eyes shut again. She wanted to wring out every remnant of her tears. She was done with feeling sorry for herself. She would change her life, rid herself of her illusions. Suzie would help her, tell her what clothes to buy, show her how to redo her hair. Most important she'd teach her not to care, how to think only of herself.

But then she cried again—she couldn't help it. It was too awful if life came down to that, if everyone was cold and hard and selfish and if love was found only in books. The tears now were streaming down her face. *Oh, God,* she thought, *do I have to be a bitch?*

Sounds. Something was happening. She wiped her eyes and peered outside again. The underwater pool lights were on. She heard laughter, then a splash. She strained to see, but her tears obscured her view. Then she recognized Suzie's voice jeering in the night. She was standing naked beside the pool. She threw something at the water, then placed her hands on her hips and laughed. "That's it, *fetch*—"

More motion. Jared swam to her. Penny could just make him out, kicking with his legs, causing the water to ripple and catch the turquoise light from underneath.

Suzie reached down. Jared seemed to have something in his mouth. Suzie took it, patted him on the head, stepped back, threw it out again. It hit the water and bobbed, something white, some sort of ball.

Penny saw Jared turn, then lost sight of him. He was probably swimming under water, she thought. Suddenly he emerged with the ball again. Suzie clapped her hands and laughed. Penny felt sick and looked away.

So—Suzie had turned him into a dog. Now he swam for her and fetched, and she patted him on his head as a reward. What degrading games her sister liked to play. She was really sick, and now Jared was like all the others—foolish, pathetic, weak.

"What's the matter, loverboy? Tired already? *Bored?*"

There was something too derisive in Suzie's tone, something too taunting, too full of scorn, contempt. She was going too far. No one acted like that. She was overplaying. *Why?*

All that summer she had carried on in what had seemed impossibly over-heated ways. Just what was the point of this exhibition with Jared? *Does she know I'm watching, listening?* she wondered. *Is she doing all this for me?*

Suzie went back to the porch of the poolhouse, turned off the pool lights, and disappeared inside. Penny heard a splash as if Jared were still in the water floundering around; then there was silence except for the wind rustling in the pines.

Later she wasn't sure how long she slept, or even if she really had. She remembered closing her eyes, wanting to sleep, wanting to shut off her mind and her misery, wanting to stop thinking, to forget, and she had, or at least she'd dozed for a while in her rocking chair until she'd heard the noise. It wasn't loud, only a moan, a faint one, agonized enough to nudge her into wakefulness but hardly intense enough to jar her wide awake. She blinked a little, turned her head, then heard it again, more piteous this time, more agonized, something like the weakening helpless whimper of an injured animal in pain.

She looked out the window. Everything was dark. Suddenly she heard a slamming sound and a shout, then a thud. She saw a flash of light, so quick she barely caught it, the sweep of a hand-held light. Someone rushed from the poolhouse, then paused just in front. Penny blinked and in that moment the figure disappeared into the shadows of the trees.

Everything was quiet for a moment. She remembered feeling confused. Then the screaming began, a series of short, sharp, shrill terrifying cries, and then the dogs began to yelp, and she heard people moving in the house, talking, calling, running around. Someone switched on the floodlights mounted on the roof. All the grounds, the tennis court, the garden and the pool, were set ablaze, and the burglar alarm siren began to screech. As she watched the scene with a growing terror, Jared stumbled out of the poolhouse, and her parents, the gardener and his wife, and the dogs converged around him on the lawn.

The floodlights must have blinded him, for as he stood there, naked, screaming at them for help, awkward and unbalanced, his body wet and spattered with blood, he raised one hand to shield his eyes. In his other he held the shears, their long, glistening, pointed blades hanging open by his side.

Afterward Penny would have no memory of her flight down the stairs, her own mad rush out onto the lawn. But she would never forget the sight that met her at the poolhouse door. While Jared stood behind her shaking, and her mother's incoherent sobs were lost in the siren still screaming from the house, she looked in at Suzie lying torn and dead upon the slashed waterbed. Her thick red blood was still gushing from the deep wounds in her breasts and stomach and cheeks, spreading into the surrounding flood, staining it an ever-thinning pink.

Turning, she saw Jared drop the bloody shears onto the tiles. Then she lunged, knelt, and vomited into the pool.

II

I sometimes wonder if Child will ever get her shit together. I sure hope so. Otherwise she's doomed. I know she's watching me all the time now, sad-eyed, hurt. I think she's trying to figure me out. (Well, best of luck, Child!) I guess she thinks I'm crazy, and maybe I am. Maybe someday, too, I'll be able to explain it to her. In the meantime I have to do what I have to do—

SHE HATED being recognized.

Once she was sitting alone in one of those New York pub-type restaurants with track lights and bare brick walls and hanging plants and out-of-work actors serving steaks to convivial foursomes when she heard someone talking at another table, heard "Maine" and "sisters" and "shears." They'd seen her, recognized her, begun to talk about the case. She called for her check and left.

Another time she was window-shopping on Fifth Avenue, staring at a pair of expensive Italian shoes, when a well-dressed young woman with an intent expression on her face came up to her and said: "Excuse me, I don't mean to be rude, but weren't you involved in something a few years back?" She recoiled and walked away as fast as she could.

Still another time she was jogging around the reservoir in Central Park early in the morning. The sky was blue, and the buildings were reflected in the water, and she was feeling wonderful, feeling as if she could run on and on and even merge with the wind, when a young man running toward her began to stare and scan her face, and then he said, "I know who you are!" and then he grinned. She felt like she was a freak or something who had to live out the rest of her life as this character in the Suzie Berring Murder Case, and then she ran all the harder, but the joy of it was gone, and she ended up in front of the Metropolitan Museum, panting and sweating and depressed, and, worst of all, remembering, reliving that awful time.

Robinson had terrified her. Schrader said he wasn't a class-A trial lawyer, but he had scared her anyway. Tall and grim, he reminded her of a cruel gym teacher who browbeats awkward students for the amusement of the class. He was politically ambitious, a small-town prosecutor hungry for a conviction in a once-in-a-lifetime murder case.

"You say it was foggy?" he asked her the second day of his cross-examination.

"Yes."

"And you were sleepy?"

"Yes."

"Then you heard something?"

"Yes."

"And you opened your eyes and saw this person running out, and then he disappeared?"

"*Yes.*"

"Can you describe him, Miss Berring? Was he short or tall? Fat or thin?"

"I couldn't see."

"You couldn't *see?*"

"I couldn't tell."

"You're *sure* you saw someone?"

"Yes."

"Well, I'm glad you're sure about *that*." There was snickering then, a little ripple of snickers across the courtroom. She looked at the jury: Schrader had told her to do that whenever there was a pause. Some of them were smiling, the two lobstermen and the pharmacist. The postmistress was as inscrutable as ever. The farmer's wife, who worked summers as a maid, stared off into space.

"Now tell us, so we can all understand—just how did your eyes adjust so quickly to the light?"

"There wasn't any light."

"Really?"

"I caught a glimpse—"

"Ah! A glimpse! Earlier you told us you opened your eyes suddenly. Do you suppose you might have blinked?"

"Maybe."

"You *did* blink, didn't you, Miss Berring?"

"I don't remember—" She had the feeling that he was setting her up.

"Think back. You dozed off, and then you heard a noise, and then you opened your eyes, and you had to adjust to seeing in the dark. Now, to make that adjustment, didn't you *have* to blink?"

"I guess I blinked. I think anyone would."

"I think so, too. And that brings us to an interesting point—the miraculous disappearance of this 'intruder' who, according to your testimony, was standing there one moment and was gone the next. But now, couldn't this person have been standing there, and then, when you blinked, just stepped back inside?"

So, that was the trap. "That's not what happened," she said. "That's not what I saw at all."

"But you didn't *see* anything. You just told us you blinked."

"You're twisting my words."

"No. I think you really did see someone—*the defendant*."

"I didn't see him!"

"How can you be so sure? You can't describe him."

"I would have recognized Jared."

"*Oh?*"

"I knew his shape, his build."

"Yes," Robinson laughed. "I'm sure you knew his body very well, Miss Berring. We're quite prepared to stipulate to that."

There were more snickers then, many more than before. She looked at the jury, injured, confused. Schrader stood up. "I think Mr. Robinson can spare us his sarcasm."

But they were still snickering. The reporters were smirking and the artists who were sketching her were smiling as they drew. Robinson nodded to the judge and then turned back to her, that awful grin, the gym teacher's grin, still on his lips.

He started in on the flashlight beam and tried to befuddle her with that, but, shaken as she was, she knew that she was on firm ground, knew that she'd seen the beam and that matched Jared's story of an intruder who'd shined a flashlight in his eyes. So she stood up to him. Schrader told her later that Robinson had made a mistake—he shouldn't have given her that chance to regain her confidence. Robinson must have realized his blunder because he turned savage at the end. "Isn't it a fact, Miss Berring," he demanded, "that you hated your sister because she stole your boyfriend away? Isn't it a fact that you're perjuring yourself now because you still love the defendant and would do anything to help him, including lie to this court, if you thought that would get him off?"

Schrader objected. The judge instructed the jury to ignore the question. Robinson turned away, satisfied he'd made his point. But she was angry then, so angry she answered anyway. "No, those aren't *facts,* Mr. Robinson," she said. And then in a level voice: "Just cheap shots from a bully. That's all they are."

She couldn't believe she said it even when people started to applaud. Schrader beamed. Jared shook his head in victorious disbelief. Robinson turned, stared at her confused. Her father, who'd been sitting grim-faced in the first row like Charles Lindbergh at the Hauptmann trial, smiled at her and winked. The judge pounded his gavel as reporters rushed out to file stories. That night she saw drawings of herself on network TV, her face twisted, creased with rage. "A dramatic turn of events at the Berring murder trial," the commentator said.

That had been her single heroic moment. Even now she looked back on it with pride. It made up, she thought, for all the awful things, the headlines that had brought her to tears (Slain Heiress's Father Grim As Ugly Duckling Sister Testifies), the terrifying chases by the camera crews as they tried to outrun her to her car. The savage unsigned letters, the ghoulish stories in the national newsprint weeklies, the lurid ones about Jared and Suzie and herself, the one which speculated that she was the killer and Jared was sacrificing himself to save her from prison—even these, somehow, seemed balanced off by that time she'd stood up to Robinson.

It had been a turning point. Her father had acknowledged it. "You're doing good, kiddo," he told her. "I still think that boy's guilty as hell but I like the way you handled yourself today."

She hated the crowds, the stares, the flashbulbs popping in her eyes, the hyped-up press reports that played upon the wealth and status of her family, the sordid gossip about a "deal"—her testimony in return for

Schrader's promise not to expose Susan Berring's "nymphomania."

It was one of *those* cases, people agreed, the ones that catch the country's imagination every several years. "A fancy-schmancy murder trial," Schrader called it, though to her it seemed more like a carnival in which she played the geek. People were fascinated by her position: sister of the victim acting as witness for the boy who everyone was certain had stabbed Suzie with the shears.

"Does defense counsel really expect us to believe," asked Robinson in his summation, "that the defendant, having engaged in numerous sexual acts with Susan Berring, and then heavily drugged, asleep out on the diving board, suddenly was awakened by her cries for help, swam to the poolhouse, burst in upon an 'intruder' in the act of stabbing her, and then simply *stood there* while this 'intruder' blinded him with a flashlight, threw him to the floor, and then just"—he flung out his hands—"disappeared? Does he expect us to believe this corny intruder-with-the-flashlight story even though the police found no trace of any 'intruder'— not a footprint, a fingerprint, a sign of a break-in, any sign at all—and when the defendant was himself seen by at least five other people stumbling out of the murder room with the murder weapon in his hand?

"No, Mr. Schrader wouldn't dare ask us to believe a word of this if it weren't for the so-called 'corroborating testimony' of Penny Berring. It's her testimony that's at the crux of this case. The question is: Can we believe Penny Berring? I submit that there are at least five good reasons why we cannot."

Had there really been five? She couldn't remember now. She could only remember how she shuddered as Robinson strove to show how the lonely, unattractive sister who lived pathetically in a world of imaginary characters out of books had finally managed to catch herself a boyfriend, only to have her sister steal him away.

"And what a boyfriend," Robinson said, "a slick, good-looking, clever actor who'd taken a summer job up here to, as he put it to Penny, *'hone* my actor's craft.' He told her he'd acted in films, but he didn't mention what kind—disgusting, degenerate hard-core smut which I haven't been allowed to show—"

"Objection!" Schrader stood up, the tufts of gray hair on either side of his head quivering with fury. "Mr. Robinson's trying to inflame—"

As she watched and listened she pretended she was an observer, outside the case rather than at its core. It was the only way she knew to distance herself, keep from crying out.

Good characters, she thought, a classic confrontation of personalities and styles. Robinson, young and tough, playing the sarcastic brute. Schrader, subtle and urbane, the veteran warrior reveling in a hopeless cause. The judge seemed made of granite, the very personification of the State of Maine. The grim father. The opaque jurors. The eager, salivating representatives of the press. The porn-star defendant and his ally, the Ugly Duckling Sister. The case had everything— money, drama, sex.

"Yes, ladies and gentlemen, it is the sister, Penny Berring, whose motives we must suspect. She claims she saw the elusive 'intruder' though it was the middle of the night, the fog was thick, and she was dozing beside a window a hundred fifty feet away. She claims she saw a 'flashlight beam' though no flashlight was ever found. She tells us she just 'happened' to be watching at the exact moment when the 'intruder' just *happened* to appear. What we have here is a jealous young woman, still smarting from the rejection of the defendant, who now comes forward with a farfetched story in an hysterical attempt to win him back. But what is so sick in all of this is that she does it after the vicious murder of her sister, whom she always hated, and still does hate, despite the fact that Susan Berring is now dead, carved up, slashed to pieces, no longer in a position to compete with her for paramours—''

She found herself nodding to his rhythms. It was as if Robinson were speaking about someone else, a terrible lying envious girl who had nothing to do with her at all. She found him persuasive. She began to hate this Penny Berring, too. What sort of person was she to have done all those wicked things and then to have conspired with a homicidal fiend to tip the scales of Justice with her lies?

But when Schrader stood up and began to talk she found him convincing, too. His rhythms were much less emotional than Robinson's, more rational and mathematical, and his phrasings were cool and precise. They suggested he had no interest in rhetoric, in anything but the truth. The Bar Harbor police, he showed, were amateurs who'd bungled their investigation and destroyed crucial evidence. A mad killer was now loose in the country while an innocent young man, whose story was fully corroborated, was being hounded by a prosecutor out for blood.

"As for Penny Berring," Schrader said, "contrary to what Mr. Robinson has told you, she has every reason to hate the defendant, no possible motive to help him now. But from the start she's never wavered from her story, which, it so happens, fits perfectly with his. Despite attempts to confuse her and break her down she's been consistent about what she saw. She has emerged from a brutal cross-examination as a totally credible eyewitness who, at the very least, raises reasonable doubt about events which at first seemed so clear, but which now we see aren't clear at all."

Which version, she wondered, would the jurors believe? She wasn't sure which she'd believe herself. As the hours went by and she waited for the verdict, she knew they were discussing her, whether she'd lied or told the truth.

Her father waited with her. They didn't speak much, just sat together side by side. He'd come to the courthouse every day, taken the same seat in the front row as if he were daring the jury not to give him justice, defying them to refuse him his revenge. His grimness, the certainty on his face, was silent testimony. Would that stern paternal silence be more convincing than her words? There was a side of her that hoped it would, that wanted to see him satisfied.

"You've showed a lot of class through this, kiddo," he said. "Must have gotten that from your mother's side." A couple minutes later he turned to her again. "They say 'class will out,' you know, but I haven't usually found that to be the case."

She could find no answer for him, couldn't imagine what was in his mind. The two of them had come to Maine for the trial—her mother had been left behind in Greenwich under psychiatric care. In Maine they had been drenched in sadness. Their tragedy seemed reflected in the ruined birds' nests in the bare-limbed trees around the house, the angry brown seas of late autumn, the chilly, pallid skies. And they had stuck to their respective views. Since her father believed Jared was guilty, she assumed he blamed her for everything. But he never said that, never told her she was deluded, never tried to persuade her to change her testimony. He only smiled and offered strange compliments.

When, finally, they heard the jury was coming in, more than eleven hours had passed. She sat still, rigid, her hands sweating, her pulse racing, waiting for the words which would stigmatize her for life. "Innocent on all counts." Even Schrader looked stunned, and there were sighs, some moans, then an undercurrent of angry whispers while the jurors were polled. She couldn't believe it, nor, she could see, could anyone else. Her father's expression never changed.

Afterward there was a strange sort of dance enacted on the courthouse lawn. A pile of leaves was smoldering in one corner; the aroma wafted back and forth as the principals strolled from interview to interview, trying to avoid each other, pausing longer where the network camera crews were set. Robinson announced that the system had broken down, that if the judge had allowed him to show Jared's films there'd have been a different verdict and right would have prevailed. The chief of the Bar Harbor police scoffed when asked if he'd reopen the case. "This verdict doesn't change anything," he said. "It doesn't create an intruder who was never there."

Schrader held forth from the steps, forcing the cameras to come to him. Since he was short, he stood a step higher than Jared, laying one hand upon his client's shoulder, resting the other on his hip. "A dicey case," he said, "but I took it anyway. Don't like to see guys go to the slammer for stuff they didn't do." Jared said he wasn't bitter. Did he have any plans? "Yes. Grow a beard," he said. Everybody laughed.

Her father was grave. No, he wasn't disappointed. Yes, he believed his surviving daughter. Yes, he found the verdict fair. If it was true that the police were no longer interested in looking for the intruder, he'd hire private detectives and pursue the investigation on his own.

Then, it seemed, they all turned suddenly to her, began asking their questions all at once. "What are you going to do now, Penny?" "Where are you going to go?" "Back to college?" "Back to Wellesley?" "Have you spoken to Jared?" "Will you pose with him on the steps?" She shook her head, was about to turn, when a woman with crazed blue eyes and wild gray hair ran up, and planted herself a foot away. Penny, surprised, started to ask her what she wanted. "Liar! Slut!" the woman hissed, then spat ferociously in her face.

It was six months after that, after she'd left Wellesley and secluded herself in Greenwich for a while, then moved to New York, changed her name, found a job, and began taking college courses at night—it was then, that spring, that she first began to run.

Weekend in Greenwich. Child comes down from Wellesley, tight-lipped as usual, tight-pussied no doubt, too. I want to grab her by her ears and shake her till she pees. "Let it flow, Child," I want to tell her, "let Thy Juices Flow." Dear Mother (or should I say Mother Dear?) looks me over like I'm a tainted fish. Her nostrils quiver. She smells naughtiness, decay. Not my bod, I know—my epidermis is immaculate. I use feminine hygiene spray, keep my underarms pristine, rinse out my mouth with pucker-power. No—what she smells is deep inside—my unhappy putrefying soul. But when I check myself out in the mirror, I can't imagine how she knows. I'm gorgeous, stunning. My face alone could raise ten thousand cocks.

Daddy-O, on the other hand, reveals nothing. He, on the other hand, pretends we're all just happy WASPs. I'm sure he has a mistress, some dusky lady stashed away in town someplace, in a little tax deduction of a penthouse he rents for her on the sly, a pied-à-terre near Sutton Place filled with shiny plants, sexy jungle plants with oily leaves, and there, on a tiger-skin rug, they fuck away in time with drums. It's all very Afro, very outré. He pinions her hands above her head, lowers himself slowly, taunting her, making her strain upward to flick her tongue against the steel-hardness of his shaft. It grows. At every lick it grows. She strains. He smiles. And then the sweet cream cascades upon her face, a river of perfect foam spreading slowly upon her dusty skin. Afterward—off to the Racquet Club for thirty minutes of squash with the hardball boys, then a long hot shower—wash away all the sweat and sex—and back to Chapman Int to gobble up some little company or country, and then, finally, The Long Ride Home. What the hell does he think we are, anyway? Does he think any of us is really sane? WASPs! God, how I loathe us, so hard and pure, so squeaky-clean!

Anyway, the weekend is the purest shit. Awful sessions at the dining table, the phony old dark carved baronial groaning board. He slices the roast so thin it curls up in shame. The pan juices are as pale as mother's family's blood. Two straight-up candles, church-type,

45

flickering, illuminate our faces, bring out all the smugness within. I sit opposite Child. She's talking about her new Comp. Lit. course. The reading list's exhaustive—her eyes glow as she lists the books. Proust, Joyce, Mann—ugh! Mother nods like a zombie. Daddy-O evinces a mild interest. Mandy passes the roasted potatoes. The peas are so green they're either frozen or dyed. Finally I can't stand any more, want to make my distaste evident to all. Mother provides me with an opening. "Now that does sound like quite an interesting reading list," she says, and, turning to me: "Don't you think so, dear?"

"Well," I say, laying down my flatware, "since you're asking me I assume you want the truth." "Yes, of course," says Mother Dear. Daddy-O, knowing I'm about to unload some shit, glances over and narrows his eyes. I say: "All right, since you want my sincere opinion, I have to tell you that it all sounds—well— a bit jejune." "Jejune, dear?" Mother, deeply perplexed, begins to shake her head. "She means barren," says Child. "She means it sounds like it's all a bore." "Is that what you mean?" Daddy asks, in his slow hushed inimitable tone. "Actually," I say, "I don't know what

jejune means. It just seemed like a good word to use at the time. Forgive me, Child—I really don't think those books are a bore at all." Child looks at me. She knows we're crazy. She's GOT to know. A long silence. Mandy appears with floating island. Hurrah, hurrah—

WALKING OUT of Central Park, turning down Fifth Avenue, she realized why she hadn't seen another jogger on the track. It was Labor Day, 6:00 A.M. Even the earliest regulars were out of town or still asleep.

It had been three years since Suzie's death, a little less since Jared's trial. She no longer called herself Penny Berring. She'd taken her mother's maiden name and was Penny Chapman now.

Her apartment was on East Eightieth between Madison and Park, in a brownstone owned by a woman psychiatrist who encouraged her patients to care for great quantities of cats. Dr. Eleanor Bowles, herself, kept quite a few of the beasts in the duplex she inhabited on the upper floors. Penny could hear them meowing whenever she entered the house, and, on certain hot days such as this holiday morning, the stench of them wafted down the stairwell to sicken her slightly as she came through the door. Still, despite the meowing and the odor and Dr. Bowles' strange patients— who turned up at odd hours, often with a cat-carrying case or two in tow—Penny was content with her home.

Her rooms were pleasant, and the location was good for using the park and getting to work.

She glanced at the card above her mailbox. "P. Chapman," it said. Looking at that name, she couldn't quite connect it with herself. It seemed to speak more of a Cosmo type than a depressed stay-at-home editorial trainee.

She unlocked the inner door and started up the stairs. The cat smell hit her like a blow. Perhaps Dr. Bowles had taken the holiday off, leaving her pets' litter boxes to ferment and overflow.

Her own flat, one floor up and in the back, consisted of a small living room crammed with books, a windowless kitchenette, a tiny bedroom and a bath. It was a typically over-priced single person's Upper East Side apartment, plagued by seasonal infestations of roaches, with a classic, grunting air conditioner stuck in the bedroom window and two dead-bolt locks arrayed on the entry door. But there was something special about it, a three-sided bay in the living room, with a window seat and leaded panes that looked out over the private gardens behind the houses. She'd had a cushion made to fit the seat and had hung some plants above the windows. She liked to sit there reading or staring out at the scraggly trees.

She peeled off her jogging clothes, took a long, hot shower, and watched the soapy water swirl down the drain. Thinking of Hitchcock's *Psycho*, the shower-murder scene, she wondered why she so often had the feeling that something terrible was going to happen to her, that she was destined for suffering and pain.

She dressed and went directly to the window seat where a stack of manuscripts waited to be read. These were her share of the "slush" that poured into Brewster & Angles every week. The sensible thing would have been to return them unread, but sometime in the sixties an ambitious B&A secretary had taken home a slushpile novel for the weekend, sniffed something commercial, and promoted it onto the best-seller list for forty weeks. Though the odds against this happening again were probably no better than a million to one, all trainee editors at B&A were now assigned to read everything sent in. Penny found this part of her job saddening. Her weekends and holidays were consumed by the fantasies of inept people who scribbled away at hopeless books. She longed to find something good—a graceful line, a character who lived, an authentic author with something interesting to say—but instead she found incoherence, private madnesses, stories better left untold.

Her mother called from Connecticut late in the afternoon, a holiday ritual, to ask her how she was. "I wish you'd come out here for a weekend, dear. We love to see you, you know. We don't see you much at all these days—"

There was a pause then, the sort of awkward pause that occurred regularly when they spoke. Penny thought her mother didn't sound too badly crocked—just a trace of slur. There was something odd in her voice anyway—beneath the mellowness of her affection something high-strung, almost frenzied, that seemed to have grown in the years since Suzie's death despite the care of paid companions and the dryings-out ("stints," her mother called them) at various expensive clinics up and down the New England coast. Penny loved her mother but couldn't bear contact. The formal, icy arrangement between her parents, the tautness between them which spoke of terrible scenes left unplayed, her mother's looniness and drunkenness, made visits to Greenwich sorrowful and strange.

"I miss you, dear. I worry so much about you living alone in the city, with all the violence and anger there. I wish you'd move to a safe doorman building. I wish you didn't go off running in the park so early, with all the muggers about, and no one around to help. . . ."

She'd heard it all a thousand times. "The muggers work at night, mother. By the time I go out they've gone to bed."

"Yes, I suppose, but still—here's your father, dear. I'm going to put him on."

She felt tension then, as she imagined the telephone being passed. Her parents would be careful, she knew, not to touch. Her mother would hold out the receiver by the mouthpiece, her father would take it by the earphone, then her mother would slip out of her chair as her father turned and stepped aside.

"Hi, kiddo—everything OK?"

"Fine, daddy. Just catching up on work."

"Job OK?"

"Sure. Nothing new."

She felt so stupid with nothing to say, hated the limpness in her voice. She could just imagine him, the crinkles around his mouth and eyes, his smile, his squared-off jaw. And of course the shock of hair that hung across his forehead and made him look so boyish, light-brown copper hair like Suzie's, now slightly grayed around the ears.

"Want to play some squash this week?" He hadn't asked her in months.

"Sure."

"Still running?"

"Yeah."

"In great shape, huh?"

"I guess."

"Well, I'd better watch out, kiddo. Call me Wednesday. We'll set something up."

It was small talk, empty, inane, but still she was touched because he tried. Things between them had been difficult the last three years. He'd been angry when she told him she was going to change her name.

He said that wasn't "right," that she couldn't run away from things, and in the soft hushed tone he used when he was truly furious said: "I don't think she would have changed *her* name if things had been reversed." She'd been nearly crushed by that, had turned away, felt tears rising to her eyes. Then he'd put his arm around her, held her close. "It's your life, kiddo. Do what you have to do."

Things had gotten a little better after that. At least now he seemed to want a relationship: occasional squash games, lunches at his club, father-son type stuff. She went along with everything he suggested, never turned him down. She wanted desperately to get to know him, break through the aura of coldness and self-absorption which always surrounded him and made her feel cut off. If only she could be like Suzie, she thought; if she could be fascinated by his business dealings, turned on by his power plays; if only she could take Suzie's place and give her father back the daughter he'd loved the best. But it was impossible. She didn't know how to be like that, wasn't interested in business, couldn't have faked interest if she'd tried. She sometimes thought that if he'd had a choice of which of his daughters he must lose, he would have chosen her.

After the call she stared out the window for a while. Then, annoyed at herself, she decided to go out. The city seemed to be full of young people in tank tops and track shorts wandering hand-in-hand. There was a black kid standing on the corner of Lexington and Eighty-Sixth. "Smoke, smoke, smoke," he whispered again and again under his breath.

She wandered into a discount bookstore, prowled the tables, picked up novels, speed-read dust jacket copy, glanced at authors' photographs. All the male writers under forty sported beards; all the women stared out defiantly as if to say that their pens were mightier than the men their novels flayed.

After a while she felt dizzy—too many books, too many covers competing for attention, most of them second-rate, a waste of energy and trees. Like a lot of English majors she'd gone into publishing because of her love for literature. Publishing, it turned out, wasn't about literature at all. It had to do with a product—"books."

Back on Eighty-Sixth the black boy was still purveying dope. Gimbels was open; a Labor Day Sale was on. She went in, rode the escalators, looked at tennis rackets and jogging shoes and close-outs on designer sheets. She stayed in the store until it closed, then walked over to Carl Schurz Park where she stood by the balustrade, watching the scows go by and the holiday traffic jam up on the FDR. When the sky turned dark she looked for a restaurant and settled on a coffee shop, where she ate a hamburger and drank a glass of milk.

When she wandered back to Eightieth Street, she found a dark van parked in front of her brownstone and a small group, whom she recognized as patients of Dr. Bowles, standing around on the sidewalk amidst a heap of boxes and sacks. They stopped talking when she came close, nodded cautiously. There was something cliquish about them, something smug, as if they possessed special knowledge, knew the secrets of the world.

Upstairs her unread slushpile manuscripts confronted her with reproach. She couldn't even bear to skim them. Instead she turned on TV and watched a talk-show, a group sitting around in Saarinen chairs arguing fiercely as they puffed on cigarettes. She wasn't interested in what they were saying but was intrigued by their intensity. She felt numb, cut off from that sort of passion. She felt she was waiting now to be renewed, released.

Yes, she thought, *I'm waiting, waiting for something to happen, an author to discover, a wonderful manuscript that will sweep me away to another world. Or perhaps I'm waiting for something to happen in my life, someone new to come and free me, a lover to appear and take me in his arms.*

It hadn't been, Penny decided at 4:00 P.M. on Friday, one of her better weeks. The temperature had risen into the nineties, the worst September weather New York had seen in years. The holidays were over. Subway rush hours were a nightmare. The city seethed with sweat and rage.

At dawn on Tuesday, running through the humid mists around the reservoir, she was suddenly confronted by a middle-aged man with thinning hair who jumped out from behind a bush, pulled down his pants, wagged his genitals and grinned at her. "Oh, gee whiz," she said, pretending she was shocked, nearly knocking him over as she sped by. For another hundred yards she endured his screams: "That's right! Run! Run! Ha, ha! Fuck you!"

That night when she answered her phone someone started breathing heavily at the other end. She hung up, and then it rang again. "I know who you are," said a soft Hispanic voice. "I know where you live. And I *know* when you're going to die." There were no more calls, but she contacted the telephone company anyway. Her number was already unlisted; now she'd be unlisted once-removed.

On Wednesday she called her father and arranged to play squash with him late that afternoon. She left her office early, took the subway home to retrieve her racket and her shoes, took another subway back to midtown, rushed on foot through the sultry New York streets in order to meet him at the Racquet Club at five. She arrived just in time to receive a call from his secretary: He was tied up in a meeting—would she mind if they postponed their game?

All was not going well at B&A, either. Today she'd been informed that Roy MacAllister, the editor-in-chief, wanted to see her before she left. There was something ominous in that, a summons late on a Friday afternoon. Was he going to fire her? Had she done something wrong?

More and more lately she had the feeling she was being left out of things, lunches with authors, meetings where important projects were discussed. She wouldn't have been as bothered by this, or by her numerous assignments to menial tasks, if it weren't that the other trainee editor with whom she shared a cubicle, Lillian Ryan, seemed to be included when she was not and lately had started bossing her around.

"Finish this up for me, will you, Pen," Lillian had said, stopping at her desk at noon on Thursday, dropping off a sheaf of handwritten author's corrections and the manuscript into which they had to be typed.

"Why me?" Penny had asked.

"There's no one else, and it's got to be done. I've got a lunch date with this guy from the Literary Guild, and Mac wants this stuff by four."

Penny had accepted the extra work with resignation, took the elevator down to the coffee shop in the basement, bought herself a cream-cheese-on-rye, returned to her desk, ate her sandwich, and dutifully completed the task. She tried not to resent it, but when Lillian stuck in her head at three forty-five, glanced at what she'd done, nodded her approval, snatched the papers off her desk, and started into the hall, Penny called her back.

"Hey—wait a minute."

"Huh?"

"Aren't you forgetting something?"

"What? Oh, yeah—thanks for helping out."

Lillian Ryan was her adversary, a competitor she couldn't seem to beat. A plump, earnest eager beaver, she wore an inordinate amount of blue eye shadow and plum lipstick that made her mouth look like a bruise. She sashayed down the corridors puffing on cigarettes, a mistress of office politics, a dragon-lady of belles-lettres. She did not intend, she told Penny many times, to remain a trainee editor very long. Penny didn't either, if she could just find a way to push herself ahead. She hated the role of doormat, longed to be aggressive like Lillian, but not so obvious or cheap.

Now she was worried. The summons from Mac-Allister did not bode well. "Mac" could be charming but also ruthless; she was impressed by him, drawn to him, but sometimes he scared her, too. He wore black leather jackets over black turtleneck sweaters and was successful on account of his manipulations rather than his taste in books.

When Penny arrived at his office promptly at a quarter to five he was on the telephone and didn't bother to look up. This was one of his favorite office tricks. Another was to terminate an interview by picking up something to read, leaving the person standing there, not knowing whether he or she had been dismissed.

"—and you can tell that son of a bitch," MacAllister was saying in a tone Penny knew he reserved for minor agents, "that he's never going to get that kind of deal from me because that kind of deal is utter crap." He slammed down the phone.

"Sit down, Chapman," he said, waving her to a chair. "Do you like working here? I want the truth."

"Yes, of course," she said. *She was going to be fired.* "Why do you ask me that?"

"Why on this terrible sweltering Friday afternoon

55

do I call you in here and ask you *that?* Very simple, *Ms*. Chapman. I'm sick and tired of your little elfin bullshit, this feeling you give me that you're always on the edge of tears. If you don't shape up I'm going to transfer you someplace far away out of my sight." He sat back and stared at her. She felt crushed, didn't know what to say. Then he was roaring with laughter. "Just a joke, Chapman. Just a joke."

He was so full of tricks, rapid changes of mood—warmth and colleagueship but unnerving vulgarity, too, insults and put-downs contrived to ruin one's day.

"Look, I've always liked your guts, the way you stood up for yourself at that nutty trial. You do good work. Keep your snotty nose clean. You're steady and reliable, and your readers' reports make sense. Your problem is you're too passive. Publishing's a business, not a seminar in American Lit. Look, I want you off that slushpile. I want you out meeting agents, the young hungry ones, the independents, the kids your age. I want to know what's going on with them. And the young writers, too. Village Voice. Soho News. The whole underground thing. Let's get them in here, get a look at them, sign some of them up for a couple of grand and see what they can do."

He paused, then gave her a flashing smile. "I'm making you an assistant editor, and I'm giving you a small expense account. Not much—take them to lunch at spaghetti joints. That's what they like anyhow. Starting Monday you're running with the big boys. Now get out of here. I got to make some calls."

Penny, head reeling, nodded her gratitude, then wandered back to her cubicle in a daze. It was nearly five o'clock, and as usual she found that Lillian Ryan had already divided up the slushpile, keeping the manuscripts that looked interesting for herself, piling the rest on Penny's desk.

"God, you were in there long enough," Lillian said. "What did he want anyhow?"

"I must be dreaming," Penny replied. "He made me an assistant editor." She shoved the manuscripts back at Lillian. "He told me I'm off this stuff."

Lillian winced. "Gee, Pen—that's great. Really great." She tried to smile but her eyes betrayed her injury. "I mean, you deserve it. You really do."

People were rushing back and forth on Third Avenue, heading for bus and subway stops, anxious to get home, change, start their weekends. Some would be heading out to Connecticut or Long Island, while others would be staying in town to go to singles' bars, discotheques, encounter groups or off-Broadway plays, or into lovers' arms. And she, what was she going to do now that she was so suddenly and wonderfully unburdened of her weekend load of illiteracy? *Maybe I should celebrate,* she thought, *buy a dress, go to a movie, eat out someplace decent for a change.*

There was a subtitled French film playing at the Fine Arts. She stood in line among waiting couples, feeling detached. Everyone else had a partner, lived with someone, went out on dates. When the people who'd been in the theater started coming out she tried to read their faces. Was the film happy, sad, suspenseful, profound? Maybe, she thought, it's one of those pictures to which you're supposed to have a confused response.

Afterwards, back on Third Avenue, walking past people standing in lines at the various cinemas, she felt despondent, listless, sad. Thoughts and memories started crushing in: Robinson glaring at her as she faced him from the stand; her father's face, grim, square-jawed, as he stood in the cemetery in Greenwich watching Suzie being lowered into the ground; Jared, entering the visitor's room at the jail, his face expectant, curious, perplexed; and Suzie strutting beside the pool on a cloudless windless day, throwing back her head, her copper hair catching the Maine sun, laughing, hawing, her chin stuck out crazily—

She was hungry; she decided to go to Chinatown. The subway rattled and roared. Across the aisle sat a young black couple, arms about one another, sneaker-clad feet entwined. On Mott Street she wandered through crowds more intense, more feverish than the movie and discotheque people uptown. The alleyways smelled of incense and garbage and herbal tea. She finally settled on a little restaurant on the second floor of a tenement on Pell Street. *I'll never be recognized here,* she thought as she mounted the narrow stairs.

A waiter with a jack-o'-lantern smile showed her to a booth. She studied the menu, chose a dish, sipped some tea then stared at the empty seat across.

"Penny."

Someone had just whispered her name, someone standing close. She looked up warily.

"I thought it was you, babe."

Jared. She couldn't believe it. She immediately lowered her eyes. What was he doing here? He was supposed to be a continent away, on a commune in California, or an oil rig in Brazil.

"Hey, don't you recognize me?"

In Chinatown of all places, in this tiny obscure restaurant out of all the thousands she could have chosen, on this night of all nights she'd decided to wander aimlessly looking for a place to eat.

"Join you?"

She looked up again. It was him, no mistake, his face dark as ever, the same black stubble on his cheeks and chin. His smile was the same, too, engaging, warm. What was he doing here? Why was he standing beside her table? *What did he want?*

"Well?—"

She looked back at her menu, feeling her pulse begin to race. She could sense him standing there, waiting for her to invite him to sit down. He was very still. She only wished she could tell him to go away.

He sat down just as the waiter appeared. She ordered "Buddha's Delight" and Moo Shoo Pork. After the waiter scuttled away, she stared at him, trying to find the proper words. "Look," she said finally, "I didn't ask you—I really didn't want you to sit down."

"Waiting for someone?" She shook her head. "What's the harm then?"

"I just don't feel up to this."

"I can understand that. But maybe you'll change your mind. I saw you out on the street. I was wandering around, I saw somebody, I thought it was you, so I followed you a couple of blocks. I saw you come up here and I thought: well, go ahead, follow her in, sit down with her if she's alone. What'll be the harm?" She looked down at the vinyl table top, shook her head. "Come on," he said. "We haven't seen each other in—how long has it been? Almost three years, right? Jesus—you saved my life. At least let me buy you dinner. We don't have to talk if you don't want."

Then she didn't know what to do. It seemed childish to walk out on him, uncouth to ask him to go. Anyway, she thought, maybe he's right: what difference did it make?

"Where were you? I mean—where have you been all this time?"

"Oh—everywhere. Texas mostly, bumming around. Odd jobs, stuff like that. I came back because I'm an actor. I finally realized New York's where an actor's got to be." She nodded. "Haven't found anything yet. Don't know—maybe I won't. Had some résumés printed up, some photos, too. Sent them around. Nothing's happened yet, but that's usual, I guess. There're some cattle calls next week. Think I'll show up, check out the mood." He toyed with a matchbook. "I could get back into porn easy if I wanted. My face's famous now. But I've sort of been through that already, I guess. Yeah, it'll probably be pretty rough."

He paused and smiled. "You should see this crummy dump I'm in. It's a real dive, around the corner from the Port Authority. Swarming with hustlers, whores. Hey, I'm poor, remember? 'The poor boy knocking on the portals of the rich.' Isn't that what they said? God—" He shrugged. "Hey—you're not feeling hostile anymore?" She shook her head. "That's good. I've thought about you a lot."

There was something so disarming about him that she couldn't help herself—she was moved. He was the same boy who'd made love to her so beautifully, so romantically on a cliff overlooking the sea on a hot summer day so long ago.

"Tell me about yourself," he said. "What've you been up to all this time?"

What could she say? Where should she begin? "I changed my name."

"Yeah, I can understand that. They wouldn't leave you alone otherwise, I guess."

"I still get recognized sometimes."

"Me, too. I had a beard for a while, let my hair go long. I don't know—sometimes I think people are staring at me, but then maybe they just like my looks."

He grinned. She began to feel more relaxed.

"I wanted to talk to you after the trial. But you disappeared so fast, and then there wasn't any way to reach you. I called a few times. The person who answered said you weren't there. Anyway I just wanted to thank you for going out on a limb for me, the way you handled yourself on the stand."

"I only told the truth."

"I know. You don't have to explain. I know what you did, the kind of person you are. I just wanted to say 'thanks for being you'—you know, something like that."

60

He reached across the table, placed his hand on top of hers. "I really mean it," he said.

He ordered some food, and they ate in silence. He was expert with his chopsticks. They had ice cream for dessert, and when the fortune cookies came he shook them in his fist, then offered first choice to her. They groaned at their banality; he crumpled up the little slips. "Maybe you ought to go into the fortune cookie writing business. Do you think you'd like it? I bet all your fortunes would be nice."

He began to talk again as they sipped their tea, of someplace he'd lived in Texas, a job he'd had, people he'd met. Listening to him she found herself liking the way he spoke, his earnestness, his vulnerability, the warm timbre of his voice. She'd always liked him, she remembered that; he was an attractive person, not sly or insincere the way some of the papers had made him out. It was hard not to like him. He had a quality which now she could see more clearly than before. He was a sensitive rebel with dark liquid eyes and an uncanny ability to evoke feelings of tenderness. She looked at him, barely listening to what he said, and found herself caring about him, wanting to help.

"I'm a better person than I was," he said suddenly. "I honestly believe that—that out of all the bad some good has come."

She looked down. "I just wish I could forget it all."

"You can't," he told her gently. "And it doesn't matter. You don't let it gnaw at you. You just pick yourself up and go on."

They walked on the streets of Chinatown for a while that sweltering September night, then up to the subway stop on Canal. He rode the train with her to Eighty-Sixth, walked her to the door of her brownstone.

"Well—" he said. "I'd like to see you again if that's OK."

She studied him, then shook her head. "I'm sorry,

61

Jared, it's nothing against you, but I just don't think we should.''

"Yeah," he said, nodding. "I guess you're right. Well—I'm glad I spotted you anyway. It was real good to see you, babe. Goodnight."

They shook hands, then he walked away. She waited until he turned the corner, before she turned herself and went inside.

Saw him on Fifth Avenue today, walking the other direction, face abstracted, blank. Impossible to know what was in his mind. Was afraid he'd see me and set my face quickly in case he did, but then he walked by as I was hoping, and, natch, I began to feel hurt. Decided to follow him, actually did for five or six blocks through the lunch-hour mobs. A crazy lady with a monkey passed—he didn't give her a glance. A gaunt street violinist with crudely lettered cardboard sign ("Please help me continue my lessons") serenaded him with Mendelssohn, but he didn't even pause. I kept saying to myself: hide, hide in case he turns. And then I thought: don't let the others know, all these people passing—don't let them read your face. Finally I lost him. Think he turned on 56th where there're a zillion restaurants.

On Monday morning she overslept and didn't make it to the reservoir till seven. There was a herd already jogging when she arrived—gays with Afghans, Farrah Fawcett look-alikes, interracial couples, the Columbia University track squad. She ran past fancy Fifth Avenue ladies trying to trudge off excess flab, was passed in turn by handsome lawyer types with tanned and rippling backs.

She spent most of the morning on the phone, contacting young agents, introducing herself, setting up appointments for lunch. Lillian Ryan came in and started typing her reader's reports. She acted secretive, shielding her papers whenever Penny passed her desk. Had she actually discovered something in the slushpile, or was that what she wanted Penny to think?

There was some excitement in the office in the early afternoon. The subsidiary rights director was wrapping up an auction; it looked as if a B&A novel would go to paperback for half a million dollars. Penny hung around the corridors picking up the gossip, sharing in the excitement of the junior staff. Later in the afternoon, as she was writing some letters, her telephone rang.

"Babe?"

"Hi." She was a little surprised to hear from him so soon.

"That was fun the other night."

"Yes," she said, wondering how he'd gotten her number; she hadn't told him where she worked.

"Look, I understand what you said about not seeing each other. I respect your feelings on that. But I kind of hoped—well—I'd like to see you again." She was silent, and then she felt resentful. What right had he to bother her now, after everything, all those silent years? "I'd like to see you again," he repeated.

"There's no point, Jared. I don't think there is."

"Come on, babe. I want us to be friends."

"It's too late for that. Don't you understand?"

"All right—listen to me." His voice suddenly took on an edge. "I understand plenty. You bet I do. I understand I did a lousy thing, and you have plenty of reason to be pissed—"

"I don't want to listen to this!"

"We got to talk it through. You owe me that."

"How did you get my number?"

"What?"

"I didn't tell you where I worked."

"Yes you did."

"No, I didn't. I made a point of *not* telling you, because I didn't want you to—" She stopped. A thought flashed into her brain. "That wasn't any accident, was it, your meeting me in Chinatown Friday night?" Silence. *"Was it?"*

"No."

"You lied to me, goddammit."

"Don't hang up, Penny. Please."

She hung up. She felt sorry for him, and anger, too. He had no right to bother her, follow her on the street, pursue her, lie. They'd had their talk. Why couldn't he just accept the fact that she was done with all that now? *Owed him?* She'd stood up for him when all the world believed he was a killer. Now it was he who owed her, owed her respect for her wish to be left alone.

She was still upset at five o'clock. There was something about the situation she didn't understand. She thought about it as she waited for the elevator. Could he have gotten to her, somehow attracted her again? She couldn't accept that, not after so many years. What was it then? Was she going to feel awkward about him all the rest of her life?

She didn't notice him at first. He was leaning against a column in the busy lobby, watching the elevators disgorging people hurrying from offices, rushing to beat the rush-hour mobs. He was at her elbow before she realized he was there, was reaching for her arm.

"Babe—"

She jumped. "Don't touch me!" Some people nearby turned and stared.

"Relax, babe. OK?"

He was wearing a denim wrangler's jacket. His jeans were cinched by a cowboy belt.

"Just relax. *Hey. Relax.*" She nodded. The people who'd been staring turned away.

"What are you trying to do?" They were standing in the middle of the lobby, away from the elevator banks still disgorging crowds.

"I'm not trying to *do* anything. I just wanted to see you—that's all. I just want to sit down with you someplace peaceful and talk. Is there any crime in that?"

"I told you—"

"I know."

"And you don't care what I want?"

"Sure I care. For God's sakes I *care.* I'm not asking so much, you know." He stood back from her and let his arms hang at his sides. "OK, babe, anything you want. Just tell me to go away now, and I'll never bother you again."

She examined him; he looked resigned and hungry. "OK," she said, "there's a fairly decent bar around the corner from here." He looked so happy then, beamed so warmly, she felt incredulous at her power to affect his moods.

The bar wasn't much, dark and overly air-conditioned, an after-work pub, the sort of place where executives get chummy with their secretaries before

66

heading for the railroad stations and their commutations back to wives and kids. There were booths along a mirrored wall, and they sat in one. He ordered a bourbon, she asked for a glass of wine.

"I just can't get over seeing you again."

She nodded. She'd resolved not to say much, to let him talk himself out.

"How was work today?"

"So-so."

"You're going to make it big. I can tell." She smiled. "No. I mean it. You got that special thing. You know—the executive look." She laughed. "Like your dad. The power look. You know—*class*."

She couldn't tell if he was being bitter or ironic, or just transparently insincere. "Look, Jared—I don't like being lied to. That was very neat, your pretending to run into me. Now I want to know what really happened. Otherwise, I'm going home."

"All right. I got to New York a couple of weeks ago, and I called Schrader and asked about you. He told me where you worked. I was going to call you a couple of times, but I didn't have the nerve. So on Friday I went over to your building to wait, and then I saw you and, I don't know, you looked so happy, triumphant, so sure of yourself, and I just couldn't—well, I thought I'd follow you a couple of blocks."

"You followed me into the movie?"

"Yeah. Wasn't much of a picture, was it?"

"For Christ's sake, Jared—you were stalking me. How do you think that makes me feel?"

"Uncomfortable, I guess."

"*Very* uncomfortable."

"Yeah, I guess it would."

"And then you followed me on the subway?" He nodded. "How did you manage that?"

"I just stood in the car behind, kept an eye on you

67

through the door. You were so wrapped up in your thoughts you didn't notice anything.''

"And then you followed me into the restaurant?"

"I already admitted that."

She stared at him, shaking her head in amazement.

"You're not afraid of me, are you?"

"Of course not."

"I'm glad. But when you look at me now, I guess you sort of think of me as a bum."

"That's not true."

"Isn't it? That's what I am, right? What did Robinson say? That I took you all for a ride? Yeah—I did, I guess. Except nobody ever understood. I wasn't some crazy sex fiend like they tried to make you think. That wasn't why I did those films. It was to live on, because I was hungry, and I needed to eat, and somebody offered me the deal, so I took off my clothes and fucked and sucked, and so what anyway? I mean, what the hell? I never harmed anybody. Those pictures never hurt a living soul."

"I never cared about that."

"Sure you did. You thought I should have told you. You were right. But how could I? What was I going to say? 'Gee, babe, I've done some porn, you know, like this far-out flick, *Pussy Ranch.*' ''

"What?"

"*Pussy Ranch.* Pretty good, right? It was about this kid who—well, never mind. The plot wasn't much anyway. I took it seriously, though. Did the best I could."

"How many of these things were you in?"

"Six or eight. I don't remember now. They shoot them so fast, a couple of days at most. Then they cut them together or split them apart. You never know how many pictures they're making. They pay you by the day."

"How much?"

"Hundred and a quarter. More now I guess. Hey,

why are we talking about all this crap, anyway? It's just something I did." She shook her head again, trying to contain her smile. "What's the joke?"

"Oh, nothing. When I met you, the first time I saw you, you were reciting Gerard Manley Hopkins, and if anybody had told me then you'd been in something called *Pussy Ranch*—"

He started to laugh, too. "You wouldn't have believed it, would you?"

"Nope."

"Remember that poem? '. . . how he rung upon the rein of a wimpling wing—' "

"Yes," she said. "I haven't forgotten that."

He was quiet for a while, and as she looked at him she began to feel something strange. Was it a melting, like that first time on the cliffs? How crazy, to feel that way now.

"You were great."

"What?"

"At the trial—you were really great. To think that I was worried about you. We were all worried, actually. Schrader, his people, especially me. But you socked it to them, babe. You got up there and *performed*."

He was looking at her with such admiration that she felt embarrassed and lowered her eyes.

"You were really something else."

Finally, when she realized it was seven o'clock, and that she'd devoured four saucers of peanuts and drunk five glasses of wine, she told him she had to go. She paid the bill, and when he offered to escort her home she told him firmly she'd manage by herself.

"Well," he said as they parted ways, "I hope we can do this again sometime."

He called her the next afternoon. They met again in the lobby and returned to the same bar for drinks.

Afterwards they bought pizza slices at a storefront stand and ate them on the street. She told him about her running. He said he understood why she did it and that he admired her for leading such a disciplined life. She asked him if he still practiced throwing his voice.

"Yeah," he said, "every night, with gravel in my mouth."

She looked at him sharply. Was he really bitter, or just kidding around? She still couldn't tell, and she wished she could. There was something in his grin—something caustic and rebellious, yet vulnerable and mellow, too.

He was waiting for her in the lobby on Wednesday, and again they had drinks. On Thursday they went to a Philippine restaurant. The food was awful, but they laughed about it anyway.

"This is sauteed pig's navel," he said, "stuffed with goose shit."

"And this," she said, holding up her fork, "is goat's tonsil in extract of mildew sauce."

"You're disgusting."

"You chose this place," she said.

He didn't call on Friday and didn't show up either. She searched the lobby for him, waited half an hour, then shrugged and started home. It had been a week since they'd met. Already he'd become a part of her life. Why hadn't he come? She didn't know, and didn't know why she cared. She spent the evening staring at TV, feeling lonely and confused.

Just before she fell asleep she tried to think things through. She liked him—she admitted that. They were friends. She liked his company. He made her feel happy, made her forget she was chronically depressed. Why hadn't he come then? Maybe he'd been busy auditioning for a part. Maybe he'd tried to call her but it was too late; maybe the switchboard at the office was closed, and he hadn't gotten through. He couldn't call her at home because she hadn't given him her unlisted number. It could all be as simple as that. Or maybe he'd just decided he'd had enough of her. He'd felt that way about her once before.

Something's rubbed off on me. I'll never be rid of it—NEVER! What? Love of fucking, passion for fucking? No. Something else. Deeper. Primitive. Has got to do with power. Seduction. Thrill of the hunt. Ecstasy of the kill. Blood on the knife. Rituals. Magic. Want to be torn. Tired of wriggling like an insect, pinned down, twisting, working up a little set-of-tennis sweat. My pussy shrieks like the baby they forgot to feed. Crying, shrieking in my crib, spitting out my pacifier. In need of milk. Hungry, hungry—thirsty, too, staggering in the desert, drying out, shriveling, dying beneath the cruel sun—

SHE ROSE early Saturday morning and walked up to the reservoir. She felt empty and sad, lethargic, too. She wondered if she could do a lap, if she even had the will. Then she saw him standing in front of the pumphouse at the southern tip, wearing a pair of cut-off jeans, a faded "I Love New York" T-shirt, and a pair of tattered sneakers held together with tape.

72

"Hey, babe. I've been waiting here since five."

"What?"

"Yeah. To work out. Waiting here for you to teach me how. Sorry about yesterday. Would have called, but we didn't exactly have a date."

"That's OK," she said. "I figured you were busy."

He nodded. "Well, which way do we go?"

She showed him how to stretch, which they did together against the little iron railing at the entrance to the track. They started off then, running slowly side by side.

"Great view," he exclaimed as they rounded the northeast tip. "The city just there waiting to be conquered, right?" She looked at him. He was breathing fairly hard. "Tired?" He shook his head. By the time they'd run three-quarters of a mile she could tell he was about to drop. "Take a rest," she said. "I'll pick you up when I come around again."

He nodded with gratitude and dropped back. She sped up her pace, was soon off running by herself. How miraculous, she thought, the way he turns up at the oddest times. She felt good, energetic, almost joyful as she reached out with her legs. When she was done she found him sitting on a bench beside the pumphouse. She stood before him, hands resting on her hips. "Now *I'm* tired," she said.

"Don't look it. You're barely breathing hard. God— I wish I could keep up with you." He asked her how long she thought it would take him to get into shape. She told him three or four months at least. When she first started out, she said, she hadn't even been able to run a mile.

"Yeah, I remember. You were the bookworm," he said. "Suzie was the jock."

It was the first time since they'd met in Chinatown that he'd used Suzie's name.

73

"I wish I'd never let her turn my head," he said softly after a moment. "I wish I'd stuck with you."

"Jared, please—"

"It's true. I've thought it a thousand times."

"Please—"

"Come here, babe." He motioned for her to sit beside him on the bench. She hesitated. She was wet. Her shirt was sticking to her back. Also she felt afraid, of something in him and in herself, too, a weakness, a longing she didn't understand. "Penny, Penny, Penny—" He took her hand. "You have perfect form. You run like a pony. You're so beautiful—" He was gazing at her, admiration in his eyes. His smile beckoned. She stepped back slightly, and her hands slipped from his.

"So," he said, "what's next?"

"I go home and take a shower."

"I want to kiss you."

"Please—"

"Well?"

"Don't."

He nodded.

"I don't know—" She turned away, took a few steps, realized she was starting home. She stood still. Jared came up to her, placed his hands on her shoulders from behind.

"I feel this attraction. It's too much. Can't shake it off." She stood very still then. "I always felt it. *Always.*"

He turned her around so she could look into his eyes. They were serious, sincere. He pulled her gently to him, slowly brought his lips down on hers. Then she was lost in his kiss. The weakness she'd felt now filled her, rose up in her as she pressed her perspiring body against his.

"Do you remember?"

"Yes."

"God—it's been so long. You're not afraid now, are you?"

"No."

"Yes, you are. I feel it. Let it go, babe. Let it go."

Walking back to her building she felt as though she were in a trance. She was haunted by that time three years before, and she kept saying to herself, over and over: *I can't believe this is happening to me; I can't believe it is.* In his arms she'd felt as she had on the cliffs, as if she were crossing a line, stepping into a world from which she'd never return. Then she was falling, yielding to something too powerful to resist. He was like a magnet in whose presence the compass point of her mind twirled round and round. Her will went slack; her brain felt fuzzy. Nothing mattered— certainly not her thoughts. She was merely flesh, and now she was walking with him to her apartment. They would go to bed. He would fuck her. *Yes*—she savored the word—*he will fuck me; we will fuck.*

"Smells like a cathouse," he said when she opened up the lobby door. But when she unlocked her own apartment, and he went inside, he turned to her and smiled.

"Great, and the window seat—just like you said."

She was pleased he liked it. She wanted him to like everything about her. As she showed him around she realized he was the first visitor she'd had in months. He sat down on the bed, them motioned for her to join him there. When she paused, he reached out for her and brought her down beside him, and then they were lying side by side.

"I ought to take a shower," she whispered.

"I don't want you to take a shower. I want to make love to you while you're still hot and wet and slippery in my hands."

He drew her T-shirt up and over her shoulders, then left it there so it covered her face. Inside the tent she could smell her body. *He's going to fuck me,* she thought again; *we're going to fuck.*

She raised her arms so he could pull off her shirt, then watched as he peeled off his own. Then it was as if the years had never passed and the two of them had just met upon the cliffs. He made love to her as he had that afternoon, showing the same intuition, knowing just where to touch her, knowing when he should be gentle and when he should be rough. Everything was the same, the same sense of melting, of intoxication, the same rising, the same hunger for skin. She was lost in waves of pleasure, she could smell the pines again, the spray, and feel the summer sun. She squirmed against him, and all the time the same thought kept coming: *It's happening to me again.*

Afterwards, in the shower, he washed her body tenderly. Then, while she stood in her underpants cooking breakfast at the stove, he stood naked in the center of the room watching her.

"You've got good tits," he said in the sweetest voice she'd ever heard him use. "And you've got one terrific ass."

She turned, looked at him. He was smiling at her, shaking his head in wonder. "I think you're serious."

"I am."

She couldn't believe how happy she felt. His comment was vulgar, but it thrilled her just the same. Men weren't supposed to exclaim over women's bodies anymore, weren't supposed to refer to intimate parts as things. It was the sort of statement she'd expect to hear from a truck driver or a steeplejack. But she loved it, loved the idea of being thought of that way. It had never occurred to her that her tits were anything much, and as for her ass, she'd never dared hope it would catch a male eye.

"A terrific ass—you really mean that?"

"Great ass," he said. "Just looking at it turns me on."

"And my tits are good."

"Not great but good." He moved against her, caressed her breasts as she fried their bacon, gently stroked her nipples. "I like them. Maybe they are great after all." She felt him grow hard against her buttocks. "See how you make me horny. After we eat let's screw again." He paused. "I love you, Penny. I love you, and I always did."

They spent the rest of the morning in her bed doing things she'd barely fantasized before. He made ingenious love to her, and taught her how to love him back. Without his asking she did the unthinkable and took his cock into her mouth. *He's wonderful,* she thought. *He makes me feel desired, alive.* Afterwards they lay on her window seat—hot, perspiring bodies. She lay her head down on his chest. *Yes, he's gorgeous,* she thought.

That afternoon they took a taxi to his hotel. She waited downstairs while he packed his bags, then gave him money to settle his bill. They taxied back to her place and found space to store his things.

"You're sure you want me to move in?" he asked.

"You already have," she said.

She told him about her job, about Dr. Bowles and the strange people with cats he'd be running into on the stairs. She told him about the neighbors she'd observed from her window seat, about the slushpile manuscripts she'd been reading so many months, her ambition to discover new great authors, her depressions and her efforts to run them off. She talked on and on and he listened to her, the two of them sprawled out on her bed. Every once in a while he would reach out for her, to touch one of her legs or thighs or cheeks, or to stroke her hair.

"God, I love you, babe," he said during a moment

when she paused. "You're so special—I've been waiting so long to tell you that. And so beautiful. You're so beautiful, too."

She stroked his body and marveled at its perfection just as she had three years before in Maine. "Do I really have a great ass?" she asked. And when he nodded she said: "Well, you have a great ass yourself."

He laughed. "That's what they used to tell me, when I auditioned for those films."

"And this?—" She fondled him. "Did you have to show them this?"

"Absolutely. When you try out for those things, you have to strip. If you're too big, it makes the men in the audience envious, and if you're small—forget it!"

She was amused. "So, what did they think of you?"

"They more or less agreed I was perfect."

She stroked him again. "Yes," she said, "I can see that. I agree."

They watched television. There was a "celebrity roast" and they hooted at all the corny jokes. They turned off the lights and drank wine in bed, then made love one more time in the strange light cast by the TV, pretending the applause of the studio audience was in appreciation of the beauty of their feat.

The next week the weather changed. The sweltering haze that had settled on New York so many weeks lifted, and the sky turned clear and blue. It was as if someone in the heavens had pulled a switch, and now suddenly it was autumn, the air was clear and clean, people wore sweaters as they walked their dogs, and the subways were bearable once again.

She ran with Jared every morning. They always gasped together when they reached the northeast tip of the reservoir and the city was revealed. "Let's go out there today, babe, and knock them dead," he'd say. "Yeah," she'd agree, "bring the city to its knees.'' His endurance was improving; after a while he was able to match her stride for stride. After their workouts they walked back home, arms tossed about each other's waists. Then they made love before they bathed, while their bodies were still hot and moist. She didn't think she'd like this very much at first, but very soon she found she did. She savored the idea that they were like animals, copulating creatures driven by demons in their genes. She'd look at his legs when they were running, the strength of his calves, the hairiness of his thighs, and think: *soon he'll fuck me, and I will fuck him back*. Where did such thoughts come from? She'd always been so repressed. Now she found herself savoring the most pungent words.

Afterwards, in the shower they'd soap each other between the legs. Once, with the water running hot, a thousand burning needles stabbing at her back, she knelt upon the tiles before him and, grabbing onto his legs, hard as pillars, while his strong fingers massaged her dripping hair, she sucked him until he came. He'd go down on her while she lay back on the bed staring at the ceiling, her head swinging in wild delirium side to side.

Sex was glorious, she decided. Just the notion of his hard, lean body on top of her filled her with desire. *I've missed so much,* she thought. *Now I must make up the time*.

When they'd scrubbed and dressed, he'd walk her to the subway stop at Eighty-Sixth. Waiting for her train she'd do her best to appear demure. She wanted people to see her as a well-dressed, reserved young business person pondering her schedule as she waited to go to work. When men tried to catch her eye—and now, it seemed, many men did—she'd turn away haughtily and think: *If only they knew what a fox I am; if only they knew how fabulously I've learned to screw*.

The autumn went well for her at B&A. She brought

in some young writers, signed up a couple of books. "You're doing OK, Chapman," MacAllister told her. "You look better now, too. Not so mousy as before."

After he said that she went straight to the women's room and stared at herself in the mirror. It was true. She didn't look drab anymore. There was something on her, a glow, and the haunted look, the look of a person afraid of being recognized, was gone.

I look good, she thought, and then she said it aloud: "I look like a girl who's getting screwed a lot."

Shocked at what she'd said, she looked around to be certain no one else had heard. Where did such notions come from, she wondered, such language, such vulgarity? From Jared, perhaps, or perhaps from deep within herself, a dark place at the center of her being, a place she was just beginning to explore.

She and Jared went often to the movies and to plays at little theaters in the Village. One night they attended a by-invitation-only nude production of a Greek tragedy held on the upper floor of a warehouse in Soho, and then to a loft party afterwards given by one of Jared's friends. He was trying hard to find work, warming up all his old contacts, reporting dutifully to all the cattle calls, auditioning for everything, no matter how small the part. A couple of times he came close, but in the end the role would go to someone else. He'd get depressed, but she'd continue to encourage him. "You're going to make it," she'd tell him, and at last, in late October, it happened; he got a small part in an experimental workshop production, twenty-five dollars a week plus delicatessen sandwiches for lunch.

The director, he said, was a madman, and the playwright a raving egomaniac. Also, he said, the play didn't make any sense; it took place in the desert and also some farfetched "desert of the mind." But he didn't care. He was grateful to be working at last. No one in the cast bothered him about the Berring case, though they all knew who he was. His one regret, he told her, was that he wasn't earning very much. He felt bad living off her, he said, but she assured him he shouldn't worry about that, that her money was inherited, and as far as she was concerned he had as much right to it as she.

The same week that Jared got the part Lillian Ryan was finally promoted to assistant editor. Penny was relieved, for though she'd taken some pleasure in being promoted first, she'd found Lillian's resentment hard to take. They were still rivals, of course, out hustling agents and trying to sign up books, but their slushpile days were over, and with that their competition cooled.

It was a beautiful autumn, the best that she remembered, the best, many people said, that New York had seen in years. It was a pleasure to live in the city, to jog around the reservoir early in the morning, to watch the days get shorter and Central Park turn gold and red. Sometimes, from as far as a block away, she could smell the aroma of the burning chestnuts sold at the stand in front of the Metropolitan Museum. The clarity of the air amazed her, the crispness, sharpness of the light. All sense she'd had of oppression and danger in the city dissolved in her joy in being alive.

On Saturdays she and Jared explored on foot, visiting the Madison Avenue galleries, taking the bus to the Cloisters and to the Botanical Gardens in the Bronx. Sometimes, when there was no movie they wanted to see, they'd wander over to Lincoln Center at night, sit by the fountain, watch the people pouring in and out of the theaters, and stare up at the Chagall murals in the arches of the opera house. One Sunday they walked all the way from Eightieth Street to City Hall, then crossed the Brooklyn Bridge on foot and spent the afternoon on the Brooklyn Heights esplanade gazing back at Lower Manhattan, its magical towers and spires.

As the autumn deepened, the leaves changed and fell, the city became truly idyllic and Penny thought: *I am happier now than I have ever been.* At last, she thought, it had happened; that lover she'd been waiting for, who would enter her life suddenly and swirl her away, had come, and he wasn't even a stranger but someone she'd known before. He'd reappeared as if by magic. They were together; he made her cheeks glow and her eyes brighten with delight. No more depressions, no more dreads. Now she didn't wait in movie lines alone or walk the streets envying others, people in pairs, lovers holding hands. Now she too was paired, had a lover, walked hand in hand, slept against the warmth of another body, was kissed and stroked and adored. Sometimes, looking through a restaurant window and seeing a girl sitting at a table eating alone, she thought of all the drab years she'd endured and how her time now had come.

*Thinking a lot about Child, lately—
wondering what's in her head. Why did
we turn out the way we did, me as me
and she as she? Could things have been
reversed? What would that be like? Hard
to imagine, but I wouldn't wish my life on
her, yet I feel she's studying me so she
can imitate me, as if I'm worth imitating,
as if my life is anything but the purest
shit. JESUS. Yes, I feel she'd take my
life if she could. I fear for her, for all of
us. The world's merciless, love's hard
and dangerous and everything goes flop-
doodle in the night—*

SUDDENLY NO task was too small or menial
for Lillian Ryan. Could she help Penny with some extra
typing? She was going out for coffee—would Penny
like some, too? She left notes on Penny's desk, telephone messages signed with drawings of a smile as if
to confirm what a happy pleasure it had been to take
them down. Penny assumed that having been humbled
by her less rapid promotion, Lillian was trying to re-

form herself by showing sincerity and good will. But one day early in November another motive emerged, one that caught Penny off her guard.

That morning Lillian arrived at the office and announced she'd quit smoking cigarettes. "I know it irritates you," she said, as if perhaps Penny's irritation had brought the decision on, "and I've decided to take up jogging, too."

Penny was pleased; she detested the smell of exhaled smoke and was disgusted by the ashtrays around their cubicle overflowing with Lillian's lipstick-stained butts.

"Got to give up coffin nails," Lillian said. "Got to get in shape. Taking a week in Jamaica this January. Want to look good on the beach." She raised a corner of her blouse, pinched a roll of skin, then turned so Penny could see it too. "Look at this! A real spare tire, right? How long do you think it'd take me to run it off?"

"Probably not by January," Penny said, "but you might be able to make a dent."

"Sure hope so. I'm tired of dating creeps. Last spring when I went to Tahiti all I could come up with was that *ape*."

Lillian had written a little story about her adventure in Tahiti that had been published in a feminist magazine. She'd met a man at a Club Med village with whom she'd spent a pleasant week swimming, canoeing, playing tennis and telling jokes. But all had turned sour the final night when Lillian had invited him to her cabana for a drink. She was in the midst of changing into a caftan when, quite unexpectedly, he'd lunged. "Didn't he understand," she wrote, "that I was a *liberated woman,* that changing clothes in front of him was an act of trust, not an invitation to treat me like a whore?" Her article had inspired a lot of ridicule around the office, but the derision did not matter to Lillian. She was now, she proclaimed, a "published writer," which meant that special value should now be given to her views.

At noon that day she asked if Penny were free for lunch. "Sure," said Penny. The invitation surprised her. "Sure. OK, if you want."

"Great. You can fill me in on jogging. I've got a couple of ideas, too, so maybe you'll let me pick your brains." Lillian led her to a fancy-looking bistro, the sort of place a senior editor might take a successful author he was trying to impress.

"Looks kind of expensive," Penny said.

"So what? This one's on me."

They ordered Bloody Marys at the bar, then Lillian twisted in her seat to see who else was there. "Look, there's Henderson, trying to steal that Jackie Susann type away from Dell. She lives in Dallas, pounds out crap and makes a mint. Watch Henderson play footsy. What an operator he is. Next thing he'll have her out to his place in Connecticut, get her in the sack, steal her from Dell, then quit B&A and take her to some other joint."

Penny was impressed. She asked Lillian how she knew so much.

"Wire myself in. Stay late and read the files. Sneak around and look on people's desks. Get chummy with the secretaries. Hang around the corridors and listen in to calls. No one ever tells you anything, so you got to hustle information for yourself. I'm developing sources outside the house now too. I'm not planning to stay at B&A forever, you know."

After they were seated she got Penny onto the subject of running, asked a lot of questions about shoes and leotards and stretching exercises, all the obvious stuff that was explained in dozens of running books. "It's getting colder now. I'd better get over to Saks and look at warm-up suits. All I want to do is lose some weight, not join the sweaty undershirt crowd."

Penny thought of making love with Jared, the two of them dripping with sweat. Somehow it was hard for her to imagine Lillian reveling in perspiration. She was the antiseptic type who'd paint on lipstick before going out to run.

Near the end of the lunch, when they were waiting for dessert, Lillian suddenly changed the subject. There wasn't any transition or pause; she started out with a sentence about running and ended with the non sequitur comment that she didn't think the nonfiction novel was dead, the way MacAllister had said it was, at an editorial meeting several weeks before.

"So everyone's done those things—so what? *In Cold Blood, Blood and Money,* and *Helter Skelter* are classics, plus I don't know how many more. People eat them up. The stories are true, and all the detail, the procedural part, there's an endless fascination with that. I got a call the other day from an investigative reporter. He's done a lot of police reporting. Now he wants to do a book. Since this guy's really talented, I started thinking up ideas. We had drinks a few times, kicked some things around, but nothing we thought of really stuck. He kept telling me 'I need an angle, a way in, someone who's never talked before,' and I was thinking, well"—she locked into Penny's eyes then lowered her voice to a whisper—"I was thinking, *Jesus Christ,* here I am sitting right on top of something, something so big it could maybe make a real killing for everyone involved."

Lillian lowered her voice even more to imply extreme confidentiality. "Look—here I am sitting next to you all these months, sharing the cubicle, practically living with you, if you see what I mean. We're like sisters. We both came to B&A the same time, we've had our ups and downs, but we're both in the same boat, anxious to get on with our careers. So I was thinking: nobody, *but nobody* knows more about your sister's story than you. The background. The bringing up. All the details, those little nuances that can make this sort of book so good. You know the leads, who to see, who to talk to, *everything*. I mean you're an absolute goldmine just waiting to be tapped.''

Penny felt unnerved. She couldn't imagine being party to a book like that.

"You and I could edit it together, maybe work up a proposal freelance, then shop it around. If Mac's interested—great. But he's going to have to *pay*. If he can't come up with the right sort of dough, we can quit and go half a dozen other places where they'll snap it up real fast.''

"Listen, Lillian—is this why you invited me to lunch?''

"Don't you see? You know *everything*, and with this writer it could really come alive. *Your* point of view, everything *you* always wanted to say. People still talk about it, you know. Everyone at the office— they're fascinated by the case. People haven't forgotten. They'll see this thing, hear about it and think: 'Yeah, I remember that. Who really killed her? What really happened anyhow?' ''

"Lillian—''

"I'm telling you . . .''

"Listen to me.''

"—could be *very big*.''

"Will you just shut up, Lillian. Will you just please shut up.''

"Sorry. Guess I got carried away. But you see what I'm talking about, the scale—''

"Shut up!"

Lillian finally caught the anger in her voice, because she suddenly snapped her mouth closed, then reached into her purse for a cigarette.

"Oh, shit,'' she said after she'd lit it. "I really was going to quit.'' She started to put it out, then stopped and took another drag. "What the hell? I guess one more won't do me that much harm."

Penny just stared at her, appalled by her venality, her crude attempt at manipulation, the transparency of all her attempts to ingratiate herself over the past few weeks. "You must really take me for a fool," she said.

"Huh? Take it easy. What's the matter anyway? You think I'm trying to get the story away from you? I'm talking about a fifty-fifty split."

"You really don't understand, do you?"

"Actually I think I'm pretty savvy."

"Good, because I'm only going to say this once."

"What?"

"I think your idea stinks."

"Don't you want to meet the writer?"

"Absolutely not."

"Well, think about it. I bet you change your mind." She suddenly stopped fidgeting with her cigarette, stared with deep curiosity into Penny's eyes. "Funny— I didn't think you'd take it this way at all."

"You miscalculated. Maybe we're not 'like sisters' the way you thought."

"Oh, cut the bullshit, Penny. I know what's going down. Everybody knows. The whole office. You think we don't know who calls you all the time, meets you downstairs after work? Someone told me he's even moved in. I mean, talk about taking people for *fools*—"

Penny pushed away her plate of chocolate mousse. "I can't believe I'm listening to this."

Lillian took a deep breath. "Like I said, Pen—everybody knows you're shacked up with Evans. You really ought to think it through. What's *that* all about? What are the *implications,* if you see what I'm talking about."

Penny pushed back her chair. *"Leave me alone,"*

she said, her voice trembling, her hands shaking too. She strode out of the restaurant. On the street she paused, then walked around the block to quiet her nerves. She'd have to face Lillian through the afternoon, would have to sit beside her, only a foot or so away, and transact her business as if a confrontation hadn't taken place. *Implications*—it was pretty clear what she meant. Oh, yes, the *implications:* that she and Jared were in the thing together; that one or the other of them had killed Suzie and then they both had covered up; that now that a decent interval had passed they'd felt it was safe to resume their affair. Lillian said the whole office knew. People were buzzing about it, thinking the worst as people always did. How naive of her to think she could have a private life, that people would ever leave her alone.

Lillian was cool through the afternoon, distant but polite. Penny envied her sang-froid, for she herself still felt tense and hurt. One time, when she came back from the women's room, she found Lillian whispering into the phone, cupping the mouthpiece with her hand. Lillian left soon after that, then reappeared just before five o'clock.

"Sorry I upset you," she announced from the door, after clearing her throat. "I really didn't think my little idea would set you off."

"Let's just drop it, all right?"

"Sure. Fine with me. It was just an idea anyway." She lit a cigarette. "Look at me—smoking again. Just a bundle of nerves. Well—see you tomorrow." She waved cheerfully and left.

Penny waited until she was sure Lillian was gone. Then she did something she'd never done before in her life: She opened the drawers of Lillian Ryan's desk and started rummaging around.

There was all sorts of junk in there, bits of paper with unidentified phone numbers, a half-eaten Hershey bar, even a wad of used tissues bearing lipstick stains. In the center drawer she found a file folder marked "Ideas." She opened it and riffled through the papers until she found what she was looking for: a single, long yellow page from a legal pad entitled "Berring Case." She read the notes scrawled out in Lillian's hand: "$100,000 advance. $25,000 expenses for investigators. LR, author-editor—80%. PC—20% for full release."

The "investigative reporter" was to be Lillian herself, and as for the "fifty-fifty split," that seemed to have been improvised over lunch.

There wasn't much else, a crude outline, some lurid chapter headings, a few tentative titles—*Death in the Poolhouse; Murder in Maine; To Kill the Heiress*—scrawled out on the back. It was disgusting, worse than she'd imagined, a cheap attempt to market Suzie's death. She replaced the folder, then noticed something else, carbons of some letters Lillian had written to agents initialed LR/pc at the bottom, as if Penny were a typist and Lillian her boss. *What a bitch,* she thought.

She was disappointed in Jared's reaction—he didn't seem outraged. "Just relax," he told her. "Who cares? She's just trying to make herself a buck."

"But don't you see how exploitive she is?"

"Sure I see. But that's her problem, not yours."

"I'd say it could be our problem if she ever does the book."

"But she can't do it. She knows she's not going to get anywhere with you, so she'll have to drop it, and that's the end."

She had expected him to be angry. He didn't even think it was so terrible that Lillian had put her initials on her letters in lower case. He said everyone did things like that; it was the sort of thing ambitious, pushy people did.

"But *you* wouldn't do anything like that."

"Maybe. If I really wanted to land a part. People screw people. That's how the world works. Publishing's no different. When they try to screw you you can always screw them back."

"Like how?" she asked. "How can I screw her back?"

"I don't know." He laughed. "Put itching powder in her jogging shorts. Put glue on her typewriter keys."

"You're making fun of me."

"I'm sorry you're upset—that's about all I feel. And if anybody's going to do a book I think it should be me. But there's nothing I can write—that's the trouble. The only person who knows what happened is the guy who did her in. I'm not exactly holding my breath waiting for him to come forward, though I've thought about that a few times—what might happen if he did."

"We'd be free of it. The case would be closed and we'd be free."

"We *are* free. Don't you see? This whole thing about living under a cloud—all that's in your head."

Maybe he's right, she thought, though Lillian's comment about the "implications" upset her still. She'd always had a fantasy that someday there'd be a similar crime, another girl would be murdered and this time the "intruder" would be caught. He'd confess to having murdered Suzie, and then, finally, the whole miserable case would be closed.

Lillian was perfectly correct the next few days though there were more of those cupped-hands-over-the-telephone-mouthpiece routines, and coverings-up-of-pages-in-the-typewriter when Penny walked by her desk. She was obviously cooking up a great number of schemes and guarding all her secrets as an ambitious young editor should. They didn't talk much, though Lillian mentioned she'd gotten up early and run a couple of times around her block, and that she hoped the effort would soon begin to burn off flab. Penny nodded, then turned back to her work. The permutations of Lillian Ryan's flesh didn't interest her very much.

She'd nearly forgotten the whole ugly business when, a few days later, she returned home to find Jared lying on the window seat depressed. He barely greeted her. When she asked what was wrong, he handed her a copy of *Backstage,* the actor's weekly, opened to a middle page where a small item was circled in ink.

"Jared Evans," she read, "exonerated defendant in the famous Berring murder case, is back at work in New York playing a small role in the Soho Workshop production of *Deserta.* The former film actor is, according to one member of the cast, 'quiet and hardworking.' One female member of the company said 'at first it was kind of creepy, but the guy's really serious and we all think he's OK.' The experimental production will open in another week."

"Well, that's not so bad," Penny said.

"That's not what the playwright thinks."

"Why? He knew who you were."

"Sure. But he says this'll distract from his play. He says now people will come to see me. His 'masterpiece' will turn into a freak show. Something like that."

"That's ridiculous."

"That's what I told him."

"What did he say?"

"He turned his back and walked away."

She touched his shoulder. "Worried?"

"I could get canned."

"I don't think that's going to happen."

"Yeah," he said. "Maybe not."

Jared didn't say much the next few days except that everyone at the Workshop was acting edgy, and that there was a lot of whispering going on. The next morning she'd barely settled down at her desk at B&A when he phoned her to tell her he'd been fired. "When I came in for early rehearsal," he said, "they were all sitting around looking at the *News*. There's a big item in David Denver's column. Seems it's syndicated, sixty-eight papers coast-to-coast."

He was calling from a phone booth. He gave her the number so she could call him back. When she did, he read her the excerpt from Denver's column. It was so vicious she wanted to scream, but he read it in a flat monotone as if it were ordinary news: "Guess who's making the same shadow these days at an Upper East Side apartment, and around the running paths of Central Park? Jared Evans, accused killer, has been seen jogging hand in hand with Penny 'Chapman' Berring, sister of the slain Suzie. You remember the case—the love-triangle abruptly ended one night by a pair of gardener's shears dripping with sexy Suzie's blood. It looks like the former snuff-porn star is back to his old tricks, worming his way into this fine aristocratic family again. Be careful, Penny! Or do you know what you're doing after all?"

"God, that's horrible," she said. "But they can't fire you for that."

"They did. Fifty bucks and a handshake. They already had somebody lined up to take my place. I'm sick about it. Think I'll take in a movie and then go home." '

After he hung up she went down to the lobby of the B&A building to buy the paper and read the item for herself. It seemed even worse to her in print than it had sounded on the phone, the sort of venomous gossip that had been out of fashion for several years but had recently started coming back. Just before noon she phoned Jared. "How do you feel?"

"Not too bad now," he said. "I was kind of expecting to get the axe, and the play's no loss. It'll probably fold in a week."

Again she was struck by his passivity, the fatalistic way he accepted so raw a deal. They talked awhile, then she asked him about Denver, how the columnist had managed to connect them up.

"Probably got a tip," he said. "They sometimes pay for that sort of stuff."

"Who knew about us?"

"Could have been anyone. We must have been seen jogging together a hundred times. Somebody probably recognized us and phoned the tidbit in."

But Penny couldn't get the notion out of her head that Lillian Ryan had been Denver's source. It was too pat—first the item in *Backstage,* and then Denver's connecting piece about them jogging hand in hand. It was the sort of thing Lillian might do to pressure Penny into helping with the book. After lunch, still angry at the thought, she confronted Lillian by slapping the column down on her desk.

"Bound to come out sooner or later," Lillian said. "You can't keep a cat in the bag in New York."

"Of course you didn't have anything to do with letting the cat out."

"Just what's that *supposed* to mean?"

"How much does the Denver office pay for this kind of crap?"

"Now look!" For a moment Penny thought she was going to spring up and attack her, but then Lillian settled back in her chair and laughed. *"Wow*—you're really subtle. I don't suppose you'd believe me if I swore I didn't have anything to do with this."

"Is that what you're saying?"

Lillian smiled. "You wouldn't believe me no matter what I said. But one thing comes to mind, and it might be worth your thinking about. If you worked on that book with me, got your side of the story out, you'd probably be able to clear the air and be free of this sort of stuff once and for all."

Penny shook her head. "You never give up, do you?"

"No," Lillian said, laughing, "I guess I don't."

"Well, I think you're going to have to now."

"Really, Penny? Why's that?"

Lillian was sneering. Penny thought of Robinson, the way he'd sneered and the way she'd finally found the nerve to put him down. She paused a moment, then looked Lillian directly in the eyes. "Those letters you're sending out with my initials—I think Mac would probably fire you if he knew. So just lay off, Lillian. No more little games, all right?"

Lillian was scared. She nodded and turned away. Penny felt wonderful. She'd stood up for herself, played "hardball" the way her father did. He would have approved and so would Suzie, she thought. "Get them before they get you," they used to chant. "Kick ass today, Daddy-O," Suzie used to say when she kissed him before he left for work.

A memory: I'm ten years old and a real pain in the ass. All day I'm naughty and selfish and rude. French Slave Girl, the au pair mother has brought over to take care of us and teach us French, has gone to her room to pack her bags. "Elle est insupportable," she mutters, referring to me. "Insupportable!"

Child's building an elaborate structure out of blocks. She's been working on it for hours, and it's been a crummy Sunday for me, and she's enjoying herself, and I'm feeling like a bitch, so, just to spread the misery around a little more I march into her room and kick it down. KICK. KICK. KICK, until every little brick is knocked across the floor. Child starts to wail. Daddy-O has finally had enough. He's going to punish me. I CAN'T believe it. He's never raised a hand to me before. But suddenly there I am being swatted right in front of Child. She's not crying anymore. I AM. I'm yelling Holy Murder. The humiliation is worse than the pain. When it's over I run to my room and slam the door.

That evening I refuse to come down to dinner. Finally Daddy-O comes to me. He walks in, sits down next to me on the bed, tells me he loves me, pats my tear-stained cheek. We talk. He asks me if I'm sorry. "Sure," I say, "I'm sorry all right. I'm sorry I got spanked." "Yes," he says, "I understand that. But I had to punish you. Let's forgive each other now." "Next time," I suggest, "why don't you punish me with kisses?" We laugh, embrace, then he kisses me good night.

JESUS! My ass has been a pillow for fucked-out heads, something to pat and stroke and lay one's head upon. (To the last one who asked if he could spank me I said: "Try it, buster, and I'll play badminton with your balls!") Jamie tells me my ass is one of my finest assets. He says he wants to photograph it close-up with a special lens that will reveal its texture. He'll make the curve into an horizon, catch the down in cross-light and make it glow. "It'll be like something in outer space," he says, "some new galaxy which everyone would want to explore. Then they'll read the title and double take. I'll simply call it 'Suzie's Ass'—"

HER FATHER called.

"Hi, kiddo."

"Daddy?"

"Course, dummy. Who else calls you 'kiddo'?" She imagined him, jacket off, trim figure encased in well-cut vest, pacing around his office with a squash racket slashing at the air, turning every so often toward the speaker phone on his desk. "Ready to take me on?"

"Play squash?"

"What else, kiddo? Want to play?"

"Sure."

"OK. Noon tomorrow. Then we shower and come back here for chow."

Their game was fierce. Her father looked good—fit and hard, agile and athletic—as he batted the ball against the wall. It was hard to believe he hadn't spent his youth playing racket sports; that, in fact, he had been the son of working-class parents and had spent his summers on construction gangs. Still he played with the verve of an Ivy League athlete, and he gave Penny no quarter—he played to win, and he shut her out.

His hair was still slick from his shower as they walked together through the lobby of the Racquet Club. His silver sideburns caught the sun and glowed as they stepped into the Cadillac limousine waiting by the curb. She could sense the aura of his power as chief executive of a multinational corporation from the obsequiousness of the doorman and the deference of the chauffeur. *He's like a king,* she thought as they drove to Chapman International, a glass and steel skyscraper at Park Avenue and Forty-Eighth. A uniformed lobby attendant ushered them into a special elevator so they could ride to the executive floor nonstop. His reception suite gleamed with glove-soft black leather, pewter fixtures, tables of darkened glass. Electronic office machines clicked and hummed as he led her to his office, which was dominated by an oval conference table and an abstract sculpture of gleaming steel.

He left her there for a few minutes while he attended to some business in an adjoining room. While he was gone she inspected the photographs and framed memorabilia arrayed on the wall. They told the story well, she thought, beginning with a picture of her grandfather, Howard Chapman, standing in front of his old Stamford, Connecticut, plant, home of the original Chapman Plow. Her father stood beside him—he must have been twenty-two or twenty-three at the time—an eager-looking boyish young man who'd come to Chapman as a salesman, then quickly caught her grandfather's eye. It couldn't have been long after that, she realized, that her parents got married, Howard Chapman died, ownership of Chapman passed to her mother, and her father began the dizzying series of mergers and labyrinthine corporate moves that turned the small plow manufacturing firm into Chapman International.

There were photos of her father inspecting the company's facilities overseas, one at a pulp mill in Brazil, another at a textile plant in Taiwan. There were pictures of him with an open-shirted Richard Nixon on a golf course somewhere in California, and another toasting the President of Korea at a dinner in Seoul several years before. The cover portrait that had appeared on *Business Week* was framed, and his honorary doctorate from the University of Minnesota praising him for "humanizing the assembly line, working for a reconciliation between the needs of capitalism and the highest aspirations of the human heart." There he was with his boyish grin receiving an award from the Association of American Manufacturers, and, again, standing with Barbara Walters, the two of them beaming, after an appearance on "Today."

But it was the family pictures that interested her the most, one of her parents' wedding, her grandfather looking worried, hovering behind; another of the four of them, her mother, her father, Suzie and herself, poised on a mountain top near Zurich where they'd vacationed one winter when she was nine or ten. They appeared the perfect image of a happy family, the parents' arms wrapped about each other, the two daughters, hair in braids, beaming at the lens. *We looked so similar then,* she thought. *The two of us were almost like twins.* When had the separation begun, she wondered; when had she and Suzie chosen their separate ways?

There was another picture, and in it everything was changed. Their father had taken it on his sailboat, she remembered, one afternoon in Maine. Suzie was a graceful seventeen at the time, looking ravishing, happy, beautiful, one hand raised characteristically to brush away a lock of hair. Penny, an awkward fifteen, was staring at Suzie, studying her, a mixture of envy and admiration and perplexity in her eyes.

She didn't hear him come back into the office and was startled when she heard him whisper just behind her ear.

"Jesus, I miss her." He was standing very close. "Some nights when I pass her room, I go in and sit on her bed and think about her, the kind of special gal she was. So vibrant, full of energy—so gay. Don't you miss her, kiddo? Well—of course you do."

She turned to face him. She was so used to other images of him, grim, square-jawed, putting on his public face, too proud to show his feelings, wanting always to be recognized as strong and hard. But there were other sides to him, too, she knew, vulnerable sides, and other aspects she'd never understood. She'd never forgotten the sight of him once in Maine when she'd seen him burning trash, staring into the flames, the fire dancing crazily in his eyes, their sockets cavernous, his features twisted, his jaw stuck out like a caricature of a warrior preparing for attack.

They took the short walk through the corridors to the executive dining room and were seated by the maitre d'hotel in a private section partitioned from the rest. The silverware was modern; everything understated, sleek. The place had a hushed and cool quality, as did everything at Chapman, even the view. The window glass shut out every sound, allowing them to gaze upon a silent city, to watch New York perform in pantomime.

"That was a good match, kiddo. Does me good to work out. And don't feel bad about losing, either. I regularly chop up men half my age." He was looking at her, she thought, without seeing her at all. "Your grandfather Chapman had a saying: 'A gentleman never sweats, except when he exercises and makes love to his wife.' " He smiled. "Grand guy. I think he'd be proud to see what we've done with what he left us, the way we've built up Chapman Plow—" She could hear other executives talking in other sections of the dining room, could hear deep male laughter, businessmen's laughter, could smell the smoke of their cigars. "Of course you never knew him. He could be a hard man sometimes, stubborn as hell. Your mother takes after him lots of ways."

A waiter brought their cantaloupe. He scooped out a spoonful, chewed it discreetly, then went on. "He didn't believe in borrowing. I spent years quarreling with him over that. You've got to borrow big if you're going to expand, I told him, but he just shook his head, said it made him nervous to be in debt. He left your mother all the stock, so then I had to fight the battle again. Happily she saw reason, finally let me handle things. Now she's a very rich woman, I'm not too badly off myself, and neither are you, kiddo, though no one would know it considering that dumpy place you live." He grinned at her.

"Do you want me to move into a doorman building, too?" she asked.

"No. I don't especially care about that, unless that's what you want to do. It's not that that bothers me, kiddo. It's your new roommate, and *he* bothers me quite a bit."

He spoke very softly, as he always did when he was mad, in hushed mellifluous tones. In *Business Week* she'd read how they scared his subordinates and could make the business world shake, how he always lapsed into a soft whispering manner of speech at those moments when he'd decided to impose his will.

"You heard?"

"Of course I *heard*. It's no secret. It's all over the papers. They put the clippings on my desk." He took another bite of cantaloupe, then pushed away his plate. "Our PR people have gotten inquiries. We will confirm or deny, that sort of stuff."

"I'm sorry, daddy—"

"We've had him under surveillance. Our security staff's been keeping tabs on him ever since the trial."

She put down her spoon. "I thought you were going to look for the other guy, the guy who ran away."

"Sure. And I did, kiddo. Spent a lot of time and money on that. But no tracks, no leads. Had to give it up."

"I don't—"

"What the hell do you think you're doing, Penny?" This time he was looking right into her eyes. "*I mean of all the goddamn punks.*"

He was glaring at her, that same crazed glare she'd

seen that time when he was burning trash. She could feel his fury; she could see it in the hard iron-gray steeliness of his eyes.

"He's not a punk, daddy," she said, trying to keep her voice level, not wanting to assert herself too much, trying to match his cold anger.

His expression seemed to relax a little. "Well, kiddo, in a sense I suppose he isn't. Maybe I used the wrong word. I could think of a few others I'd like to call him, but they wouldn't be polite, and then you might get offended, and I wouldn't want that at all. But right now he's back in our lives. He gets off a bus from Texas and a couple weeks later he's jogging alongside you. Now there's stuff in the papers, rumors going around. I'm just waiting for the market to react. A little 'adjustment,' you know—that's what they call it. A couple of points down when the insiders pick this up."

"Aren't you exaggerating? I don't see what this—"

"No, I'm not exaggerating, and of course you don't understand. If you understood you wouldn't be doing what you're doing. I give you credit, at least, for *that*." He shook his head. "We're not Chapman Plow anymore where we can say to hell with everybody else, do what we please, go our own way. We're public. Among us we hold damn near half a million shares, but there're other people who have even more, and that's what I'm worried about, you see. There're a couple groups watching us. There's been a lot of takeover talk. A little reaction on the market and people start asking questions. There's gossip, a loss of confidence in management, and it doesn't help that your mother's more or less incompetent, and the word's getting out on that. Our debt position's not too terrific at the moment. I've taken some chances, and now we're facing a confiscation in Brazil. They could really put me through the wringer on that, force down our stock, then make their move. I'd fight, of course. I've always fought when I've been squeezed. But then their natural reaction would be to play hardball, drag in the family, get the story out on your mother, dig up Christ knows what. It could get very messy. Very messy indeed."

She couldn't make much sense of what he'd said. "I don't understand all this."

"No," he said, "I don't suppose you do. I'm talking about articles, magazines, more of this gossip column garbage. How would you like it if someone wrote you were spitting on your sister's grave? Someone's sniffing around already mumbling about a book. How would you like to see Suzie smeared all over the headlines again, pictures of you and your boyfriend running around the reservoir, maybe even snuzzling a little in the Ramble, a big goddamn lovestruck smile stuck smack in the middle of your face?"

He was so angry and yet so controlled she felt as if she were in the middle of a nightmare. She looked down, saw her hands shaking in her lap.

"—That's all we need right now."

There was a long silence then. She watched him bone his fish, his movements surgical, precise.

"You still think he killed her, don't you?" she asked suddenly, regretting the question the moment the words escaped her lips.

"I confess that possibility does occasionally cross my mind."

"You never had anyone looking for the intruder. You never believed me at all."

"Oh, I *believed* you." She wanted to scream at the way he said it. "I still do. I believe you really *thought* you saw somebody else. Not in a million years did I ever think you were insincere. But until the police find this so-and-so and get him convicted, I'm betting on

104

your current boyfriend, and that's the problem, you see.''

Yes, she thought, *I see.*

"It's all about money, then, isn't it?"

"Sure, kiddo. Money, justice—you name it—you tell me where's the bottom line. But in case you're thinking I'm a monster, and I guess that's what you're saying in a way, let me tell you it comes down to a lot more than that for me. It's *you. Your* life. I've lost one daughter, it hurt a lot, and I'm not all that anxious to lose another." He looked her in the eyes again. "Got me, kiddo? Getting the picture now?"

They spent the remainder of the lunch discussing her mother. He urged her to come out to Greenwich for a weekend visit. He said he thought it might lift her mother's spirits if she did.

"I'm not really capable of doing much for her in that regard anymore," he said. "I just wish we could find somebody who could keep her off the sauce."

It was all very civilized, she thought, as she stood in the executive elevator alone, hurtling to the street. But out on Park Avenue, when she looked back at Chapman International, the building's severity, its sharp angles and polished lines, she was appalled. It was brutal. And she thought: it wasn't civilized at all, the squash game, the lunch—they were hard and nasty and cruel.

Suddenly, for one bewildering moment, she found herself wishing she'd been killed instead of Suzie. *Then maybe he'd miss me*, she thought.

Jamie's got this thing for wet. "The wet look." He wants to shoot models with their T-shirts wet so the fabric sticks to their stomachs and their boobs glow through the cloth. He likes their hair wet, too, and sweat on their faces, and wet spots under their arms. He tells them to run in place. "Work up a sweat, kids," he yells, "get yourselves wet while I move around the lights."

WET. Everything has to be WET. Wants the skin to glisten, cream on their bare arms, cream on their calves so they're shiny and catch the light. WET! WET! Every other fucking word is WET! Finally I figure it out. WET like a woman. WET like a pussy, lubricated, full of need. I ask him if I'm right. "You're learning," he says. "WET and creamy and shiny and eager, just like you, Suze, just like you." I give him the finger and he laughs. "Just wait till after work."

Wow! Can't wait! All afternoon I think about it. So just when everybody's gone home, and I'm all ready for it, already

WET, practically dripping in my pants,
this guy turns up at the door. "Oh,
Jamie," he squeals, "I've been twitching
my ass all the way down Madison just
thinking about what we're going to do."

"Yeah," he says, "well, we'll all get it
on together, OK?" "With HER?" squeals
the guy. "Sure. Why not?" says Jamie,
"she's a person, too. She's got her
needs." NEEDS! I can't stand it. NEEDS!
What the fuck does he know about my
NEEDS? By this time the queer and I
are glaring at each other. Then it hits
me: Jamie had all this planned.

I decide to play along. "Look," I say,
"I want to be reasonable about this. If
what's-his-name here—" "Dave."
"Yeah—well if Dave has been twitching
his ass for God knows how many blocks
down Madison, then far be it from me to
deprive him of his fantasy."

Dave looks kind of squeamish, but I'm
acting very relaxed so I figure he's
thinking maybe it won't be THAT
HORRIBLE after all. "Good girl," says
Jamie, "I've got some darkroom work.
Why don't you two go upstairs and get
acquainted. I'll join you in twenty minutes
or so."

We all grin at each other, then Dave
and I go up to the balcony. "Look," I say

soon as we're alone, "I can see you're really not too keen about sex with chicks." "Well," he says, "he and I did have a date." "He had a date with me, too," I tell him. "Obviously he was planning all along to get in the sack with us both. That's his screwy thing. He's into these bi scenes, and he manipulated both of us to set this one up. We can't let him get away with it. We have to teach him a lesson, so he doesn't pull this kind of crap again."

He loves it—he's a bitch just like me. "I'm going to fix HIM," he says, standing up, loosening his belt. "I'm going to jerk off right now onto this lovely suede couch. Thing must have cost him a couple of grand." "Thirty-five hundred," I tell him, "AT LEAST." I discreetly disappear into the powder room, then take a quick peek back. He's standing there, this dreamy expression on his face, pants down around his ankles, pumping away. Then this stuff starts spurting out and a mass of it goes spurt right onto the center of the couch. He moves a little and keeps pumping and shaking until he's got a pattern of drops going from one end to the other. Just then I hear Jamie coming up the spiral stairs. I move fast, get down on my *hands and knees and start sucking away. It's PERFECT. "What the hell is this?" Jamie screams. "And look at my couch. What have you animals done to my couch?" Dave pulls up his pants and zips up with great dignity. "Sorry, Jamie," he says, "guess we just got carried away."*

Jamie's completely freaked, still can't believe his eyes. "But my couch," he screams, "it's all wet, for Christ's sake." And thus he sets himself up. "Right," I clamor in, "that's the way you like things, isn't it? Wet—right Jamie Sweets? Wet! WET! WET!!!!"

And then I start to cry. Can't stop, just gushing on. Everyone's solicitous. "It was just a gag," says Dave. "Just a stunt." But I weep and weep—can't control myself. Jamie hugs me. "It'll be all right," he says. "Whatever it is it'll be all right—"

SHE WAS enraged at the way Jared responded when she told him what her father had said at lunch.

"Don't you see—he never had people looking for the guy. He had them watching you all these years. He says he's still 'betting' on you. You've been spied on.

Spied on. It's as if they're waiting for you to kill again so they can catch you and have you put away."

She was sitting in her window seat. He was on the floor, his arms wrapped around his knees. "Kind of a waste of time," he said.

"But the point is no one's looking for the creep."

"I never thought they were looking for him anyway."

"Didn't that bother you?"

He shrugged. "Everybody does his thing. Your father does his, and I do mine. That's the way things work."

She just couldn't fathom him, the resigned way he accepted things. She looked at him now, saw how different they were. He lived day to day, he didn't suffer and smolder the way she did.

"Maybe someday they'll catch him," he said.

"Sure," she said, "like they're really trying. The police, the FBI, Chapman security—they're out there conducting this big manhunt. They know who he is and there're wanted posters and now it's just a matter of time. Meantime you can't keep a job."

"Well, babe," he said, "Jesus Christ! We'll just have to live with it. Why get so riled up?"

"Because I don't *want* to live with it. For three years I *lived* with it. I walked around like a zombie, afraid of being recognized, afraid of people and what they thought. Then you came along. I didn't feel numb anymore. Now you say we've got 'to live with it' and 'everyone does his thing' and 'maybe they'll catch the guy' when you know damn well they never will." She wondered if he were moved by what she was saying. "How can you be like that? It's your life, too. You can't go around acting like a victim, getting fired because of some lousy column item, letting people say you got off on a technicality, or whatever they seem to think."

He was smiling. "Never seen you so upset before."

"Surprise you I'm so upset?"

"A little. You want to play hardball, don't you—play hardball with your old man?"

"I'd like to prove to him you didn't do it."

"How do you expect to do that?"

"I don't know."

"Play detective maybe?"

"No, Jared, not play detective."

"Well—sounds like the Hardy Boys to me."

"You're mocking me. Don't you care at all?"

"Not really. I got caught in the middle of something, and I almost went to jail. Now I don't give a shit what your father thinks, or anybody else." She wanted to scream at that. It was so dense, so self-absorbed.

"I'll tell you something else," he said after a pause, his voice taking on an edge. "I think you're hung up on your dad."

"What do you mean by that?"

"You care too much what he thinks. He says something crummy and you really care."

It was true. She *did* care. She knew that, knew she wanted to break through to him and inspire the warmth he and Suzie used to share.

"I'd like to show him he's wrong. That's important to me."

"I think it's more than that."

"What?"

"You think he really thinks I'm going to kill you, and there's a side of you that thinks he's just waiting for that to happen because when it does it'll prove that he's been right. You're so hung up on that it's pathetic. Then there's this thing you have about Suzie being his favorite and him thinking it was you who should have been killed since you were the one who had the relationship with me. That's bugging you, too."

She was stunned. "Maybe," she admitted, "maybe that's part of it."

"Sure it is. And he's got you on this guilt trip, making you almost wish it had been you, making you think you deserved it and Suzie didn't. That's what's so crazy—that somehow he's got you thinking that. Probably he doesn't mean to. I can't imagine him deliberately trying to put that in your head. But whatever the reason it's total bullshit, because the truth of the matter is that, in a way, Suzie *did* deserve it. She brought it on herself." He stopped, gazed at her. She sensed he had said more than he meant to. "Hey, let's get out of here. I feel all cooped up."

They decided to run even though it was late in the afternoon and she'd already played squash. Running seemed the only way to clear their heads. They changed and went outside. It was a good autumn day. In Central Park there were mothers wheeling baby carriages, youngsters walking dogs, old people bundled up in sweaters feeding pigeons or sitting on benches reading carefully folded copies of the *Times*.

"One thing I know," he said as they warmed up. "It wasn't any damn intruder. I never believed that. I told Schrader, but he said forget that part of it and concentrate on getting off. But it wasn't some stranger or a burglar or someone who just happened to stop by. Burglars don't walk into poolhouses, discover somebody sleeping there, pick up a pair of shears and stab a girl eighteen times."

She looked at him. He was talking about it at last. He had always avoided the subject when she brought it up; he had always said he didn't want to talk about it, or wasn't in the mood. Now, it seemed, he wanted to talk; she found that an encouraging sign. If he'd just tell her what happened that night, everything he could remember, then, maybe, she could begin to fill in the

112

blank spaces that made her own recollections so vague, so like a dream.

"No," he said as they started to run, "the way I see it, whoever killed her had to know that she was there. He probably came by to see her, then something happened and set him off. That's what I always thought. I never thought it was premeditated. But whoever did it knew her, knew she'd be in there and knew his way around. He knew that house, the woods, all the ways on and off the place—otherwise he couldn't have slipped in and out without a trace."

They ran in silence for a while. She felt her perspiration begin to rise, the rhythm of her heart increase. She was dying to ask him why he thought Suzie brought it on herself but was afraid he'd stop talking if she did.

"Sex," he said, "it had to have something to do with sex. That's what Suzie was all about anyway. The way she was carrying on that summer, the stuff she was doing, the way she treated us—like shit, you know—like we were all shit, and she was . . . well . . . whatever she thought she was. Maybe someone couldn't take it, got really pissed and—" He glanced at Penny. "It had to be a sex murder. Nothing else makes sense. It was someone who knew her, someone who was jealous or crazy or whacked out completely by what she was doing, what she'd done to him. Too many taunts. Too many humiliations. Couldn't take it finally so one night he steals in there thinking she might be alone. He didn't see me on the diving board, had no idea you were dozing by your window upstairs. So he creeps around the lawn and first thing you know he stumbles on those lousy shears. There were a couple of pairs of them around, remember? That fishy gardener, Tucker, with his iron-clad alibi—he was queer for shears. He had all these sets of them, remember, and he left them out all over the place even at night because he said your father was

113

rich, and it didn't matter if they got rusted because your father could always buy some more."

She remembered that—Schrader had brought it out. He'd been trying to throw suspicion on the gardener in order, he'd explained, to muddy up the jury's mind.

"So he finds those shears, OK. Maybe he stumbles on them by accident in the dark and reaches down to see what's biting against his shoe. He picks them up, but then what's he supposed to do? Can't heave them away—might wake somebody up. You see I'm guessing he just came by to gaze at her. He's in love with her, so that's not so strange. But if he wakes up the dogs or someone in the house he might get spotted, and that wouldn't be too cool. So what's he supposed to do with those shears? He doesn't want to drop them back on the ground because he might stumble on them again when he leaves. In the end he just picks them up and carries them toward the cottage thinking maybe he'll set them down on the concrete or someplace out in the open, out of everybody's way. Or maybe it just feels good to have some protection in his hand in the dark. OK, he's creeping around the cottage now, the shears in his hand, and then he's gazing in at her through the door. He watches her sleeping in there with that weird angelic expression she always wore when she wasn't putting on her act."

He was getting angry, she could see. His face looked tormented. She reached out, touched him, and that seemed to calm him down. He shook himself as if he were shaking off his anger. They ran like that for several paces, hand in hand.

"He's gazing in at her for a while, a few seconds maybe or twenty minutes—we don't know how long. I was stoned and you were dozing, so we don't know how long it was between the time she went back inside and the time she moaned." Penny nodded.

"OK, he's gazing in, and then he starts to react.

Suddenly there're all these conflicting feelings rising up inside. Like the way she treated him. The way she made him feel special, made him feel she cared. Then the way she kissed, the soft way she'd bring up her lips, the cushioning of them, the warm slow teasing lappings of her tongue. Jesus, she was something! Not like you—not at all. You're real. You're a person. She was just this *thing*, this hot teasing cunt. It's an ugly word but that's really what she was. *Cunt. Pure cunt.* Just oozing sex, oozing it out all over us. We saw her, felt her, kissed her, fucked her and then we were blind to everybody else. It wasn't that I ever consciously sat down and decided I was going to dump on you. There wasn't any choice. Suddenly she was there. I stopped thinking; everything centered on my cock. She could lead me around and there wasn't anything I could do about it. We were her victims. That's the way I felt." He sighed. "So this guy, this creep in the bushes, he's the same way. He's staring at her, gazing at her incredible angelic sleeping face, and he's thinking about all the things she's done to him, the way she's led him around, what a cock-teasing cunt she is, and all the pleasure he got out of it, too, and then the way she treated him afterwards, after she let him stick it to her a couple of times, the shitty way she made him feel. And he feels like such an asshole now, and what the hell, he asks himself, what the hell am I doing out here creeping around her cunty cottage, hiding in the shrubs at night, gazing in on her—I mean what kind of weird power does she have over me anyway? *Why am I doing this? Why am I being such a jerk?* And then something happens. He starts getting really mad. He starts hating her because she's turned him into such a jerk, and there's nothing he can do about it. And the worst part, the part that hurts the worst, is that he knows he's acting like an asshole, and if he knows it then, he knows, everybody else knows it too, and it's all her fault, it's all the fault of that fucking little cunt in there. So he starts to move in. He's not thinking 'I'm going to murder the bitch.' No, nothing like that. It's not a conscious, premeditated thing. It just starts happening to him, this weird crazy blend of fury and lust and lust for blood. Maybe he thinks he's just going to pounce on her. Like he's thinking 'I'm going in there and rape her. I'm going to fuck the shit out of her, then I'm going to slap her around a little and walk out of there and that'll be the end of it. Then I'll be free.' Maybe that's what's in his head—I don't know. Maybe he just wants to scare her or something innocent like that. Anyway he starts in, and he's still got the shears in his hand, and he's not thinking anymore, just crazy with this wild lust. Then before he knows it he's standing over her, and he can't control it anymore. It gets too powerful—I don't know why. Maybe the anger just gets too big. Something happens, though—something snaps for sure. Instead of his cock he plunges at her with the shears, and then it's all confused, he doesn't know what he's doing. It's just blind rage, hatred, lust, the whole bit combined, and he stabs her—*again*, and *again*, and *again*—''

They were running hard, pounding the path, nearly sprinting, and Penny looked at him and was scared. It was as if every time one of his feet hit the ground he was imagining he was stabbing Suzie, too.

*Why doesn't he pay attention anymore?
After everything, everything—why now
so cool? Doesn't he know that
forgiveness isn't necessary? That we
operate on another level? That we're
special people? Lawless people? That
when you're gods the rules don't
apply?—*

IT WAS strange the way his story, his imagined
tale of how Suzie had been killed, stuck with her over
the next few days. He seemed to understand it so well,
as if the emotions were part of him, as if he'd felt them
himself. There was something chilling about that, as
if, living with the crime all these years, he'd solved it
in his imagination, and now only lacked the killer's
name. If she hadn't seen that figure, seen the flashlight
beam and then the person who'd paused at the poolhouse door, she might think he understood the murder
too clearly, had solved it all too well.

But that was impossible. She *knew* he hadn't done
it. She'd *seen* the other man. Their stories were perfectly matched. It was all so strange as she tried to
play the moments back. She'd tried so many times,

117

and always the action had been the same: that rapidly moving light, that stranger pausing outside the door. Thinking of it was like watching a movie, fascinated by a horrible thing that was happening to someone else. She'd seen replays of boxing matches on TV when they'd played the knockout punch over and over in slow motion so the viewers could see the fist smash against the face, the mouth twist back in agony, the legs wobble, the body begin to slump. Over and over, slower and slower, until sometimes they froze the frame at the moment of supreme impact. What if Robinson was right and she had in fact blinked at a crucial instant—and had lost something, a definitive frame, a moment that could have told her who he was? Jared had to be right. It had to have been one of Suzie's lovers. But which one? *Which one?*

She could barely remember their faces, let alone their names. When she tried to recall them, she could only come up with a composite, someone whose first name was Ashton or Carter or Prescott, who went to Princeton or Dartmouth or Yale, whose hair was dirty-blond and whose body was tanned and sleek and lean, unlike the paunchier, hairier Bar Harbor townies who pumped the gas and mowed the lawns. She tried to list them, even wrote down several names as they came to mind but she knew the task was hopeless, that they'd been interchangeable even then.

What would Lillian Ryan's imaginary reporter friend do now, she wondered, if he were going to write a nonfiction book about the case? How would he go about it? How would he scrounge up their names? Lillian said he was looking for an inside source; she was supposed to play that role. But she didn't know anything beyond what she'd seen that night—that unrecognizable figure, that intruder, whom she'd barely glimpsed and could never identify.

It was then one morning later that week, riding to

work on the subway, that it suddenly struck her that there *was* someone who knew them, someone who'd known them very well. She was standing near the door swaying back and forth, squeezed from six different directions by fellow strap-hangers as the train hurtled its way to midtown when, for no particular reason, she thought of Cynthia French. Cynthia had been Suzie's closest friend that summer, had known all the boys, had probably slept with most of them, had even taken part in orgies with Suzie several times. No question— she'd be the perfect source. What had happened to her? Where could she be found?

She'd left Bar Harbor right after the murder. Her family had a place up there, but she hadn't stuck around. There was talk at one point of calling her as a witness, but the prosecution hadn't bothered, and Schrader said it wouldn't be worth the time and expense to dig her up and interview her since she hadn't been there that night and couldn't contribute positively to Jared's defense. Penny doubted she'd thought about Cynthia two or three times in the intervening years. Where was she from anyway—Philadelphia? Wilmington? She'd done some modeling at college; maybe she'd taken that up as a career.

When the subway reached her stop, she fought her way out, then let herself be pushed toward the exit by the mob. She started right in at work when she reached the office, and it wasn't until she took a break at eleven that she thought of Cynthia again. On a hunch she opened the Manhattan directory. There was a C. French at a Greenwich Village address.

"C. French"—that meant a woman listing herself ambiguously to avoid the sickies who get off making obscene calls. It could just be Cynthia, though there was no particular reason to think she was living in New York. Penny wrote down the number on a B&A message slip, and stuffed it in her purse.

The whole day she contemplated the possibilities: what would happen if she called and it did turn out to be Cynthia after all? Suppose they arranged a meeting, got together, talked. How was she going to explain what she wanted without appearing foolish, sounding like an amateur sleuth?

She waited until five, and then, after the office was deserted, she took the slip out of her purse, dialed the number and let it ring. No answer, which wasn't surprising—"C. French" probably had a job like everybody else, in which case she was probably still en route home from work. Penny waited fifteen minutes then dialed again. This time someone answered.

"Hello?" It was a girl's voice, but not Cynthia's—she was sure of that.

"Yes, hello," said Penny. "I'm trying to reach Cynthia French."

"Uh-huh—"

"Is this her number?"

"She lives here—yeah."

The girl sounded petulant. Penny wasn't sure, but she thought she might be black.

"Could I speak with her please?"

"Not just now, sweetie. Leave your name and number. She'll buzz you when she gets in."

"When would it be convenient to call her?"

"So—we're playing those kinds of games."

She was trying to think of what to say to that when the girl suddenly giggled. "OK, honey. Have it your way. Cindy ought to be back and available for personal calls let's say after eight." She clicked off.

Later at the apartment, after dinner when Penny and Jared were lying on the floor watching the evening news, she turned to him and asked if he remembered Cynthia French.

"Who?"

The news was a gory story about a hillside strangler in L.A.

"The blonde one—Suzie's friend."

"Oh yeah, that one—sure."

"She's living in New York now."

"Big deal for her." He turned to her, smiled. "OK, babe, let's hear it. What's up with Cynthia French?"

"She knew all Suzie's boyfriends. I thought of calling her, getting her to help me make a list."

"Forget it," he said. "You won't get anywhere with that."

"Maybe not. But I thought I'd try anyway."

He shrugged, turned back to the TV. A little after eight she went into the bedroom, closed the door, and dialed Cynthia again.

"Penny *Berring*—I don't *believe* it." It was Cynthia all right, the same snooty Main Line accent, the same hard emphasis that reminded Penny of corridor talk at a college dorm.

"I've changed my name now."

"Yeah, heard about that. Just read something about you, too—the other day. Well, well, when Fiona said some cutie called, I sure didn't expect her to turn out to be you."

"Fiona?"

"My roommate. She thought you were some kind of trick."

Cynthia must have turned away from the phone; Penny could hear her talking to someone else. "Yeah," she was saying, presumably to Fiona, "a girl I used to know. A voice out of the past." She came back on the line. "Sorry," she said, "Fiona's a little paranoid. Thinks I hang out at the Sahara picking up models, or something." Penny could hear giggling in the background. "So—it's really been a long time. What's on your mind? Don't be shy, Child. Speak up."

She called her "Child," as only Suzie had used to

do. Was there something about herself, she wondered, something diminutive and cuddly that made people call her "babe" and "child" and "kiddo," an aura perhaps that inspired the kind of affection people normally lavished on children and little dogs?

She said she wanted to get together, discuss something she couldn't talk about on the phone. Cynthia paused, then leapt for the bait. "Come on down tomorrow after work," she said. "We'll sip some wine, talk about old times."

When Penny returned to the living room Jared was lying on his back watching a game show in which second-rate celebrities, seated in boxes, made jokes and squirmed while colored lights flashed on and off.

"Ever hear of the Sahara, some sort of pickup spot?" she asked.

"Yeah," he said. "It's a fancy lesbian joint."

That fucking pussy-eater Cynthia—she really ticked me off today. Couldn't keep her cotton-pickin' hands off me, couldn't keep her dykey tongue inside her mouth. "Love you so much, Suze. Love you so much. Just want to kiss you all over. Just want to lap you up." Pig! Caught her staring when I was playing tennis with Paul. Turned around suddenly and there she was sprawled out on her sunchair, legs spread, hand resting on her yucky crotch. When our eyes met she wagged her tongue around, slurped it over her lips. I could have killed her. It was a hell of a big mistake letting her get off on me all those times. Now she's panting after me like all the other assholes around here. Tried to sic Carol T. on her but it didn't take. Shit! Thing is I got to stay cool, not let that creep mess up my plans—

THE BUILDING was an old West Village tenement on Bank Street near Abingdon Square. The place looked run-down, and though it didn't exude an odor of cats like the lobby of her brownstone, there was a certain essence present in the hall that spoke of unfinished novels and unsold paintings, films that would never be shot and music that would never be performed. It was the smell of Greenwich Village: stagnant pot smoke, decayed plumbing, lasagna casseroles. Penny was surprised to find Cynthia living in such a place, a long way from Bar Harbor, she thought, a long way from the Main Line.

Cynthia greeted her from behind a chainlock. "My God—it's really *you*." She unlocked the door, took Penny in her arms. She was braless in a boy's white T-shirt, tight faded jeans and battered Wellington boots.

The apartment was humbly furnished. There were a few throwaway pieces, the sort of stuff people in the Village pick up off the streets, and big blowup posters of butch-looking women in leather jackets astride huge motorcycles. There was a board-and-brick bookcase stuffed with the usual books on acupuncture and vegetarian diets, ecology, Carlos Castanada, and novels by Erica Jong and Gael Greene.

"Come in, Child. Let's have a look at you. Take off your sweater and turn around." She stood back while Penny did a turn. "I can't *believe* it. You look so *grown-up.*"

Cynthia flicked on a stereo. Disco music flooded the

room. Then she led Penny to some cushions where they sat down side by side.

"Just to clear the air, Child, let me say it up front. Lots of changes over the past three years. I'm gay. Fiona and I are lovers, and we both play around a little, too." Penny nodded. "I guess you figured that. I'm not trying to lay a trip on you. Just want you to know where I stand. Don't worry—I won't make a play for you. Ever make it with a chick?" Penny shook her head. "Not a bad experience even if it doesn't turn you on. You ought to try it once at least. Not with me necessarily—I mean just to get a taste." She paused. "Well, now that we've gotten through that, let me open up some wine. Or would you rather blow some weed?"

Penny said wine would be OK. She waited on the cushions while Cynthia went to the kitchen to get their drinks. She could hardly believe the way Cynthia had changed. She'd been this very snooty upper-class blonde, silly and manipulative, full of inanities and guile. Now she was completely different, a tough, direct young woman who seemed to know exactly who she was.

"Really *got* to my parents," she said handing Penny a glass. "I brought Fiona home last Christmas, and that *really* freaked them out. My mother took one look, then took to her bed. My brother Tom—remember him? That asshole finally ordered us out of the house. Couple of weeks later I get this typed letter from daddy on his law firm stationery the essence of which was that unless I went to some shrink in Philly and started cleaning up my act I wasn't going to get another cent from him. Fiona said 'screw it,' so now I'm kind of broke. Waitressing at the Trattoria around the corner, taking dance class to stay in shape, and working a gay hot line four nights a week."

She clinked her glass against Penny's, then took a sip.

"The hot line's a gas. People call in with their troubles—VD, cystitis, lover gone, coming out. You name it—they call in about it, and old Cindy just sits there advising them in this real calm telephone voice I've got. Someone tried to make a date with me the other night. Said I sounded just like Daisy Buchanan out of *Gatsby*. You know, like my voice was 'filled with money' or something. If only the poor dear knew—"

Penny nodded through all of this, increasingly amazed. Cynthia was hard, cynical, but authentic, too, not the flighty girl she remembered from Maine.

"So, Child, what brings you down here? Out with it now. Don't beat around the bush."

"I've been living with Jared since September."

"Yeah—so I read. I always figured he did it, you know, even though you said you saw someone else. He had as good a reason as any of the rest of us, I suppose."

It was a strange comment, and Penny wondered what she meant. Already, she could see, Cynthia wanted to talk. All she had to do to draw her out was to keep her on the subject of Suzie and their mutual escapades in Maine.

"Why do you say that?"

"You mean 'good reason'?" She grinned. "Well—why not? You're old enough to take it. After all the shit you've been through you're entitled to know it all. The fact is, Child, your sister was a rotten bitch. She didn't have any friends either, not real ones. I was supposed to be her 'best friend,' but now that I look back on it I realize I hated her guts. She was a seducer, old Suze. Sucked us in, made us fall in love with her, and then when she had us in her spell, made us feel like worms. She didn't want lovers. Didn't even want friends. What she wanted was slaves, and slaves was what she got." She stood up and began to pace the little living room, taking long strides, her boots clumping on the floor.

"I was in love with her. Adored her—I really did. First from a distance, then up close. I went in with my eyes open, because I knew where all her relationships finally led, but I didn't care. I just wanted to get my hands on that beautiful slinky body of hers. Started out kind of funny at Sarah Lawrence. We roomed together, you know. We'd swap clothes and stuff: shirts, shorts and jeans. We were the same size exactly, though she had all those luscious curves. So I started wearing her stuff, asking if I could borrow this and that, and, for reasons that escaped me then, I found wearing them turned me on. I wasn't sure why at first. I was denying my tendencies I guess. But then, I remember, when she'd go out on a date, as soon as she was gone I'd start looking through her drawers. I'd try on her panties and her bras—the few she had because she didn't like underwear very much. You know she used to go off campus to buy cigarettes wearing a trenchcoat with absolutely nothing underneath? I thought she was *amazing*. I'd never known anyone like that. Anyway just wearing her stuff made me feel good.

"She slept raw too, like she was a goddess or something. In the mornings I'd wait in bed, waiting for her to jump up. That's what she did. She'd open her eyes, and then suddenly when she was ready she'd leap out of bed, and there she'd be, this beauty, stark naked, and she'd do these little exercises like touching her toes, and stretching backwards, and she was the most beautiful thing I'd ever seen.

"One night, after she quit college and was working for Jamie, that photographer—he was *weird*, I can tell you, very *bi* and into all sorts of *scenes*—one night she calls me at the dorm. 'Want to make it with this stud?' she asks. 'The three of us together, a sandwich. All right?' Remember how she used to talk? Every line ended with a question—'all right?' 'OK?' So I thought, gee, this could be my chance, I'll play along and get my hands on her, too. So I took the train into town, and we end up with this very aggressive guy, this six foot six basketball player type. The three of us are in this huge bed she had at that little apartment she rented on Sixty-Sixth, and this guy's in the middle, and he's really turned on to us both. First he sticks it in her, then in me, then he goes down on her while I squirm around under him and suck him off. So we're trying all these positions, giggling away, and he gets off a few times like gangbusters, and Suze and I are eyeing each other every once in a while as if to say like isn't this *really cool*. But eventually he gets tired, sits back and says he wants to watch *us* play. This is what I've been waiting for. I smile coyly, and Suze says 'Why not?', and so we start off, and suddenly I'm getting what I want. It's all a great big joke as far as the two of them are concerned, but for me it's the whole point of the evening, the consummation of a year's worth of fantasies and dreams.''

She finished off her glass of wine, then sat down, pulled out a joint, lit it and inhaled deeply. She offered it to Penny, who shook her head.

"I liked it. God, how I *liked* it. I mean I really got off on it, and of course I tried like hell to stay cool so I wouldn't let on and scare old Suzie off. But she picked up on me right away. The next morning she was watching me, studying me, and then she touched my cheek and smiled like she'd finally figured me out. That was her thing, you see—to find the other person's weakness, then exploit it any way she could. She didn't say anything, but it was clear enough. She kissed me good-bye, and every time we saw each other after that she'd touch me or kiss me or embrace me, and show me that same little smile that said 'I know what you like now, and maybe I'll give you more of it if you're good.' One night I came into the city, and it was too late to go back to the dorm. So we shared the bed, just the two of us. She lay real close to me, and I touched her, and she said: 'It's OK, Cin, make love to me if you want. It doesn't do all that much for me, but if it turns you on, go ahead!' Of course she had me then. She knew just how to do that, just what levers to pull. I'd work on her, do everything I could think of to get her going, and she'd just lie there with that big fat smirk on her face, saying 'It's OK, Cin—keep trying. I'm getting a little warm I guess. Try this. Try that. A little more of this, a little less of that—OK?' And so there I was working my tail off trying to get a fire going in that sleek cool body of hers. It was hard work, I tell you. And that's how I ended up her slave.''

Cynthia inhaled again, then she shook her head.

''She was the *princess*, you see, the *goddess* who was doing me this big favor by letting me make love to her imperial self. I always had to do all the work. That was the game—that I had to try and turn *her* on. Never the other way around. Never mind about me. A kiss on the lips was about the best I ever got, and maybe a few pats and caresses and that was just about it. Well, after that she made me suffer all sorts of little ways. Made me go out with her on double dates, try out this guy for her, try out that guy, tell her what he liked so she'd know how to handle him, give her all the clues so she could get control. She made me run all sorts of little errands, too, like picking up her shoes and her dry cleaning, fixing her breakfast, giving her massages and backrubs, combing out her hair. Not exactly torture, but she'd make it as humiliating as she could. And sometimes she was really mean. I'd kiss her and then she'd push me away. 'Not now, Cin,' she'd say. 'I'm not in the mood right now.' Or 'Can't you keep your big fat paws off me, Cin? Like I know you got the hots for me, but like I'm really into guys, all right?' Sometimes I'd just plain beg. 'Please Suze,' I'd say, 'let me kiss you, let me go down on you.' And then if I was real humble and begged her a lot, or did a special favor for her, she'd say 'OK—you got fifteen minutes. I got a date so make it fast—OK?' She knew I adored her. I must have told her so a thousand times. And then that summer came, and she needed me to help corral those guys. 'I want to fuck them all,' she told me. 'Every last one of them. Every one of those jerks. Together we'll do it; together we'll fuck them all.' So that's what we did that summer. That was our *summer project*. To fuck every one of them like she said. *Every single solitary one*. First her, then me; or first me, then her. She'd tell me: 'Your job, Cin, is to keep bringing them in. I don't want to run out. This is an assembly-line operation. If I'm busy with one, you keep the next one warm, all right?' Then she'd say: 'If you're a good little piece of ass, Cin, I'll let you have a little piece of me, OK?' God, she was unbelievable. That sister of yours was *the end*. She had me coming and going that summer every which way, and half the time I was in a daze, running errands for her, sucking around after her, taking out her trash, anything to keep her attention, anything to get a few minutes with her alone. We did this topless act around the pool. We went out and fucked on sailboats. We humped on that awful waterbed of hers. One night during a party at the yacht club we did it with a couple of guys in the men's locker room on the floor. She *made* me sleep with all these guys, most of whom I loathed. I didn't like sex with men by then, though I still knew how to put on an act. About half a dozen times we did threesomes in the poolhouse, and twice there were four of us together, and we kept switching off, and I never even knew their blessed *names*. I'd moan or something, then I'd feel her little hand on my thigh. 'Keep the faith, Cin,' she'd whisper. 'Keep the faith, OK?' So I kept the faith—''

Cynthia had been staring down while she told Penny all of this, as if it were so shameful she didn't want to show her eyes. She looked up finally.

"Surprised, huh? Surprised to hear what she was really like? But then you must have known some of this. You were watching us, weren't you? That's what I read.''

"I was watching," Penny said, "but I had no idea. I never figured out the relationship quite like that.''

"*Relationship?* I wish there'd been a *relationship.*'' Cynthia shook her head. "It was so empty. I don't know why she acted that way. Sometimes I had the idea she was playing some sort of game, like she had a plan, or was trying to prove something or other—like there was really something she was up to, something she was trying to do. But I never knew what it was, and I was so freaked out I didn't even care.''

"What about the guys?''

"*Worse!* You should have heard some of the stuff she said to them. It's a wonder someone didn't—'' She paused. "But then someone did. Probably one of them.''

"One of her lovers?''

"Must have been. Who else? I told you—I always thought it was Jared, not only because he was there that night, holding the shears and everything, but because he was . . . I don't know how to say it exactly—''

"What?''

"Well, I thought he was sort of *crude.* Don't get me wrong. I also thought he was *gorgeous.* But he wasn't one of those Ivy League creeps. He wasn't phony, well-mannered; he wasn't a boy. You could tell by looking at him he wasn't the sort to take a lot of shit. So I just figured she went too far with him, and instead of taking it like the others he got really mad, and it was what she deserved anyway, like she was asking for it, maybe even trying to bring it on.''

"Funny—Jared said something like that the other day.'' She paused. "Do you really think it's true?''

"I don't know. She was up to something, I'm sure of that. It was as if she was deliberately walking a tightrope, trying to provoke something, I don't know exactly what. Maybe she just wanted to be beaten up. She was sick enough. I often thought she got what she wanted, like she could maybe get off on that, death being the ultimate trip, as they say.'' She paused. "On the other hand Suze was life-embracing. She was funny, split. She let herself go, and she held herself back at the same time. You never really got to know her. There was this side she kept to herself.''

They sat in silence, Penny sipping until her glass was empty, Cynthia smoking her joint down until it was barely a quarter-inch long.

"Tough, isn't it?''

"What?''

"Oh, you know—*life*. I remember seeing your picture in the papers. You were plastered all over everywhere those days, and you looked so injured. I felt real sorry for you then.''

"I survived.''

"Yeah—you did.''

"I still get recognized sometimes.''

"Sure. I read that stuff in Denver's column. What a shit he is. But it's funny, every so often, every six months or so I'm with some people and someone mentions the case. It sort of runs like an undercurrent, like Patty Hearst or Wylie-Hoffert or Valerie Percy, the one they never solved.''

"Do you tell people you knew her?''

"Sometimes yes, sometimes no. Tell me, Child—I

asked you this before—what brings you down here? Anything I can do?"

Penny looked at her. "You'll probably laugh."

"Why don't you try me and see?"

Suddenly she felt a great warmth for Cynthia, didn't feel nervous about appearing foolish anymore. "I want to find out what happened. You said it yourself a minute ago—it was probably one of those guys. Jared's got this whole scenario figured out, but he doesn't care about it anymore. He says I'm hung up and wasting my time, and I should just forget it and try to live with it and go on."

"Well, he may be right about that. Anyway, the police—"

"They never did a thing. I knew that but I didn't care because I thought my father had people investigating all this time. I just found out he didn't. He always thought it was Jared, and now he's furious because Jared's with me, and he's afraid his precious Chapman stock might go down." She shook her head. "When Jared and I got together again, I was so naive— I thought it was all over and we really could go on. But instead it just got worse. There's this undercurrent like you said. A girl at my office talks about it behind my back. Jared got fired from a play on account of Denver's column. I just can't stand it, being looked at like we're freaks, and meantime there's someone just walking around out there. It's like we're suffering all the time, and the only way out from under it is to find out what happened, which is probably just a hopeless task."

Cynthia was looking at her with compassion. Penny felt she understood.

"OK, Child," she said very softly, "tell me exactly what you're trying to do."

"Get together a list, the names of all those guys. I

can't remember much about them now. I called you because I thought you might.''

"Yeah." Cynthia shook her head. "I should, shouldn't I? I had *intimate relations* with most of them, I guess. But the truth is I was so freaked out I didn't even know their names half the time. As far as I was concerned they were just a sickening mass of hairy legs.''

They talked a little more, Cynthia promised to come up with some names, and then Penny said it was time for her to leave. She was standing out on the corner of Bank and Bleecker about to hail a cab when she heard someone calling, looked up and saw Cynthia, head sticking out of her window, motioning for her to wait.

"Hey, don't go yet," she yelled. "I'm coming down.''

Penny waited on the front stoop of the tenement. A minute later Cynthia appeared.

"Funny," she said. "I was just taking off my boots when I thought of something. Suzie kept a diary. Did you know about that?''

"No—''

"Well, it was *something*. Really lurid. More of a sex diary than anything else. She never let me look at it, but occasionally she read me little bits. It was a record of all her lovers and what she thought of them—really devastating stuff. She had all these crazy notes on the sizes of their cocks, the stupid things they said and did in bed. We used to lie on the waterbed giggling while she read. Then she'd laugh that horsey laugh of hers and tell me there was stuff about me in there too. I begged her to let me read it, which, of course, was just what she wanted me to do. Then she'd snap the book shut and stick it under her ass where, she'd inform me, I wasn't to go nosing around.

"It was so sick. She said she wanted a good record of all her 'transgressions.' Said she was going to publish it someday, when she was middle-aged and all her summer lovers were leading boring respectable lives. Told me how much she loathed Bar Harbor, and what a pleasure it would be to blow the place apart. 'Won't be able to get enough dynamite for that,' she told me. 'but this'll do it, right?' Then she'd pat the diary and stick it back under her ass.''

"What happened to it?"

"Don't know. I thought it might have turned up after she was killed, and, to tell you the truth, I was a little worried since there was stuff about me in there, and I didn't particularly want our affair aired at Jared's trial. Maybe your parents found it and burned it up. It wasn't exactly the sort of treasure you'd save as a memento of a long-lost loved daughter, you know.''

"They didn't burn it. They never touched her things.''

"It was black, leather-bound, unlined pages crowded with her tiny scrawl. She kept it hidden, of course, I remember looking for it a couple of times when she wasn't there. I wanted to read what she'd written about me, but she must have hid it pretty well." Cynthia paused, then shook her head. "I never found it anyway—"

Why do I worry sometimes I'll die very suddenly, be hit by a taxi crossing Fifth, be murdered by a madman in Central Park, then someone, Child perhaps, will stumble across this book and learn the secrets of my heart? Don't care. Couldn't give less of a shit. But then why do I leave out certain things? Why do I hide this journal every night? Compulsion? Busywork? Fear of what it tells me about myself? Surely this book is not the key to my secret garden. I don't own that key myself. The garden is surrounded by insurmountable walls, its vines and flowers mysterious, unknown—

THE IDEA that there'd been a diary and that it might still exist someplace was so tantalizing she couldn't let it go. She thought about it as she taxied uptown from Cynthia's, tried to imagine where it might be and the sort of information it might contain. After Suzie died, she remembered, she'd gone through all her things, first in Maine, then in Greenwich, where she'd holed up with her mother after withdrawing from Wellesley College. She'd found a few letters, various papers of various kinds, but nothing like a diary, nothing personal at all.

Back at the apartment she detected a glimmer of interest when she told Jared what Cynthia had said. "Maybe the police found it," he suggested. "They must have combed the cottage pretty well."

"I don't think so. Remember how they bungled everything? If they'd found it they would have had to turn it over. Robinson would have had to show it to Schrader because it might have been exculpatory, with all those other guys' names and everything."

"Yeah, well maybe they just deep-sixed it, then." Already he was losing interest.

"I doubt it. Someone would have talked. There were reporters crawling all over the place. No, I don't think the police found it, and I don't think my parents did either. They stayed completely away from the pool-house. I was the one finally who packed up all her stuff."

"Then maybe Cynthia was right," he said. "Maybe it was inside one of her speakers or someplace."

Penny sighed. "We got rid of everything—her clothes, the remnants of her waterbed, even her stereo. There was this ghoulish atmosphere, people coming around looking for souvenirs. My father asked me if I wanted anything, and when I said I didn't, he said pack it all up and have it hauled away and burned."

Jared shrugged. "In that case I guess it's gone."

"Yeah, guess so," she said.

But even after they went to bed she couldn't shake off the idea that somehow the diary might have survived. She tried to sleep but couldn't. She kept thinking of the house in Maine, its rooms, its grounds. If Suzie had kept the diary regularly, writing up all her lovers as Cynthia had said, then she would have had to keep it fairly nearby, so the cottage was the logical place. *But where?* She imagined her way around the room, and then, suddenly, a memory came to her, first vague, then sharp, like pulling an image into focus through a lens. She shook Jared awake. "I think I know where she hid it," she said.

When she and Suzie had been little, she told him, before they were allowed to go off bicycling by themselves, they'd often been stuck for weeks at a time on the estate, especially when their father was working in New York. Usually their mother took them up to Maine in the middle of June, and they stayed there through Labor Day, more or less ignored. Their father, obsessed with building up the business, flew up on occasional weekends and then took a brief vacation the last two weeks before they left. So they were stuck on the estate, and since there weren't any other kids around, and their mother rarely ventured out, they were forced to amuse themselves. They played all sorts of games, indoor games on foggy days (Scrabble, which she'd loved and Suzie had loathed, and Monopoly, which she'd hated and Suzie had adored), and on the good days outdoor games, hopscotch and tag, hide-and-seek and treasure hunts which became more and more elaborate as their mutual boredom increased. One time, she remembered, Suzie had hidden the "treasure," a paperweight from their father's desk, in a metal cookie box she'd painted aquamarine, then placed at the bottom of the pool.

"We had such fun with those treasure hunts," Penny said. "We'd work hours figuring out ways to stump each other, and Suzie's ways were always best. She was ingenious about hiding things. She had a mind for that, secret stashes and passwords and codes. One time she loosened a tile inside the cottage. The floor there is tiled, just like the area around the pool, and there're tiles, too, like baseboards, running along the bottoms of the walls. She loosened one of them, and then she hollowed out the space behind it, and fixed some white cement on the edges so you'd never know it had been touched. I never found that one; so finally she showed it to me. I was just thinking, since she was living in there, maybe that's where she kept the diary."

"Hmm," said Jared sleepily. "Could be, I guess."

"Let's go up there tomorrow and see."

"Oh, come on—"

"Let's go there tomorrow. Why not?"

"You got to be kidding. Don't you have to go to work?"

She sat up, turned on the light. "I'll call in sick. We can rent a car. It'll be good to get out of town."

He was looking at her strangely. "Hey, babe—let's not get carried away."

"Look," she said. "let's *do* something for a change. Let's get off our asses, and see if the damn thing's there."

The next morning she made breakfast while he called around to rent-a-car agencies. He finally made an unlimited mileage twenty-four-hour deal with an independent on East Eighty-Fifth. They stuffed a few things into a knapsack—extra sweatshirts because she knew it would be cold in Maine—picked up the car, and headed for the FDR Drive. It was nine o'clock when they crossed the Triboro Bridge. Traffic was light, and half an hour out on the New England Thruway, barely a mile, she realized, from her family's Greenwich house, Jared stopped at a gas station and she went to a phone booth to call in to B&A.

"Any special reason you want me to tell him?" MacAllister's secretary asked.

"Just say it's a family thing. I'll work next weekend and make up the time."

They lunched on clam rolls at a Howard Johnson's a little south of Boston, and she thought: *We're in New*

England now; Maine is getting close. She'd felt anxious in the car as she'd contemplated what it would be like returning to Bar Harbor, returning to the house. She hadn't been in Maine since the trial. She'd resolved never to stay in the old house again, never even to return to the town after Jared was released. There'd been too many lonely, unhappy summers there, and after the killing and all the blood she had never wanted to go back.

Now she wondered if they weren't on a fool's errand rushing up there this time of year on the off-chance they'd find Suzie's diary in that old hiding place behind the tiles. For a moment she thought about turning around, going back to New York, leaving the past alone. But then she knew that wasn't possible. She *had* to try. She didn't have any choice.

Jared fidgeted with the radio, tuned into stations as they traveled up the coast so that they listened to the same top forty songs over and over again, and the chatter of DJs of varying talent and panache. He drove steadily, tried to divert her sometimes, chattering about the scenery, the people in the other cars, in an attempt to break her mood. But she felt grim and answered him in monosyllables. Finally he turned to her. "I feel kind of silly about this. It's so—I don't know—Nancy Drew or something," he said.

"First it was the Hardy Boys. Now it's Nancy Drew. It isn't, Jared. It's us. We're doing it, and that makes it real."

They crossed into Maine a little after two o'clock. They followed the coast road that ran along Penobscot Bay and then north toward Mount Desert Island. It was foggy and nearly dark when they reached Bar Harbor. She'd never been there off-season, had never seen the town in its pristine state. The harbor was nearly empty, no yachts, just a few fishing boats. Most of the stores were closed, everything was dark and gray, and she felt a deep chill from the wind, the real cold of a Maine winter soon to bury the streets and fields and forests in snow. As they wound their way along the curving coastal road that encompassed Acadia Park and then turned onto roads they'd once ridden together on his motorcycle, passing the old houses boarded up by owners now snug down in Philadelphia or New York, she began to shake with cold and dread.

And then she felt the tension coming off him, too. He was as nervous as she. Something about his breathing betrayed him—it was too controlled—and the way he drove, the tight way he gripped the wheel. She'd been selfish, she thought, thinking he was lazy, thinking that was why he hadn't wanted to come. It was he, she now understood, who must feel the greater dread, returning to the scene of a killing which everyone still believed he'd done.

A hundred yards from the front gate of the estate he suddenly stopped the car. "Want to turn back?" She looked at him, but she couldn't tell if he was serious. "Of course not," she said, "but I am feeling a little creepy now."

He reached out for her and touched her cheek, breaking the tension. He started up again and pulled up in front of the gate. He got out, tried to open it, then shrugged and walked back to the car. "Damn thing's locked. Guess we'll have to walk in."

"I'll go get Tucker," she said. "He'll come down and open up."

"Want me to come?"

She shook her head. "He's going to be shocked enough when he sees me."

He gave her a boost over the gate, then she started up the drive alone. Tucker and his wife lived in the caretaker's cottage a hundred feet from the road. She was relieved to see his pickup truck parked in front, but there was no response when she knocked.

Damn, she thought, *should have phoned from town.* She knocked again, then walked around to the side. She could hear the sound of a TV, recognized the pause-filled rhythm of soap opera dialogue.

"Tucker," she called out. "It's Penny Berring." It was strange to use her old last name again. She heard the TV volume go down, went back to the door to wait. Mrs. Tucker opened up.

"Why Penny!" She didn't look particularly over-joyed. "We weren't expecting you."

"Sorry, Mrs. Tucker. Guess I should have called."

"Haven't seen you in a long time. Come in. I'll get you tea. Then I'll go fix up the house."

"That's not necessary," she said. "Just want to spend a few minutes. All I need is the keys."

"I'd better get Phil, then." She turned and started up the stairs.

"You don't have to bother him," Penny said. "I see them over there." She started toward a peg board in the hall where the keys, all neatly labeled, hung on little hooks.

"I need one for the gate and one for the cottage."

"You don't want to go in there," Mrs. Tucker said, poised halfway up the stairs.

"Yes, I do. That's why I came."

Mrs. Tucker stared at her. "I'll go get Phil," she said. She disappeared upstairs, then Penny heard them talking, their words muffled by the walls. She was about to reach over and take the keys she wanted, when she heard a heavy masculine tread on the stairs and knew Tucker was coming down.

"Kind of short notice," he growled, clumping over to where she stood. "Not so nice catching us off our guard this way, not giving us time to clean things up."

"I'm only going to be here a few minutes. You don't have to turn on the gas, or anything like that."

"Your father says—well, look who's here!"

Penny turned. Jared was standing at the door.

"Hello," he said to Tucker. "Remember me?"

Tucker grimaced. "I remember you, all right."

"We're in a bit of a hurry, Tucker," Penny said, "so if you'll please give me the keys we'll get on with our errand and out of your way."

The caretaker hesitated. His distaste for Jared was evident, his distaste for the whole situation. He looked at them, looked away, then went to the board and snatched up the keys.

"Here, take 'em." He handed them to Penny. "Your father says 'Tucker, don't let anyone in there, not unless you hear from me.' Then you turn up without notice. What the hell am I supposed to do? Well, you're in the family, though as far as I've heard he ain't in it yet." He looked hard at Jared. "Go ahead. It's your house. Lock up when you're finished. You can leave the keys on the porch."

He turned his back on them and walked stiffly up the stairs. She turned to Jared. "That's what they call New England crustiness," she whispered in his ear.

They walked back down the drive, unlocked the gate, drove in and parked in front of the house. They walked around it, then crossed the lawn. She felt the springiness of the grass and remembered the feel of it against her bare feet when she'd crossed it at dawn those mornings three years before. But now it was night, the wind was strong and the air was chilled. A loose shutter somewhere swung open and shut. She looked back at the house. Its Victorian profile seemed menacing against the blackness of the sky.

She pulled the light switch outside the poolhouse, but the lights on the porch didn't come on. "Damn— the electricity's off. The panel's in the main house. We'll have to go in there and turn it on."

"Never mind," said Jared. "I brought a flashlight.

I'll get it—it's in the car.'' He walked back across the lawn, leaving her alone at the poolhouse door.

He'd brought a flashlight—how intelligent, she thought. Then she remembered the flashlight beam, and was seized with foreboding. *No,* she thought, *that's nonsense:* it was the intruder who shined the flashlight at him. *Getting mixed up. Shouldn't do that. Mustn't let myself get freaked.*

She turned back to the poolhouse, peered in, felt the glass cold against her nose. She thought of herself that summer peering in at Suzie sprawled out with one of her lovers, their limbs entwined, the waterbed undulating as they slept. Suddenly she stood back; the memory was too intense. She looked back at the main house, found her bedroom window, thought of herself sitting up there in her rocking chair, staring down, spying, imagining Jared and Suzie making love.

''Here—'' Jared had the flashlight on and was shining it at the lock. She fumbled with the keys, found the right one, and opened the door. The air inside had a cold, damp smell.

Jared shined the flashlight around, probing all the corners of the room. There was no furniture; the floor was clean. No waterbed now, just the tile floor and the four walls. Once again she began to shake.

''Well?'' He turned the light on her. She couldn't see him and suddenly felt unnerved.

''Why are you doing that?''

''What?'' he asked.

''The flashlight.''

''Oh. Sorry.'' He lowered the beam, handed the flashlight back. She took it, stepped to the center, and pointed at the north baseboard where the tiles met the wall.

''There,'' she said, trying to hold it steady on a particular tile. ''That's the one, I think.''

Jared went to the wall and knelt. ''You're shaking

144

the light," he said. "Better give it back." She paused, then handed it to him. Then she knelt beside him, feeling the cold floor through her jeans. She knocked gently at the tile and tried to pry it loose. When it didn't budge she tapped at it again. This time it fell out. She reached for it, caught it in her hand.

Jared held the flashlight firmly while she began to pull things out. The first item was a small bottle of Amazone. Opening it, sniffing at the stopper, she felt tears rising to her eyes. Memories of Suzie flooded back, the aroma of her body, the combination of this perfume and the essence of her skin. Inhaling the odor she almost felt that Suzie was with them in the room.

The next thing was a wallet, old and worn, the edges damp and decayed. There was no money inside, just some keys and old photographs sealed at their edges with Scotch tape. They inspected them: a picture of her mother with a tennis racket across her lap; one of her father in his bathing trunks about to dive into the pool. There was a smaller print, too, from the same series as the one she'd seen on her father's office wall, of herself and Suzie on the sailboat, Suzie in profile this time, looking out to sea, smiling, her chin jutting out, while Penny stared at her with the same mixture of envy and admiration that had so struck her in her father's office the week before. Now it struck Jared too. "You always looked at her like that," he said.

"How do you know I did?"

"I remember from those times I came around." He raised the flashlight, shined it in her face again. "You're looking at the picture the same way now." He paused. "It's as if—"

"What?"

"I don't know. Like you want to be like her, some-how."

Penny's face froze. Then she pushed away the flash-light. There was more in the hiding place, a small plastic medicine bottle and a pipe. Jared opened the bottle and dumped some of its contents onto his palm. "Incredible," he said, "this must be the same stuff we smoked."

"Here it is!" She pulled out a leather-bound notebook, the pages unlined, covered with tiny script just as Cynthia had described. They thumbed through it together. "Just can't believe it," she said. "It's as if it's been sitting here waiting for us all this time."

He hugged her. "Got to hand it to you. You're a genius, babe. What do you say we get the hell out of here? I'm starting to get spooked myself."

She nodded, began to put the perfume and other things back into the cavity, then changed her mind. She decided to keep them. They belonged to her now, she guessed.

To annihilate myself. Burn. Catch fire.
Search the gutter. Screw and screw.
The sweet object of my desire doesn't
care a hoot. Brokenhearted I weep and
rage.

Maybe cruelty is the answer. To give
pain even as I suffer. Receive pain, pain
of the flesh, to burn away the pain so
deep inside.

"So you want to flirt with S&M," Jamie
says. And then in an ominous tone: "You
can't flirt with it, you know. Once you
start with that you never go straight
again."

He loves the idea that he's jaded. He
adores the thought that he can't get a
hard-on unless there's a whip in the
room or a threesome on the bed.
Anything but love. "Love gives me a
shrivel-on," he proclaims.

All very faggy, end-of-the-Roman-
Empire, Weimar-Germany, 1920s ennui
stuff. I nod anyway to show I think it's
quite profound.

Then I ask him to cook something up.

"Something heavy," I say, "I want to be—you know—scared—"
    He nods: "Leave everything to me—"

THEY DROVE quickly out of Bar Harbor. A heavy rain began to fall when they crossed Trenton Bridge. Traffic was light; the roads were deserted except for an occasional oncoming truck. Jared drove as fast as he could, but sometimes the rain was so heavy the wipers could barely clear it from the glass.

"That was crazy what you said in there," she said.

"Just being in there was crazy," he replied.

"But that was crazy what you said." He concentrated on his driving, didn't answer. "Well?"

"What was crazy?"

"Saying I looked like I wanted to be like her."

"That's what I thought."

"But it's crazy."

"Sure—sure it is. You'd be out of your mind to want to be like her."

They were silent for a few minutes, then she turned to him again.

"Why did you shine the flashlight at me, Jared?"

He glanced at her, shrugged. "Just fooling around."

"It was as if you were taunting me. You were, weren't you?"

"Just fooling around. That's all."

They drove a couple more miles.

"You wanted me to think maybe you'd done it. You were trying to get me upset."

He nodded. "Stupid, huh?"

"More like perverse."

"Well, everyone else thinks I did it. For a while after I was arrested I even thought so myself."

"My God. You did?"

"I actually did."

"Tell me about it!"

"Do I have to? Do you really want to know?"

"I think it would be better if you did," she said.

He looked at her, then back at the road. "It's not very pleasant."

"I can deal with it."

"It's an ugly story."

"Tell me anyway."

"OK." He was silent for a moment, then began to speak. "At first I really wondered. Everyone was saying I must have killed her, everyone was accusing me, and I wondered if maybe they were right. I didn't remember all that much. That night was so strange, and that dope we smoked, the same stuff we found tonight in her stash, scrambled up everything in my head."

"When you arrived I was watching you. You stood still suddenly, as if you were worried, or hesitating about going in."

"Yeah. I remember that. I thought I heard something. Maybe it was the intruder. Maybe he was down there even then."

"What happened when you went inside? I only heard some snatches now and then. You danced—I saw that."

"Yeah, and then we screwed. After that we smoked quite a bit of her stuff, and then, I remember, she started getting nasty, said she wondered if I'd performed as poorly with you as I had with her. I remember saying, 'Do you have to be such a bitch, Suzie? Do you have to be such a bitch?' And I remember her smiling when I said that as if it pleased her, and then asking me: 'I really am a bitch, aren't I? I really am—

right?' 'Yeah,' I said, 'and you're some piece of ass, too.' And she said: 'If I'm a bitch, then you're a dog, because only a dog would fuck a bitch.' And so I said: 'OK. I'm a dog.' And then she started in. 'Come, Fido—be a good doggy, a good doggy-woggie. Come here! Lap at bitch's pussy! That's a *good* dog. Oh, yes you *are!*' That sort of stuff, all that dog motif crap, until suddenly we're into this male dog, female dog routine, this weird doggy game, and it's crazy, we're crawling around on the waterbed on all fours, sniffing at each other's crotch and behind. I try to mount her, she wriggles away, and all the time we're making these dog sounds—not barks, but little whines, snorts and growls. It's pretty funny and fairly sexy, and we're laughing away, but I wasn't sure just how funny it was to her, because even when Suzie laughed that crazy jaw-boned laugh of hers, there was something serious underneath, like maybe it was more to her than just a game. I don't know. I guess what I'm saying is that her laughter didn't ring very true that night. There was something cruel about her, too, I remember, like maybe she really did think of me as a dog. Funny—I could barely remember what we did right afterwards. It was very fuzzy and all I could recall was how incredibly stoned I was. But being there tonight, being in there, even though the room was empty, made it all start coming back. I could almost see us crawling around that huge waterbed, which made me seasick, I remember, the way it swayed and rippled and you never could get a steady hold. That weed of hers was really potent, and made it all unreal, like we were floating loose on a raft way out at sea, playing dog-and-bitch, or whatever she called her little game. Then later I remember she had her fingers around my neck. 'My fingers are your collar,' she said. 'My arm's your leash.' And I'm still crawling on all fours, and she's leading me toward the door. 'Bark!' she orders. 'No,'

I say, 'I don't want to bark. Someone'll hear.' 'Good,' she says, 'let them hear. I don't give a shit. Who cares, right? *Right?*' Then we're outside and I'm flapping away at the water, and she's throwing this tennis ball at me, telling me to fetch-and-swim. 'Fetch, Fido,' she says, and, believe it or not, fetch is what I did. She turns on the pool lights, the ones under the water, and there I am swimming around in that huge aquamarine tub, swimming after a tennis ball for Christ's sake. Suddenly she's not a dog-bitch anymore—she's a *human* bitch, which was how we got started on the whole trip in the first place."

He paused and looked at Penny. "I guess you saw some of that."

She nodded. The lights of an oncoming car made streaks on the rain-soaked road.

"I must have been a pretty sorry sight. I remember feeling really nauseous, and that grass was so strong I was getting more and more stoned out. Then finally I remember grabbing the tip of the diving board with my hands, pulling myself up until just my legs were in the water. And I was still holding that damn tennis ball in my mouth. It's hard, you know, to hold a tennis ball in your mouth. Try it sometime and see. I was so tired by then I couldn't even chin myself up, so I just hung there, and then I guess she saw her little game was over because she said something nasty like 'Gee, this is *really* interesting. I'm going back to bed, OK?'— something sarcastic like that. Then she went back into the cottage and turned off the pool lights, and there I was, just hanging there in the dark, feeling like a fool, with this damn tennis ball stuck in my mouth.

"I didn't stay like that very long, maybe a few seconds. Then I spat out the ball and tried to hoist myself up. Couldn't do it, so I just let myself sink back into the water, then I swam round to the ladder, climbed out, got back on the diving board and just lay on top of it on my back. I remember the feel of that board, the rough sort of rope-like texture of it. That's when I should have left, of course, gotten on my motorcycle and charged right out of there with or without my clothes. But I didn't, I fell off—everything sort of goes blank around that point. I was wet and cold, I remember, but I didn't care. I wasn't going back into that cottage; I wasn't going to follow that bitch back in there. I remember thinking that, and then I don't know how much time went by. I heard something. Something woke me, like a dog whimpering, maybe even the sort of sound a dog might make while being fucked. I didn't know, but I could hear it was coming from the cottage, and I thought maybe she was just trying to tempt me back. I was still dazed. The dope had taken hold, and it wasn't giving me any room. And then everything's very vague. All I know is that I suddenly realized she needed help.''

He stopped.

"Then what?"

"It gets sort of ugly."

"Tell me." He shook his head. "Come on," she said. "You can't stop now."

"Well, I don't remember whether she actually cried out. I do know I was in the pool again before I realized something was going on. So I guess I was on my way back in there anyway, had decided to swim leisurely back, try and clear my head, then join her on the bed again. It's then that all the madness began. I swam across, pulled myself out of the water and stumbled toward the door. Then there was that beam in my eyes, the light shining right in them. I couldn't see. 'Turn it off, Suzie,' I said. Then I was conscious there was another person in there, and, a second later, I was hit. It happened very fast. There was this moment just before he knocked me down. I don't remember what it was exactly, except that there was something strange. Anyway there was contact. I was straight-armed in the chest, and I was off balance so I went down, and then I was on the floor crawling toward the bed. The floor was all wet and—listen, you don't want to hear any more."

"Yes, I do," she insisted.

He groaned. "I was crawling around looking for her, and everything was sticky. I was crawling on top of her, feeling for her face, and then I suddenly realized she was gurgling blood. There was water all over the place, and stickiness, and then I caught hold of those shears, and suddenly I started screaming, screaming like crazy, and then the lights came on, and the siren sounded, and you know the rest. And the thing was—*I wasn't sure.* They said I did it. Had I really seen that flashlight? Had someone really knocked me down? I had her blood all over me. I was holding those lousy shears. The police came and took me away, and it wasn't until the next day when I heard that you were saying you'd seen someone, too, that I was positive I hadn't freaked out, that that dope of hers hadn't turned me onto violence and made me kill her—" He shook his head.

"That doesn't make any sense. You must have known you hadn't done it." Penny looked at him. "You *couldn't* have—you must have known that."

"Don't be so sure, babe."

"How could you even *think* that?"

"Because I thought maybe I could."

"That's ridiculous."

"No—I think I could." He looked at her, then back at the road. "Everyone else thought so. So—why not?"

"Look," she said, "I don't understand. It's as if you want me to agree with that."

"Don't you?"

"No!"

"But you were worried when I came up with that flashlight, and especially when I shined it in your eyes." She didn't answer. "Weren't you?"

"Yes. All right. For a moment I was scared." She looked at him. "What are you doing? Playing some kind of mental game?"

He grinned at her. "I'm an actor. I'm into little scenes."

"You're toying with me. I don't understand."

"I wanted to test you, see if I could shake you up."

"But why?"

He shrugged. "You were the only one who ever believed me. I wanted to see if maybe I could get you to change your mind."

"It isn't true I was the only one. There was Schrader and all the jurors."

He shook his head. "It was *you* they believed. Not me."

"It's the same thing. You got acquitted."

"No, it's not the same."

"What are you trying to tell me, Jared?"

His face became serious. "Just that I think I'm guilty in a way." He looked at her, then back at the road. "I didn't kill her. Of course I didn't kill her. But, and this is the truth, I *could* have—given the right set of circumstances I *could*. She was asking for it. I've always had that feeling about that night. And I *could* have done it if I'd taken her seriously. I have that in me. That's why I understand what went on inside that flashlight guy. Think of it—stabbing someone you hate over and over again, someone who's tortured you. It's all gone then—all your anger. And what are you left with? Guilt, remorse, maybe punishment. But you're free of tension. You're free. She was asking for it and I could have done it. That's all I've been trying to say."

She felt for him then, his anguish, understood finally

why he'd been acting so resigned. He felt guilty. For this perverse reason he felt that he deserved all the bad breaks he'd had. Being there that night with Suzie, going on trial for her murder, all that had broken something inside of him, and though he'd been cleared, he hadn't really *felt* cleared at all.

"OK," she said, "you've convinced me. You could have done it. You feel like you did. I got all that. So let's drop it now. *OK?*"

He turned and looked at her. "It's funny," he said, "for a minute I thought—"

"What?"

"Nothing, really. You sounded just like Suzie then, that's all."

It was true; she realized it the moment he pointed it out. Unconsciously she'd done an almost exact imitation of Suzie's pattern of speech. A strange thing, she thought, considering she'd never used that "OK? All right?" mannerism before. She closed her eyes and tightened her grip on the diary in her lap. She tried to sleep.

They stopped for coffee a couple of times at deserted fluorescent-lit fast-food joints. It was impossible for both of them to read the diary at the same time so they took turns reading it aloud. Penny found it terrifying. She was entering her sister's mind, finding a new Suzie, familiar yet strange, a Suzie who mockingly described her own debasements, then cried out in vulnerability and pain.

Some of Dr. Bowles' patients were hanging around the brownstone when they drove up. A black van was double-parked in front of the house, and the patients, young men and women with sensitive faces, had formed a line and were busy passing boxes of cat food and sacks of litter fire-brigade style until they formed a neat pile beside the curb.

"Jesus," said Jared, "if you think we've had a creepy day, just take a look at *them*."

Last night was the night. Jamie arranged my "scene." "We're going to cauterize your wounds," he told me. Then, waving a finger: "Remember, whatever happens, YOU asked for it. It's all being done for YOU."

Cindy came by for the afternoon. Can't stand school, she said. Wants to drop out and room here with me. "It was a big mistake, leaving college," I told her. "Don't be a jerk. Stick it out. Get your degree." Her face fell. She just wants to be close, so cloying, such a whimpering pathetic little thing. Reminded me of myself. Am I that much of a turn-off, that ridiculous, that much of a royal pain to him?

She stuck around, ironed some blouses. "Look," I told her, "I got an important date tonight. Maybe you better go back to Bronxville now." No—she wanted to wait up for me. Finally I got cruel. "Leave me alone, Cin—Jesus! Can't you see I'm not into it? OK?"

Jamie arrived at eight, took me to Le

Cirque. He was carrying his camera bag.
"You'll be scared," he assured me. So—
it's really going to happen, I thought.
Blow my mind. WOW!

Outside the restaurant a long black
limousine. We got in, then the scary part
began. "Put your head down on my lap."
I obeyed, he stroked my hair, explained I
wasn't to know our destination, where
we were going, and even afterwards
where we'd been. The windows were
shut tight. All I could hear was the hum
of the car. "Poor baby," he said over
and over. "Poor, poor baby, about to
enter the abyss." We were driving fast,
must have been on a speedway, FDR
Drive or something, uptown or downtown
I had no idea. "Poor baby, poor little
girl—oh, what are we ever going to do
with YOU?"

We drove for an hour. The car finally
stopped. He warned me not to look. I
had to be blindfolded first. Outside I
smelled flowers, lawn, heard crickets,
distant howling dogs. We were in the
country someplace. I fantasized a
powerful man's estate.

The doorbell chimed. "You're not
Suze anymore," he whispered. "You're S
tonight, S like O in The Story of O." Was
I dreaming? Should I laugh, rip off my

*blindfold, run away giggling in the night?
As much as I wanted to flee, I wanted
even more to stay and to endure.*

*Door opened. Jamie gripped me tight,
led me across a deep pile rug. I sensed
the others. Six or seven, I thought, men
and women, too.*

*"This is S," Jamie announced. "Curtsy
to them," he whispered. I obeyed, heard
approving "oohs" and "ahs." "You're
going to like her," Jamie said. "S is
insatiable. You'll all be able to drink your
fill." Already he was unzippering my
back. Soon I was naked except for my
necklace, and of course the blindfold tied
around my head. More approving sighs,
mutterings. "Isn't she special?" Jamie
asked. "Yes. Yes she is." I don't know
why but it was the women I really feared.
I sensed they were hard, fortyish,
severe, not sweet pathetic things like
Cin, but cruel, and I wasn't pleased by
the thought that soon I'd be in their
power. It was the men I craved, the older
powerful ones.*

*CLICK. Steel handcuffs snapped
around my wrists. I started to protest but
Jamie shushed me up. "You've got to be
helpless—you agreed to that." I was led
about the room, their hands stroking,
feeling me up. Someone pinched my*

nipples. Someone else put his hand around my neck. "I think she's hot already," one of the women said. A hand thrust into my pussy, two fingers hooked in, probing up. "Yes, she's wet. She'll be ready soon." "Look how straight she stands." "She's proud, isn't she. She won't be later, though."

The bed was huge. My wrists and ankles were tied to the corners. I was open, stretched, available to be used. And they came in succession, a lone man first—he was heavy and breathed hard and sweated as he thrust. A wait then—who would have me next? Two of them, I thought, then I suspected there were three—mouths on my breasts, a tongue wagging fast and taut against my clit, fingers everywhere, tickling, stroking, a thick cock thrust suddenly against my lips.

"Deep throat," he ordered. Flashes of light. Jamie was taking pictures. Will he sell them to a split-beaver mag? The idea appealed to me. My punishment. What would HE think if he saw me like this? I struggled and writhed to enhance the effect. And then the thought of being photographed made me come.

"She's got a lot more in her," a woman said. She went down on me, ate *me for an eternity. Then they left me alone. How long? Half an hour? After that it was all cocks, each bigger than the next, hard savage ones banging in and out till I ached. I was gang-banged, ravaged, turned over, taken from behind. Jamie's flashbulbs popped. I was Greeked and then released. Jamie led me to a bathroom, unknotted my blindfold, watched me while I bathed. "Thrilling enough?" he asked. I shrugged, blasé. "Shot seven rolls," he said. "I'll make you a scrapbook as a souvenir."*

Up yours, sweets, I thought. Thanks a bunch for the trip, but I'm afraid it didn't help. The memory wasn't blotted; all I felt was dry and rather pained.

"So—?" he asked later in the car. "An experience," I told him, lying in his lap. "I'll write it up in my secret diary. I'm glad I did it, but I wouldn't go through that again. I'm more of an S than I am an M, I think. I'll tell you one thing, dearie. Being Greeked isn't all that big a charge. I feel sorry now for all you fags."

Today I snuck into the darkroom. The scrapbook he made was filled with shots of me, close-ups of various and sundry genitalia, and the backs of people's heads. He cut out the rest, evidence of

*who the people were. But I wanted to
know what I was screwed by, so I went
into his safe, found the negs and made
up a set of contacts for myself. JESUS!
The men were flabby, middle-aged, the
women lined and old. Couldn't he have
set it up with a black basketball team,
anything except this overweight
suburban bunch? The one with the thick
dick has a face like John Mitchell. The
cruel lady looks like Walter Cronkite in a
fright wig. Jesus, I've been gang-banged
by Great Neck! By Scarsdale blue-hairs
for Christ's sake! I've been had by the
sort of people you see sitting around in
airports, white tufts of chest hair
sprouting out of polyester shirts—*

AFTER PENNY read this passage she felt filled
with sadness and shame. There were many pages like
it, tales of orgies and self-debasements, scornful ref-
erences to inadequate lovers, shrieks of discontent.
The diary upset her, but not because of sex. It was the
pathos of it, Suzie's misery, that filled her with despair.

There was another thing, too, something she didn't
understand: the diary turned her on. How strange to
react to her sister's escapades as if she were reading
a pornographic novel. But that's what was happening;
she was *aroused* by what she read. Peering into Suzie's

sex life was to discover bizarre longings—to be tied to bedposts and probed by strangers, to be ravished by armies of men.

Jared said the diary just showed how screwed up Suzie had been. "There's this guy she seems to be hung up on, someone vague who won't see her and apparently feels about her the same way she feels about Cynthia. And then there's the bisexual photographer, Jamie, but she doesn't seem to like him all that much, and he doesn't come across as the impassioned killer type."

"So where does that leave us?" Penny asked.

"Back at zero, where we'll always be."

Still the diary fascinated her. It was as if Suzie were calling from the pages, crying out to her for help. Maybe it had been silly to think it would give her the murderer's name, but now she was interested in other things: why Suzie had lived this way, what had made her so unhappy, what was behind her will toward self-destruction, what she had been looking for.

She wanted to meet this Jamie Willensen, wanted to put a face on this person to whom Suzie had relinquished so much. Jared told her to leave it alone, stop prying around in Suzie's life.

"She's my sister. I don't feel I'm prying."

"She's dead now. What difference does it make?"

"I want to understand her."

"You're getting obsessed."

"I just want to understand."

"You can carry that too far."

Her interest annoyed him. He complained again that she was talking like Suzie and that her gestures were sometimes the same. "Next thing you know you'll want to start re-enacting scenes," he said.

"Sure. Why not? Why don't you tie me down and fuck me in the ass?"

"See? That's just what I mean. And you think it's just a joke."

"No. I'm serious. Maybe I am obsessed. I care about her. What's wrong with that?"

He shook his head. "Caring won't bring her back." Then he looked at her. "Maybe you ought to see a shrink."

She didn't want to see a shrink.

She wanted to see Jamie Willensen. She looked him up in the phone book. His studio was just a couple of blocks away. She asked Jared to walk over there; maybe they'd catch a glimpse of him as he came or left. Jared wasn't crazy about the idea but finally agreed to come along. They went over after work.

It was an old carriage house conversion on East Seventy-Eighth, a narrow two-story building, the kind that was cheap thirty years ago, worth a fortune now. The carriage entrance, two huge doors facing the street, was sealed up, but there was a little doorway to the side and two doorbells, one marked "residence," the other "studio." Penny knew the sort of place. She'd seen spreads on fashion photographers' studios in magazines: a cavernous downstairs filled with lights and expanses of fabric and paper hanging on rollers from the ceiling like giant shades and various props spread around; upstairs would be the apartment where he lived.

The place was shut tight, though she could see some light escaping through vertical blinds on the second floor. "What are we supposed to do now?" Jared asked. "Ring the doorbell and introduce ourselves?"

"I just want to see what it looks like," she said.

"You said you wanted to see *him*. There's a phone booth on the corner. Call him and tell him we're here. Tell him you're Suzie's sister and you've been reading her diary, and there's a lot of stuff about him in there, and we wondered if he had any of those old orgy photographs around, and if he does could we come up and take a look.''

"You know I'm not going to do anything like that.''

"You want to see him—OK. I'll call him, tell him there's a baby on his doorstep. That should lure him out and then you'll have your look. Then maybe we can get out of here and go eat dinner someplace.''

He was taunting her. She turned to him and asked why he was being so mean.

"Because this whole scene is ridiculous, standing around out here looking up at his windows, hoping by some fluke he'll come out and show his face. I know you're into that sort of stuff, but isn't it usually the other way around?''

"What?''

"Well, aren't you the one who's usually up there in the window, and aren't the people you're spying on usually standing around outside?''

She looked at him, unbelieving. "That's a lousy thing to say.''

He seemed confused. "I'm sorry, babe. I just feel like a fool standing out here. It just came out. I didn't mean it. I don't know what I meant.'' He reached out for her but she stood back.

"Things like that don't just 'come out' unless they're already in your head. Since you're so hungry,'' she said, turning, walking away, "why don't you just bug off and eat.''

He called after her. "Where are you going?''

"None of your business.'' And then, as an afterthought, she turned and stared at him. "Fuck off!'' she said sharply. And then to herself: *That's what Suzie would have said.*

They made it up later that night. He was waiting for her when she came back from a Woody Allen movie. She'd gone to it hoping some laughter would do her good, but she hadn't laughed; the picture had made her sad. Jared apologized again, this time earnestly. He said she'd been right—the idea that she was a voyeur had been in his mind, and because it was her one weakness, he'd used it against her as people who know each other very well sometimes do, to take out his own frustrations and bitterness which had nothing to do with her or even with having to stand outside Jamie Willensen's carriage house, but with the fact that he was a failed actor, maybe even a failed human being.

"There's that creep of a photographer," he said, "a piece of human garbage, if you can believe half of what Suzie wrote, making big bucks, being touted as a Big Talent, who can afford a suede couch that cost thirty-five hundred dollars three-and-a-half years ago, which means, if you take inflation into account, it probably sells for four grand today. And to top it off I was thinking about how it had 'come' dribbled on it by some asshole named Dave, and how, probably, instead of having it cleaned he's just left on the stains to make it more of a conversation piece. So I turned on you and said something lousy, probably one of the lousiest things anyone's ever said to you in your life, which puts me, I suppose, in the same category as prosecutor Robinson. And so, on that note, I was thinking maybe I should just pack up and move into the Y or someplace, or maybe better, more in keeping with the sort of bastard I am, that bug-ridden whorehouse down by the Port Authority from which you extracted me so kindly, and for which I've repaid you by acting like a shit."

Penny had begun to laugh halfway through his little speech, and Jared could barely keep a straight face himself as he came to its end.

"OK," she said. "Apology accepted. Now please, for Christ's sake, shut up."

They got into bed, and he made love to her very gently, doing everything he could to please her so she would know that no matter what he'd said it wasn't sex that held him to her, but love. When they were finished and had turned off the lights, she lay on her back and tried to sleep. But she couldn't. So many things were whirling through her mind. She turned to him and finally whispered in his ear.

"What was she like?" she asked. "What was she really like?"

"Suzie?"

"Uh-huh."

"You knew her a lot better than me."

"I mean—you know: what was she like in bed?"

"Jesus, babe." He propped himself up so he could look at her. "I don't know. Jesus. I can't remember that."

"Come on," she coaxed him. "You can remember if you try."

"There's no way to describe something like that. It was so long ago. What difference does it make?"

"I'd like to know."

He shook his head. "I want to forget it. I want to forget what she was like." He turned his back, then fell off to sleep.

Either he really couldn't remember, or couldn't bring himself to tell. In either case she was annoyed. What use was he if he couldn't tell her the things she wanted to know? *Jamie Willensen would tell me,* she thought, *if I could ever get close enough to ask.*

Jamie and I had a deal. If he satisfied my fantasy, I'd satisfy his. His is complicated, baroque, reeking of faggy S&M. But hearing him tell it gives me a charge. Humiliation—maybe that's my game!

The scenario is set. We go to The Underground on West Street Saturday night. The place is jammed, people staring, tittering. Slave masks hang from the ceiling. Rubber underwear. Leather jockstraps. Vibrator kits. Dildoes in assorted sizes. Lotions, creams, a whole wall of bondage devices, another of paddles and whips, a chart showing the "handkerchief code." Three skinny guys in T-shirts are waiting on the mob. Everyone very polite, very proper and correct. Merchandise is ordered in hushed tones. Items purchased are handed over in discreet black paper bags.

"Can I help you?" asks one of the salesmen.

"Yes," I say, quite loud enough for

everyone to hear. *"I'm interested in looking at male genital restraints."*

"Ah—" He leads us over to a counter where all sorts of wicked-looking gadgets are displayed.

"I like that one," I say, pointing to a mean-looking gismo, all black leather and chrome studs. The salesman pulls it out. *"Do you think this will fit you, sweets?"* I ask, giving Jamie a withering look. By now the entire store is silent. You can cut their fascination with a knife. Jamie shrugs, embarrassed. *"Looks like it might be a little small,"* I say. Then to the clerk: *"He's hung like a horse—can you BELIEVE it? Well, the tighter the better I suppose. Twenty-four hours in that ought to teach him who's the boss."*

I snap my fingers. Jamie, blushing to his ears, fishes out his wallet, forks over twenty bucks. *"No need to wrap it,"* I tell the salesman. *"It's going on him the minute we get home."* The salesman, I'm certain, has a hard-on. The women are incredulous. A young college couple examines us as we turn around.

"Yes," I say as we leave the shop, *"twenty-four hours cinched up tight as I can—then you'll REALLY be sorry for what you did."*

Out on the street: "God, you're
dynamite," he says.

"Get your charge, sweets?"

"Did I ever."

"Shall we go back and buy a pair of
clamps to torture your little nips?"

He's on fire now—I can tell. Back on
Seventh Avenue I feel his crotch, find
him hard as steel. "You really are an M,"
I tell him.

"Yes," he says. "Oh, yes!"

For a week we play out the charade.
He gets more and more into it—I less
and less. Finally when he asks me to
beat him with a riding crop, I scornfully
refuse. "Get one of your numbers to do
that for you," I say. "Go to a leather-bar.
I resign my role as Queen."

He's crestfallen, and I'm glad. All this
kinky stuff leaves me cold. I loathe my
brassy wise-ass act, my good-time-
outrageous-bitch routine. I long so much
for tender love, to be held and cuddled,
the great strong chest to weep upon, to
cling to in the night—

AFTER JARED'S refusal to describe what Suzie was like in bed, Penny decided to keep her thoughts about Suzie to herself. They were her problem, her obsession—no reason to bother Jared with them anymore. She carried the diary in her purse, brought it out at odd moments, reread certain passages again and again. She didn't know why it obsessed her except that by telling her about Suzie it seemed also to be telling her about herself. Why had they been so different? What had made their lives diverge? She believed that if she studied the diary hard enough the answers would be revealed.

The tantalizing mystery now, she thought, was why Suzie had lived the way she had, as if she'd been controlled by something, driven by some controlling power. As for their sisterly relationship, the more she thought about it the more convinced she became that beneath her own bookishness and voyeurism there was a lot of Suzie, too.

She didn't know why she thought this. It wasn't clear. Sex—that was part of it; she thought about sex a lot now, sometimes for hours at a time, and had begun to fantasize in ways she'd never done before. She thought about seeing Jared in one of his porno films, wondered what she'd feel if she saw him big on the screen, naked, savagely screwing someone else. And then she began to think about seeing that in real life: a threesome, a foursome, an orgy, with lots of faceless men and Jared, too, and herself, of course, being screwed by all of them, taking them on one at a time and then by twos and threes.

Maybe she and Jared should go to one of the swingers' clubs. He knew people who held sex parties—they should go to one of them. It seemed peculiar to her that she should be thinking things like this, and when she hinted to Jared what she had in mind, he said he found it peculiar, too. "That's not you," he told her, shaking his head. But then, later, she wondered: *If these are the things I think about, if these are my fantasies, then they* must *be me.*

Another thing that struck her in the diary were those points where Suzie's life had intersected with her own. That dinner in Greenwich when Suzie had said she found her reading list "jejune"; that time when they were little and their father had spanked Suzie for knocking down her blocks. She barely remembered those things, but reading about them brought them back. Differently, of course—her own memory of the jejune incident was so vague she could only remember the sting of her tears as she stared at the toppled blocks.

Suzie wrote odd things about her: "I want to grab her by the ears and shake her till she pees"—"I sometimes wonder if Child will ever get her shit together." But there was a strain of tenderness, too, a concern for "Child," a hope that "Child" wouldn't suffer the way she had. There was a cryptic reference to a conversation about Scott Fitzgerald they'd had once driving up to Maine. She remembered it as a casual bit of talk, but Suzie evidently had found it intense:

> —listening to her chatter I feel like flirting with danger, skirting close up to the edge. Child sniffs at "Let me tell you about the very rich. They are different from you and me."; thinks Fitz got Tom

and Daisy Buchanan all wrong, too, with his accusation that they "smashed up things and creatures and then retreated back into their money or their vast carelessness." Finds Baby Warren's final dismissal of Dick Diver ("That's what he was educated for") implausible.
"Fitzgerald never really understood," she says. "We ought to know, don't you think? We're rich and not like that at all." She talks on and all the time I'm touched and moved and also screaming wildly inside. Who says we're not like that! What about Devereux and Nicole? I guess Fitzgerald got that stuff balled up too—

There was something else that surprised Penny—she'd no idea Suzie suspected she was being spied upon in Maine. But there it was in black and white: "I know she's watching me all the time now, sad-eyed, hurt. I think she's trying to figure me out. (Well, best of luck, Child!)"

She'd been so careful, but now she saw how easily she'd been found out:

Feel the prying eyes, the glowing eyes, staring out of the darkness, watching me with envy in the night. The cottage is my stage, but where is the applause? Nothing coming to me from my audience, no tears or laughter, not even a snicker or a hiss. I can only imagine

the effect, and it's very spooky.
Someone sitting there watching me,
envying. The more wildly I perform the
more tightly hands grip the chair. Jesus!
I'm giving a sex show! Where are my
watchers? Where are the faceless men?
Where are their hoots, their pants? Do
they whack off silently to my noisy
humping on the stage?

There was something mystical about that, and other passages as well, a wild leap from Suzie's awareness of being watched to her fantasy that she was giving a sex show for an audience of men. But Suzie had been uncanny in her accuracy, had guessed at details she could not possibly have observed. It was true: Penny's hands *had* gripped the rocking chair and she *had* been stimulated, afraid to make the slightest noise, even afraid her chair would squeak. How could Suzie have known about that? Had she possessed the "genius of the mad"?

Yes, there were strange passages, and lurking always in the background was the unnamed indifferent lover, the "Dark Man" of the diary, the one who'd be sickened by her love-sick eyes just as she was sickened by Cynthia French:

Whenever we see each other he's so
goddamn cool. All those nights I spent in
his arms—it's as if they mean nothing
now, as if they're part of a deep and
ancient past. What is it that makes him
so special? Why do all other men seem

*so meager by comparison? I make up
prints from the orgy, send them to him
wondering what he'll think. Will he call
me in the middle of the night? Tell me
he wants me? Will the sight of my pussy,
spread out, hungry and wet like a
skinmag model's, like a whore's, a
cunt's—will that turn him on again? Or
will he be disgusted? Enraged? I barely
sleep the next three nights, so great is
my suspense. Then my envelope comes
back. It's been misaddressed. Such an
obvious slip—I'm totally disgusted and
don't send it off again—*

One morning, a week after their crazy high-speed
journey to Maine, she and Jared had another argument.
It started over something trivial—she asked him to turn
down the radio so she could read the *Times* in peace.
But soon it escalated and then she called him lazy, and
he accused her of being selfish and acting more like
Suzie every day.

"Sorry," she told him, "you'll just have to take me
as I am."

"I love you as you are. It's what you're turning into
I can't stand." She stood up, placed her hands on her
hips, gave him a mocking look. "That's just what I
mean," he said.

"What?"

"The way you're looking at me now. Your stance.
Everything."

She laughed at him, put on her running shoes, and
went out to Central Park to jog alone. It was pleasant
to run by herself for a change, to get out of that claus-

trophobic apartment, away from Jared too. They were spending too much time together. They never saw anybody else. They never did anything. He just sat around and made feeble efforts to get a job. She at least had a career. He was jealous of her for that, and over her interest in Suzie, too. He couldn't stand the way she studied the diary, her questions about Suzie and everything she'd done. It was important, she realized, for her to get away from him, preserve some privacy for herself. From now on, she decided, she'd run alone, find her own pace, use the time to think things over and unwind.

She started getting up earlier, going out without him, when the track around the reservoir was still uncrowded and the dawn had barely come. There were fewer runners then; the cold air and late autumn sunrises had chased many of them out of Central Park. She liked the solitude, the sense of freedom, and also the chance to look at other people, meet their eyes.

She'd never done that before; she had been too shy, had always looked down at the ground when she passed someone, afraid she'd be recognized, afraid of people's stares. But now she welcomed those encounters, so fast, intense, these mutual inspections of faces and bodies, these rapid comings-together and drawings-apart, these momentary intimacies when she could hear the person's breathing, smell his sweat.

Seeing a male runner coming from the opposite direction, she'd scrutinize him closely, examine his face, perhaps even smile just a moment before they passed. Meeting him again she'd smile more broadly, and sometimes, at the last moment, subtly lower her eyes. Spotting a bulge if his running pants were tight, she'd turn after he'd passed, admire him from behind. Sometimes he'd turn, too, and then both of them would laugh. *I'm becoming a crotch-watcher,* she thought. *I'm cruising guys. I like it; it's harmless and it's fun.*

Then the same thing started happening to her in the subways, waiting in the stations or standing in the cars. She'd find herself examining men, wondering about them, what it would be like to touch them, how they'd look undressed. It was the sort of thing Suzie used to do, looking at men as if they were hunks of meat. She remembered the way Suzie used to do it, the expression on her face, the way she'd hold her body, the cool appraising stare in her eyes. She could sense men responding to these inspections, too. They made her feel powerful. "Think sexy," Suzie'd always advised. Now, thinking sexy, she felt sexy and confident.

As the days passed her new-found interest in male bodies spread from the jogging track and the subway into office hours, too. Looking at the Puerto Rican boys who handled interoffice mail at B&A she wondered what they'd be like as lovers, how big, how long, how hard, how rough they'd be, whether Suzie would have liked them, whether they'd be better than the Ivy League boys she'd had. And she started looking at the editors, MacAllister especially. What lay beneath his black leather jacket and black turtleneck? Was he hairy or smooth? A stud or a washout? What, she wondered, would Mac be like in bed?

She'd always felt herself drawn to him. Now, suddenly, she'd look at him and begin to fantasize. There was something so attractive about his maturity, the authority in his manner, his decisiveness. His voice was strong, his intellect was powerful, and he radiated sexual power, too. She tried not to fantasize too much—it made dealing with him too complicated, made it difficult to concentrate at editorial meetings, think about books, do her job. But she couldn't help herself, and then she felt guilty, as if somehow she were being disloyal to Jared, betraying him by having fantasies about Mac and other men. Suzie, of course, would never have felt guilty.

Why, she wondered, couldn't she be like that? She realized she still had lots to learn. In a funny way, she thought, Suzie would teach her—through the diary. The diary could be the key to many things.

I've been injured, bruised. My psyche is agog. I'm obsessed and miserable and self-hating and heading for the gutter. If only the gutter were really pleasurable. If only orgasms were enough.

Thinking more and more lately of getting away from here—the city, Jamie, all the crap, the threesomes and the dildos, the S&M. I need the kind of men whose sweat smells good, muscled Nordic meat, brainless, faceless—the storm trooper look, thick blond fuzz on their legs and thighs, the kind of men who, when they go down on you, you don't have to look at grease.

If only he knew how promiscuous I've become, and also how depraved. Would love to ram it in his face. Got an idea about that. Make an arena and act. ACT. Engender great anxiety. Flaunt it madly. Fuck away till something pops or breaks—

For MONTHS she'd been postponing a visit to Greenwich. She dreaded it, suspecting that things were getting worse there and that if she went home she'd have an awful time. It was hard to imagine how things could get worse; the last time she'd gone, before the summer, the tension had been terrible, the mood so cold it had made her shake. She'd decided then not to visit her mother unless her father was away.

She chose a chilly sparkling Sunday afternoon in early December when he was on a business trip (Seoul and Taipei; some sort of textile deal), and went out carrying Suzie's diary to read and relieve the boredom of the train. She caught a taxi at Greenwich station. The town looked forlorn to her, the expensive little shops so chic and yet so empty of anything of value, decorated already with Christmas things, pine cones and miniature Santas and red bunting, which depressed her as Christmas always did. When the taxi entered the estate area, passing the stone walls and gates to long, curving drives, she caught glimpses through the bare trees of big houses set behind, and it occurred to her how false the architecture was—fake Palladian villas and pseudo Norman chateaux, great rambling Tudor monstrosities with leaded glass windows and crenelated towers. She passed a group of girls on horseback. They were in their early teens, dressed in handsome riding habits, shiny black boots, protective bowler hats, carrying crops that made them look arrogant, though she suspected they really weren't, and she thought: *This is how the American aristocracy lives; this is the veneer.*

At first approach her own house was impressive. One passed through gates, then up a long drive of white pebbles which meandered through the landscape. But when the slate-roofed house came into sight, she was struck as always by its ugliness. It was huge, luxurious, and out-of-scale, too large and dominant for its property. It always looked to her as though it had been dropped there gratuitously from the sky. It spoke to her of her father's willfulness and his need for heraldry.

She paid the taxi, walked up the steps, tried the door, and found it locked. How strange, she thought, pressing the bell, to have to ring to get inside. An unfamiliar woman let her in. She introduced herself as Mrs. McIver as if that were enough—she was a nurse or paid companion or whatever the current euphemism was. Penny had met many such women. They were always middle-aged and rather strongly built, they had kind eyes, and they didn't seem to last too long—got fired by her father, or quit out of boredom, or left because her mother wearied of them and ordered them dismissed.

Mrs. McIver led her into the living room, then went out to tell her mother she'd arrived. Penny looked at the Oriental rugs, the furniture upholstered in English chintz, the phony coat of arms carved in stone above the fireplace, and wondered at how her father's taste had changed, how the appetite for this huge pretentious house, which he'd bought with such pride because it symbolized landed gentrydom and wealth, had given way over the past fifteen years to the taste represented by his offices, austere and hushed modernity, glass and steel.

"Oh, Penny dear—" Her mother seemed almost to be scooting toward her, arms outstretched, ready to clasp her to her breast. "Dear, *dear*—it's just been *ages*—'' The embrace was firm, and her mother looked good, she thought, her skin pink and fresh, her eyes alert, her gray hair glossy and alive. As they kissed and hugged Penny noticed Mrs. McIver watching them from the door. She smiled and nodded, then disappeared. "But you're so *skinny,* dear—almost like a boy.''

"It's the running, mother.''

"Yes, the jogging. I forgot. Everyone's doing it these days. I see them around, old men sometimes, in those funny pajama suits. I always pray they won't have heart attacks.''

She turned to the fireplace. "I *told* them to light the fire, dear—I wanted the room to be all cozy and warm when you arrived. Well, no matter. I have a little project for us this afternoon. I thought we might get out the Christmas things, dust them off together and chat some while we work.''

It seemed a nice enough idea, better than sitting on the sofa while the talk wound down to silence. Penny let her mother lead her up the staircase, grand, carved, imperial, and to the attic where the Christmas decorations were stored. "So many rooms, Penny—so many unused rooms up here. This house was built for a dozen servants. Costs a fortune to keep it heated now, but your father won't hear of moving to a smaller place—''

They walked down a hallway, past extra servants' bedrooms with dormer windows, then into the real attic where the beams showed, the walls were dark and unfinished and the lighting came only from a few bare ceiling bulbs. Penny had been scared of this part of the house when she was little, and Suzie, knowing she was scared, had often hidden in it during their games of hide-and-seek.

"He was quite upset, you know, dear.''

184

"What, mother? I mean—who are you talking about?"

"Your father, dear. He was really quite upset. Tucker called him, and he was very irritated about what you'd done."

"Tucker?"

"Yes." She turned, looked straight at Penny. "I don't know why you're pretending you don't know what I'm speaking about."

"My trip to Maine?"

"Yes. Of course. Tucker was quite put out, you see. At least that's what your father said. 'Quite put out'— I believe those were his very words, though they don't much sound like Tucker's vocabulary, do they?" She glanced at Penny again. "I doubt he'd use an expression like that, don't you?"

"And daddy was angry?"

"Did I say that? I don't believe I did. I believe I said he was irritated and upset. You should have checked with him first before you went up there, he said. He'd given Tucker instructions about not letting anybody in, and then you turned up and intimidated the poor old man—I think that was the gist of it—and then Tucker got scared, thought he'd better call down here and let your father know. After all, he'd disobeyed his orders, he didn't want to be sacked. I guess he wanted to be the one to tell your father, rather than risk his hearing it from someone else." That made Penny smile, the thought that she'd intimidated the "poor old man." "Yes, dear, I'd say your father was quite *concerned.*"

"If he was so concerned, mother," she said—they were bending over, both of them, picking up cardboard boxes labeled "Xmas Decorations Fragile"—"why didn't he call me up and bawl me out? I never knew I wasn't supposed to go up there."

Mrs. Berring smiled, and it was then, because of

something in her smile, that Penny first began to suspect she wasn't as healthy as she appeared.

"That's not your father's way, to bawl you out. You should know that by now. It's not a question, dear, of your not being allowed to go up there. You must never think a thing like that. It's just that he wants to be kept informed, so he can tell Tucker to have things ready for you when you arrive."

"I was there exactly fifteen minutes."

Her mother nodded as if she already knew.

"Maybe the reason," she suddenly whispered in a tone that changed the whole tenor of the conversation, "maybe the real reason he was so concerned was that he couldn't figure out what you'd gone up there *for*." Yes, it was as if there was suddenly a conspiracy between them, as if her mother knew more than she was saying, and the two of them were now allied. *But then, how could she know about the diary?* she asked herself.

"Do you know why I went up there?"

"No, dear, I don't. And I don't want to know. But I do know one thing, and that's that your father was *upset*." She laughed a little, looked at Penny. "So maybe he knows, or he suspects. You can never be sure with him."

Penny decided to let the matter drop; her mother seemed content to do the same. They had the boxes open and were looking at various types of lights and bulbs, discussing which ones they should use on the tree this year. Her mother seemed immersed in the problem, was chattering about what a lovely Christmas they were all going to have while Penny was thinking about how dreadful it was going to be and how much she'd rather spend the holiday with Jared instead.

Her mother produced some dust rags and they settled down to pulling glass balls out of boxes, dusting them off, then carefully replacing them when they were clean. "I imagine a very simple Christmas," her

186

mother said wistfully. "Just the three of us. We never see anyone, never have friends to the house anymore. Just a family thing, and Mrs. McIver of course."

"She seems nice, mother."

"Oh? Do you really think she does?"

"Well, I *hope* she is."

"She *isn't,* dear. She isn't nice at all."

"Why? What's the matter with her?"

"She's in it with the rest of them."

"In it? What do you mean?"

"She's in your father's pay, my dear. A person in another person's pay is loyal to that person, not to the person she's pretending to be loyal to."

"Is she really disloyal? She's not mean, is she?"

"Of course not. She wouldn't *dare* be mean."

"Then what's the matter, mother? Tell me, for God's sake. Tell me what's going on."

The conspiratorial whisper again; "They're trying to get me to sign papers. Stock proxies. All sorts of things. And I won't *do* it." She giggled. "I simply won't do it. And your father's furious, but of course he doesn't show that he is. He's got some trick now, some way he's going to get me to sign, surrounding me with all these people he pays, like her, and then—well, we'll just see if I sign or if I don't."

She'd been rummaging through another carton full of objects for the crèche, when suddenly her hands seemed to freeze. Penny looked into the box, saw their old Christmas stockings, the stockings with their names stitched on, which they used to hang in front of the fireplace and which were always stuffed with little gifts on Christmas day.

"Here's yours, dear, here's *his*—" She held up her father's stocking as if she wanted to keep it as far away from her body as she could, "—here's mine, and here is *hers.*" Penny looked and felt a needle press against her heart. It was Suzie's stocking. The name Susan had been beautifully stitched onto it in a script she recognized as coming from her mother's hand. "Poor thing, poor dear," her mother sighed. "We shouldn't keep this any longer I suppose. We really should dispose of all her things, once and for all, don't you think?"

She stuffed Suzie's stocking into a pocket of her dress, and then it seemed as if everything became sane again—they chose a star for the top of the tree, and Mrs. Berring talked about Christmas cookies and Christmas punch, and how she thought she could handle a cup or two of that, and maybe even some eggnog, though she knew she really shouldn't drink.

"Of course, mother." Penny put her arm around her shoulders. "Of course you can handle an eggnog or two, or you could have a virgin eggnog, like a Virgin Mary—how about that?"

"Oh, Penny, you're the only one."

The only one who trusted her, or who was nice to her, or who wasn't in her father's pay? Penny wasn't sure what she meant exactly, but she guessed all three, and then she felt as though she might begin to cry and wanted to run away.

"I'll tell Mrs. McIver to have one of the men bring these things down when the tree arrives. Come." She stood up. "We have something now to do ourselves." Penny followed as they left the attic, retraced their way down the hall, down two flights of stairs to the main floor, then through the kitchen and down the cellar stairs. She couldn't imagine what they were going to do down in the cellar, but she followed meekly, sad and curious, and anxious, too.

"See *that?*" Mrs. Berring pointed at the wine cellar. "He's got it padlocked. Afraid I'll get my hands on some of his precious Burgundies. Afraid I'll drink them to the dregs." There was a new note in her voice now. Anger had replaced the confidential whispering of the attic, and Penny became worried for she saw they were moving toward the furnace room.

"Your father's a dangerous man, Penny. Take care of yourself. *Beware*." And then, as they entered the furnace room where two old-fashioned coal furnaces blazed away, her mother began her tirade.

"*Dangerous*. Very *dangerous*. And *slippery*, too. Imagine—trying to get me to turn over control. He's got control anyway, he runs the damn company like he owns it, even if he doesn't, you know. I called a lawyer. He told me: 'Don't sign anything. Don't give up anything.' 'But what if they force me?' I asked. He said they couldn't, it'd be invalid, that they couldn't get me to sign over anything unless I was represented by counsel, so that was that. I told your father, told him to his face. You should have seen him. He turned purple. Then he started to whisper the way he always does when he gets mad. 'How dare you call a lawyer?' he demanded to know. Dare! *Dare!* What the hell did he mean—how did I *dare?* 'It's *mine*,' I told him. 'My father left the shares to *me*. How easily you've forgotten. Howard Chapman was *my father*.' But what if something happens to me? The shares would go to you, of course, and then they'd be after you—you'd be their victim, because all he wants is *power*. He's not content just to run everything. He has to own it, *all* of it. *God damn!*"

She moved forward then, moved so quickly Penny couldn't hold her back, moved between the two great furnaces, picked up an iron poker that was hanging there, and used it to unlatch and pull open one of the furnace doors. She stepped back then, in the face of the fire and heat, and suddenly she looked mad to Penny, crazed, like her father when she'd watched him burn trash that time in Maine, but maybe even crazier, like a madwoman, the flames dancing in her eyes, her flesh orange, reflecting the fire. And then she reached into her pocket, pulled out the stocking, Suzie's Christmas stocking, and flung it into the furnace. The two of them watched it incinerate, shrivel in an instant to ash. Her mother pushed the poker viciously at the furnace door and slammed it shut.

"Well, that's the end of that," she cried. "That's the end of the Christmas stocking of that miserable little *slut*."

Penny was horrified, gasped at the wild expression on her mother's face, but almost immediately her mother became docile, her body sagged, and Penny had to guide her up the stairs. She turned her over to Mrs. McIver who said it was time for Mrs. Berring's nap.

"Is she always like this?" Penny asked while she was waiting for her cab. Mrs. McIver gave her a quizzical look as if she weren't sure what Penny meant.

"She seems so normal, then suddenly these strange personalities appear."

"She's been excited about your coming out. She's tired now, and overwrought."

"At least she was consistent when she was drinking."

Mrs. McIver shrugged. "That's an illusion. Family members often say things like that. The alcohol just covers things up. She was drinking herself to death."

On the train, riding back to the city, Penny thought about the afternoon. It had been the most painful visit she could remember. To see her mother like this, to see the range of her disturbance, her hatred for her husband, the loathing and the ways she coped with it, the blandness interrupted by the conspiratorial smile, interrupted in turn by open rage, and then that cry as she'd thrown the stocking into the furnace—all the hurt of Suzie's death was in that cry, she thought, all the mourning, the sense of loss, bound up in that act, as if she could exorcise Suzie and the horror of her murder by burning up a sentimental reminder and calling her a "slut."

What a sham, she thought, as the train pounded back into the city, through Harlem, past tenements which she knew had no heat, were full of roaches and rats, where people lived huddled six, eight, God knew how many to a room. *They envy us, rich white people out in Greenwich and Scarsdale and Westport, but they have love and soul and body warmth, and we're just cold and cursed with madness and filled with cruelty and pain.*

She and Jared had planned to go to a movie that night. She'd told him which train she'd be on, and he met her, as arranged, at Grand Central. But she was so depressed about the afternoon that they decided to go back uptown and spend the evening at home. It was dark as their taxi sped up Park Avenue, and though she wanted to explain it to him, describe the afternoon in all its gruesome detail, she found it difficult. She was stuck on that image of Suzie's Christmas stocking shriveling in the furnace; she could focus only on that, and on her mother's exclamation: *"slut!"*

"It was like *everything* was burning up," she said. "Of course she's been dead for more than three years, but in her diary she seemed to come alive again, and then watching that stocking go up in flames and hearing mother speak of her like that—it was like she was dead this time for good."

They got out at Eightieth, he put his arm around her, and they walked the remaining half block to the house. The heat was on in the building and the lobby was as pungent as ever with the smell of cats. He got his key out as they mounted the stairs, but then, when they reached the apartment door, they both stood still in shock. The door was open a couple of inches, and the "unpickable" locks she'd paid a hundred fifty dollars for were drilled out. At the sight of that, the broken locks, the metal filings on the floor, she began to tremble.

"Shhh." Jared brought his finger to his mouth. "I'd better go in first and check." She nodded, knowing how dangerous it could be to confront burglars in the act. He appeared half a minute later. "All clear, but you're not going to like the mess."

She followed him in to find every single thing she owned in disarray. Every book was tumbled out of the bookcases, every plate and glass had been swept off of every kitchen shelf, every drawer had been turned over and emptied, the mattress was upside down, the rugs were pulled out, and the cushion of her window seat, the treasured cushion upon which she'd passed so many happy hours, had been ripped open with a knife. She felt violated.

"Fucking addicts," Jared said. "Funny—the TV and stereo are still here. And your typewriter. That's the kind of stuff they like to take."

Penny stared at the mess, moving carefully from room to room. It seemed to her that, somehow, everything was wrong.

"I don't know why they bothered," Jared said, pointing at the cushion. "Pure hostility, I guess. We could call the police but it won't do any good. Funny they didn't take the TV."

A thought flashed into her mind. "Maybe they were looking for the diary."

"Oh, come on. That's a lot of crap."

She pulled it out of her purse. "I took it with me to read on the train. Maybe there's something in it. They wanted to get it, see what we've found out."

"You're crazy. You're so hung up on that thing you think everyone else is, too. What do you mean 'They were after it'? Who exactly is this 'they'?"

She asked herself the same thing. She wasn't sure, didn't know whom she meant. But she was sure the break-in wasn't the work of appliance thieves. Her apartment had been ransacked. Whoever had broken in had made a search.

"There's something in here," she said, clutching the diary.

"Babe—" He took her hand. "No one knows about the diary. We're the only ones. Even if there is something there's just the two of us, and Cynthia, of course. But she doesn't even know we got it, so what you're saying doesn't make much sense."

"Then why is everything still here? My Nikon. My jewelry."

He shrugged. "Maybe they were scared or something. Maybe they heard a noise, got scared and ran." He started picking things up while trying to calm her, but she was dialing the phone before he noticed she'd walked away.

"Who—?"

"Shhh," she said. It was ringing now at the other end.

"The police won't give a shit. There's nothing stolen."

She motioned for him to shut up. "Hi. Cynthia. This is Penny. Yeah—there's something important I have to know."

She knew right away there was something; she could tell by the way Cynthia paused. There was a shyness, an embarrassment in her voice. No, she'd never told anybody about the diary before, but yes, there was something, and she'd been meaning to call Penny about it, had wanted to call her but had put it off, and was a little embarrassed about it actually.

"What, Cynthia? Just tell me what you're talking about." Jared had stopped trying to wrestle the mattress back into place and was standing in the center of the bedroom watching while she listened to Cynthia explain.

"Couple days after we talked these two guys came around. Very polite, you know, middle-aged, sort of uncley types, and they flashed these IDs, private investigators' cards. Said they were looking into the Berring case. Said they knew you'd been to see me, and then you'd left town suddenly, had driven up to Maine. Asked if I had any idea why you might have left like that, whether it was connected to our talk."

"And so you told them about the diary, right? *Right?*"

"Yeah, I did. But then I pooh-poohed the whole thing. I guess I should have kept my mouth shut, but they were so nice and everything that I thought, well, you know—what's the harm." She paused. "I would have called you, but then I sort of felt ashamed. I don't know how deeply this thing goes. I'm really sorry, Child. Hope I haven't screwed you up."

"Never mind, Cin," she said. "It's OK. Really OK."

It hit her then, even before she replaced the phone. It all came together, everything, like the blocks in one of those mind-twisting puzzles when they suddenly fall into place and the puzzle is revealed and you could kick yourself for not seeing it all before. Middle-aged private investigators—that sounded like retired cops, the sort who staff out corporate security departments, like the security department at Chapman. Her mother saying Tucker had called her father and told him she'd been up in Maine. Her father telling her the day they'd played squash that his people had Jared under surveillance, which meant, of course, that they were watching her as well. And now this break-in just when she'd be away in Greenwich. It was so pat, so obvious, the events so neatly linked. They'd learned about the diary from Cynthia; they knew she'd gone to Maine to get it; they knew from Tucker she'd only spent fifteen minutes in the poolhouse. So they knew she had it now. All they had to do was wait until she left for Greenwich, then break in, find it, find out what it said.

She was explaining all this to Jared as rationally as she could, and then it started jumbling out of her in a mad rush of words, and then he was staring at her, listening intently, incredulous at first, not quite understanding what she meant.

"The lover," she said, "don't you see? The Dark Man of the diary—so cold, aloof, and Suzie's terrible hurt, her pain. Then her crazy summer project, trying to catch his attention, punish him by flaunting herself, or maybe win his sympathy and inspire a renewal of his love. I knew she was carrying on too loudly, exaggerating her behavior, making sure she was heard and seen. The audience—Jesus! Listen to this." She had the diary open, was flipping through the pages, looking for words and clues. "She calls the cottage 'my arena.' On the next page she calls it 'my stage.' She writes that she's 'performing.' All the time I thought she was doing it for me, but now I see she wasn't doing that at all."

"Then what was she doing?" Jared asked, sitting down on the bed.

"Don't you see? Put yourself in front of the cottage then look back up at the house. *All* the bedrooms look down on you—not just mine, but my father's and mother's too. God—she tips it off all over the place, even with this stuff about Fitzgerald, 'Devereux and Nicole.' It was *him* she was in love with. It was him, for Christ's sake. My father."

"Wait—you're going too fast. Who's this Devereux? Who's Nicole?"

"Characters in *Tender Is the Night*. Devereux Warren and his daughter, Nicole. He freaks her out by taking her to bed."

"You're saying your father and Suzie—"

"It *had* to be. Look at this stuff." She opened the

diary to another part. "She imagines him being sucked by a mulatto mistress. How could anyone imagine her father like that? She was always his favorite. They had these games, these little sayings they used to chant. They'd whisper together and hold hands. Then something happened, messed her up, and she quit college and started to go berserk. She did all those crazy things with Jamie Willensen, went to that orgy in the suburbs, tried to destroy herself, burn away her memories. Listen to the way she longs for him: 'Why doesn't he pay attention anymore?' Listen to this: 'Brokenhearted I weep and rage.' God—what agony! It's all here. She wanted to destroy herself. She wanted to be dead."

"That's what I always said."

"Cynthia thought so, too. Said Suzie had her own game going, that there was something she was trying to do. Listen to all this cryptic stuff: 'do what I have to do'; 'something's rubbed off on me'; her fascination with a cold and powerful man, her worry that Cynthia will 'mess up all my plans.' She sends him photos of the orgy hoping to infuriate him. She follows him on Fifth Avenue, weeps and rages, then searches desperately for someone else. She tries S&M to 'cauterize my wounds,' but that doesn't work—she can't shake him off. He's cold to her. Always cold. After their affair he won't touch her, so she dreams up the 'summer project,' to fuck everybody she can find right in front of him, under his windows up in Maine. Jesus—even when she's little she asks him to 'punish me with kisses.' In Maine she wants him to come down and punish her. Listen: 'Punish me for being bad.' What she really wants is for him to come down and make love to her again, cradle her, make it right. But he just sat up there watching her in silence. Just watching. And then she snapped."

She started to cry then; she couldn't help herself. It was so sickening and perverse, and also so very sad.

That's what made her cry—the awful *sadness* of it. Suzie's terrible misery. The diary was one great cry of pain. Thinking of Suzie writing it, trying to sound tough yet crying out, then pining for her father, pining away for him, going through all those mad gyrations, torturing herself, degrading herself, waiting for him to come down and hold her, or punish her, or scream at her, or, as she'd written, waiting at least for his "applause"—all that made her cry.

It was eight o'clock and she was still crying, sitting on the bed amid the wreckage of her apartment, weeping, weeping, while Jared held her and whispered to her and rocked her back and forth. She couldn't control herself—the tears just flowed. She couldn't stop, so she wept on, gasping sometimes, thinking she would never stop. They must have spent another half-hour like that until finally she sat up and looked at him, and then they set to work ordering the apartment.

They put everything back where it belonged, and what was ruined—the cushion, the broken glasses and plates—they packed up into garbage bags which Jared hauled downstairs and set out on the street. Then she tried to make a salad of some leftovers in the refrigerator, but it didn't taste very good and they weren't hungry anyway, so they threw that out, too. Jared said first thing in the morning he'd call a locksmith and have an iron-rod lock installed. He suggested, too, that she Xerox the diary, and maybe put the original in a safety deposit box or someplace, because if people from Chapman Security pulled black-bag break-in jobs like this, then there was no telling what they might do next if they wanted that diary enough.

She nodded while he was saying this, still dazed by what had happened, all the revelations, and now by thoughts of incest—what that really meant. Jared was still talking, and she wasn't really listening to him until she suddenly realized that what he was saying was really terrible, much worse than anything she'd even begun to think.

"—So you see what we're up against. He could do anything. I'm thinking maybe I should go to Schrader, and have him contact the police."

"Why?"

"Well, it's damn clear now that your dad was the murderer. He shined that flashlight at me, then he knocked me down."

She wanted to scream at him to stop, but when she opened her mouth she couldn't make a sound. He was oblivious to her anyway, pacing around the apartment, talking, gesticulating, checking his points off on his fingers as if he had everything figured out, and listening to him, trying to make sense of what he was saying, she began to feel sick.

"When you said Suzie snapped, I saw it right away. Of course it wasn't Suzie who snapped. It was him. Your dad. *He* snapped. He was enraged by what she was doing down there, crazy on account of it. And afraid, too, of course, and with good reason—maybe she'd tell on him, tell what he'd done to her, and that could ruin him, undermine his position at Chapman, shake the faith of his stockholders, all that crap he worries about. So he's just like the guy I always imagined, except he wasn't a humiliated college jock. But it's the same thing if you look at it a certain way—the same emotions, the same crazy rage. One night he can't stand it anymore. She's taunting him, carrying on with all those guys, and, with my luck, it had to be me she was doing it with that night. It finally gets to him, so he comes down filled with lust and hate to put an end to it, end the whole thing once and for all. Maybe he figures he'll just have it out with her, or maybe he knew what he was going to do. It doesn't make a hell of a lot of difference now whether he killed her in madness, or very coolly just to shut her up. In the end he picked up a pair of shears, went in there and ripped her apart. And there I was, the sap, the schmuck, lying asleep on the diving board, just lying there ready to take the rap. He kills her. He stabs her again and again and again. Then she cries out and I wake up and swim back to see what's going on, and then he blinds me with the flashlight, shoves me down, runs out, pauses for a moment—that moment when you saw him—then fades into the bushes and sneaks back around to the house. While I'm grasping around in there, slipping around in all that blood, he regains his composure, washes up, turns on the siren and the lights, and then comes back out playing his father-of-the-victim role just in time for everyone to see me stumbling out with those fucking shears."

"That's not true." She'd finally found her voice. "That's not what happened," she screamed.

"Isn't it? You saw him, didn't you?"

"It wasn't him. I know it wasn't."

"You're awfully sure."

"Jared, this is crazy. You're getting off on something crazy here."

"The way I remember it, it was dark. You blinked. You could barely see. You don't know who you saw."

"You're coming on like Robinson now."

"Yeah? Well, maybe Robinson was right."

"What is this? I'm telling you it wasn't him."

"I say it *had* to be."

"It wasn't. I know it wasn't. Just like I know it wasn't you." She looked at him and saw he didn't believe her. Then he started rattling off more points.

"Look, babe, you figured it out about the two of them. But you don't take it where it has to go. Like why? What happened? Why did he cut it off with her? Out of guilt, maybe, or boredom, or, most likely, because he got tired of her, or maybe she just grew up too much and he likes them young and wasn't turned on anymore. I think she got to be a nuisance with all her pining around. I think she threatened him, told him she'd tell people what he'd done. He didn't have much choice after that. He had to get rid of her. And that's just what he did."

"I'm not going to listen to this." She put her hands up to her ears.

"You goddamn well *are* going to listen." He grabbed her wrists. "Your father's a cold bastard—you always told me that. She was threatening him, saying she'd ruin him if he didn't take her back, so he *had* to kill her if only to shut her up. Now he finds out through his goons over at Security that Suzie kept some sort of intimate sex diary. 'Jesus,' he thinks, 'got to get hold of that.' And then he figures that maybe you really found it, so he knows he's got to get it, destroy it, burn it up. That diary's hot stuff, really ruinous, like Nixon's tapes. He's got to be careful now. Got to be crafty and cool. So when you go out to Greenwich, and he knew you were going there to see your mother, his goons wait across the street for me to leave, then they bust in here and turn the place upside down. All right—they didn't find it. So tell me what happens now? Think about it. He's *got* to be worried. That fucking diary— it's still around, and he doesn't know what it says. He's gone this far, sent his goon squad in. The next step's pretty obvious it seems to me. He's *got* to find out what you know, and, well, if he thinks you know what happened, then you're as dangerous to him as Suzie ever was, and you know how he handled *that*."

He picked up the diary from the bed, began reading excerpts, excited, wildly excited, like an adventurer on a manhunt, she thought, tracking, closing in on a quarry, dizzy with the thrill. He was acting triumphant about it, *triumphant,* putting together the puzzle, filling in the pieces, talking about her father, calling him a murderer, saying he might try and murder her. It was too much. She couldn't take it, began to scream. He told her to shut up, then they fought, she scratched at him and he wrestled her and held her down, and then, pinned on the bed, she stopped thrashing and began to weep again.

Jamie says he's tired of pimping for me. "Spades, fags, Ss and Ms," he groans, "and now you want college boys in Maine!" "So, I'm tired of fetching and carrying for you," I tell him, "finding props, unloading your goddamn cameras, doing all the shitwork in the darkroom, OK?" "So?" he asks, "like what's the bottom line?" "The bottom line," I tell him, "is that I'm fed up and walking out."

A real quarrel then. "I pay you a salary," he screams. "There's this thing called professional ethics." "What bullshit," I tell him. "All the shoots we go on, the fashion photo trip, is just fucking under another name." "I'm teaching you," he yells. "Letting you see how I work, the secrets of my craft." "Well," I say, "you're not exactly Richard Avedon, you know. I don't feel like I'm apprenticing to a genius quite."

He's furious! That name, Avedon, always sets him off. He hates Avedon, though he'd kiss his ass if he had the *chance. He hates the notion that he's second-rung, because he knows that's what he is.*

"You're a spoiled little rich bitch," he says. "You're a fucking nympho. You're hung up like no one I've ever seen."

I laugh. Is that really the worst he can come up with? Of course I'm a spoiled little nympho bitch. I eat cocks like his for breakfast. What about SUPPER? What about LUNCH?—

LATER SHE'D smile as she thought of how their faces must have looked that Monday afternoon when they finally saw Schrader at his offices on upper Broadway. It would be a cynical smile, amusement at Jared's naiveté, his purity of purpose, his demands for justice, the youthful outrage in his eyes. And as for her own face, red and puffy from a night of tears and screams, she'd laugh a little bitterly at that, too, remembering how confused she'd felt, how close to madness, when the real madness was yet to come.

Jared did the talking; she and Schrader listened. Schrader had grown a goatee since she'd seen him last so that between the two bushes of gray on either side of his head and the gray point of his beard his face was now triangular. Schrader didn't say much, just threw in an occasional question to keep the chronology straight. As Jared came to the end of the tale Schrader closed his eyes and nodded at each point (the dogs hadn't woken up; there hadn't been any tracks), and then he looked at the passages underlined in the Xerox copy of the diary, and he nodded after he read each passage, too. Finally when Jared was finished, there was silence in the room.

"So," said Schrader, "I see what you're driving at. What do you want to do?"

Jared looked at her, then back at Schrader. "Reopen the case," he said.

Schrader nodded. "Yeah. That's what I thought." He turned to Penny. "You go along with this?"

"Of course she does."

"I'd like to hear it from her."

Jared shrugged. "Come on, babe."

"Well, I'm sure now they had an affair," she said.

"But you don't think your father killed her?" She shook her head. "That's what I thought." He turned back to Jared. "Forget it. You don't have anything at all." Jared started to protest, but Schrader raised his hand. "Actually what you've got is a girl's diary which doesn't prove anything except that maybe she experimented a lot with sex. It's a nice story you've told me, or maybe not so nice, but it's just a story, totally worthless in a court of law."

"Now wait—"

"You wait. I'm trying to save you a lot of pain. I got you off and it wasn't easy. Robinson had a damn good circumstantial case. If it hadn't been for Penny here you'd be in the jug right now. But with this—" he pushed the diary back across the desk, "—it'd be a picnic. Any two-bit criminal lawyer could defend against this. No prosecutor would take it on anyhow, because there's nothing here at all."

"There's plenty there."

Schrader shook his head. "It purports to be a diary, but then maybe it isn't. Maybe it's just a lot of crazy fantasies. It doesn't prove incest, and it certainly doesn't prove homicide." He paused. "What do you think is going to happen? Penny's father's going to read this and listen to your theories and then break down and gush out his confession and that'll be that— he'll be sent up, and you'll be exonerated for good? Forget it. You're free. You're walking around. No one can touch you. You can't be tried again. If it bothers you what people think, go away someplace—San Francisco, Paris, any place you want. You're young. You've got a lovely girlfriend. Your whole life's ahead of you. Don't let this eat you up.''

He spoke brusquely, but with kindness, too, Penny thought. Listening to him she felt relieved. ''Last night,'' she said, ''everything seemed so clear.''

''Sure it did. To *you*. And maybe, by some remote chance, Jared's right. But there's nothing he can *prove*. People drive themselves crazy with cases that can't be proved. I've got people waiting outside who have cases I can win. But this is hopeless, a hopeless case.''

''That's it, huh?'' said Jared. ''You're busy. You want us to go.''

Schrader smiled. ''You asked me for advice.''

''What about the break-in?''

''Incompetent burglars.''

''Cynthia said—''

''She said some people came around and asked her what you talked about. We might be able to find them, prove they work for Chapman, but what does that prove except that your father's still suspicious of Jared, and is keeping an eye on him because he doesn't want his other daughter killed.''

''OK,'' said Jared. ''OK. We get the picture. What a crock of shit.''

Schrader nodded. ''Maybe a crock of shit. That's what most things are these days.'' He shook hands with them, saw them to the door. Out in the waiting room Penny saw the anxious faces of his clients, poor people clutching eviction papers, blacks and Puerto

Ricans the police were trying to ramrod into jail, junkies who couldn't afford a lawyer, thieves, murderers, clients he knew how to defend. But he couldn't help them, or rather, she thought, he already had. He was a defender, not a prosecutor, but he knew his law: no prosecutor would take her father on.

Out on Broadway Jared stopped. "Can't believe that guy, how hard-nosed he is."

"Come on," she said. "Let's go home. I've really had enough."

"I don't want to go home. I want to go up to your dad's office and slam the diary down on his desk."

"Look," she said, "I'm tired now. Let's go home— OK?"

Though it was cold they decided to walk straight across Central Park upon grass crisp with December frost. Jared was edgy, nervous, full of anger. He stopped every so often to kick the ground. "I really want to show him the diary," he said. "Tell him we know what's going on and we're going to shout it from the rooftops. Hey—let's do it." He grabbed the envelope from her hands.

"Give that back," she cried.

"No," he said. "I want him to *know*."

"That's mine, Jared," she said, calmly, though she was angry now herself. "Give that back to me right now. I'll decide what we'll do with it, if we'll do anything at all."

"OK," he shouted. "I get it now. You want to take that bastard's advice."

"That bastard only saved your life. You're out free. I'm the one who's injured now. It's *my* father. What the hell is wrong with you?"

He stopped. "You know something, Penny? You sound more and more like *her* every day."

"Spare me, will you? We've been through all that a million times."

"Like last night, talking to Cynthia. *'Right?' 'Right?'* Just like *her*. I could have sworn your voice was just the same."

"So?"

"Yeah—so? What's happening to you? Want to protect him because he's your dad? I may be out free, but don't forget he tried to set me up. He sat there while I went to trial. He glared at me in court like I was a killer, when he knew all along—*shit!*"

"Look," she said. "I can't deal with this. I'm taking the diary." She grabbed it away from him; he didn't try to hold on. "I'm not going home; I'm going back to the office, and I'm going to try to function, and meantime I'm going to think this through. Tonight we'll talk it over—"

"Real calm like it's a rational situation we can really sit down and *discuss*."

She paused, looked at him. "You know something, Jared? You're the one who's changed. You were the one who always said 'you have to live with it' and 'let's not get carried away' and 'it's his problem, not mine.' You never cared. You didn't particularly want to go to Maine. You said the diary was a crock. You were the one who sat around on his ass all day long."

"So—it's come down to that. I'm the one who sits around on his ass, and you're the one who goes to work."

"*Jes-sus.*"

"There you go again."

"I sound like Suzie, right?"

"*Right.*"

She was standing about six feet away from him, looking at him closely, examining him, trying to decide whether she wanted to be with him anymore.

"The way you're looking at me now—"

"*Is just the way Suzie did, Right?*"

"What's wrong with you?"

"What's wrong with *you*?"

They were eyeing each other, more like enemies than lovers, she thought.

He stood back, relaxed his body, started to employ an extra calm and reasonable tone of voice.

"You know he killed her. Inside you know."

"He didn't. Schrader says so, too."

"Schrader's full of shit." He was angry again.

"Everybody's full of shit except you, and you're a genius and the rest of us are idiots. That's about it—right?"

"God—you're so hung up."

"I think you're the one who's hung up now."

"Look—"

"And you haven't been all that straight with me either."

"How haven't I been straight?"

"Oh, I don't know—holding things back. Stuff like that."

"Holding back *what*?"

"That night. Everything that happened. It took you long enough to get around to that."

"I didn't think you'd want to hear about it."

"I had to pry it out of you, that's for sure."

"What are you talking about?"

"All that stuff about how guilty you felt. How you *could* have done it. All of that."

"I don't see what that's got to do with this."

"And shining the flashlight in my eyes. Wanting to *test* me. Or so you said."

"*What are you saying?*"

"I'm not sure exactly. Just that this whole situation is very odd."

"I'll say it's odd. A father and daughter—"

"That's not what I mean."

"Well?"

"Well, I just think it's odd the way you were so

happy-go-lucky about everything until last night, and then suddenly, *suddenly* you're on this insane notion about my dad, and very hot and eager and out for blood, so to speak, as if you've been waiting for all this to come along, so you could sort of—"

"Yeah?"

She shrugged. "Divert attention, maybe. I don't know."

"If you're saying what I think you're saying, then you're full of shit, too."

She laughed. "Your vocabulary's getting kind of limited." She looked at him and shrugged. "I'm full of shit, huh? Well, that's OK with me."

"There you go again. What is this 'OK' stuff, this 'right' stuff, wanting to know about her, even how she screwed? You really are trying to be like her. Maybe you have similar fantasies. Maybe that's why you're suddenly so protective of your old man. What the hell is happening anyway? Here we are accusing each other—this is so damn crazy—I just don't—" He turned, walked over to a tree, slammed his fist into the trunk.

She left him there in the park hoping he'd calm down. She knew she'd said cruel things to him, but he'd said cruel things to her. Now she wanted to go to work. She couldn't screw up her career. Her whole life was a mess, but still, she knew, she had to keep her head.

She couldn't concentrate. She went through the motions at the office, made some calls, sat at her desk pretending to read, then went to an editorial meeting where she didn't say anything, and when Mac turned to her to ask her opinion on a novel for which an agent was demanding an exorbitant advance, she announced "I have no particular opinion on that just now."

When she came home Jared was in the bedroom. He had the door closed and was watching TV. The place smelled like a McDonald's. He'd gone out for fast food, brought home hamburgers and french fries, eaten them, and left the wrappers in the sink. It would have taken him five seconds to put them in the garbage. *Sheer hostility,* she thought.

She cooked dinner, then brought it to him on a tray. He didn't even look up from the TV, didn't acknowledge that she was there. *OK,* she thought, *he's mad.* She went back after half an hour, took the tray away, washed the dishes, then returned and sat beside him, reached for him with her hand. He didn't take it, just lay limp, sprawled out on the bed.

"OK," she said. "If you want to be like that for a while—OK."

They didn't talk any more that night. She reached for him in the dark, sometime after midnight, started to stroke his chest, but he changed his position so she couldn't continue, then finally he turned his back.

"Why do you hate me?" she asked. He didn't reply. "OK," she said, "I hope you get over this, I really do. Because if you don't then I don't want you with me anymore."

He spoke to her then, but he didn't turn. "Is that an ultimatum?"

"Sure, sure. Take it that way if you like. In the meantime I just want you to know that *I'm* the injured party. *I'm* the one whose life is messed up. *I'm* the one who ought to be hating everybody. Me. Not you. *Me.*"

Silence. She didn't sleep well and could tell he wasn't sleeping well himself. She shut her eyes, tried to will herself asleep, but she could hear the pipes gurgling as the heat subsided for the night, could hear great trucks in the early morning hours tearing down the avenue and then the garbage trucks just before dawn grinding up the trash piled on the sidewalk in bags.

She got up very early. It was still dark outside. She

made coffee, then left the house, went to a coffee shop, sat there hunched over her table, drank two more cups, ate a jelly roll, watched people come in, and thought: *I'll go to the office, get something done before they come, maybe reread that novel so I can give Mac an opinion. I'll throw myself into work today.*

She did; she had her memo typed and on Mac-Allister's desk before he came in. She advised against paying the advance. "The novel's good," she wrote, "but I don't think it's big money reprint stuff. Also there's something about this agent's demands that makes me think the author's disloyal, that even if we pay him what he wants he'll go someplace else next time. He's dissatisfied with us for some reason, thinks he's ready for a prestige imprint, something 'classier' than B&A (as if there could be, Mac!). My advice— let's pass this one up."

MacAllister called her in after lunch. "Just wanted you to know," he said, "I called the agent and told him 'no way.' Not because of your memo—I'd come to the same conclusion myself. But that doesn't take away from you at all. You're an editor, Chapman. You understand the business. You've got hunches, instincts. You're getting to be important around here."

She was overjoyed. She called the apartment to share her news. No answer. Maybe Jared was out someplace, walking in the Park, jogging maybe, or sitting in a movie house. She hated the thought that he was just lying on the bed watching TV, not bothering to answer the phone.

She came home prepared to talk things out with him, apologize first of all for her "diverting attention" remarks. Then she would put it to him bluntly—maybe the time had come for them to consider breaking up. She was annoying him with her Suzie mannerisms. She couldn't stand the idea that he thought her father was a killer. There was another possibility and she would put that to him, too—they could go away someplace for Christmas (Bermuda, the Caribbean, even Marrakech), someplace where they could lie out in the sun and try and patch things up. But he would have to purge himself of his suspicions of her father. Incest was one thing—that was bizarre and tragic and painful enough to contemplate. Murder was something else. She didn't want to hear about that anymore.

When she got home she found his note. It was sitting on the center of the bed:

Going away for a while. Need to be by myself, think things through. Will get in touch when I'm ready. Till then take care. J.

She quickly checked the closet, the drawers. He'd taken all his clothes, cleared out everything he owned. He was gone and from the look of things he didn't intend to return very soon. She lay back on the bed, looked at the note again. He hadn't even written "Dear Penny." He hadn't said that he loved her, where he'd gone or when he might return. He hadn't even called her "babe."

IV

Now, just like I figured, they're hanging around me like flies around a honeypot. Word's out I'm a nympho and every stud in Bar Harbor's getting his pecker sharpened up—

It was good to be alone for a change, free of his criticisms, his accusations that she was becoming too much like Suzie, free of him impinging upon her life. Of course she missed making love, the warmth of another body beside her in the bed, but he wasn't indispensable for that. No—it was better without him, she thought. No more distractions, catering to another person's needs. She was free now to explore Suzie, explore the Suzie in herself.

She ran every day at dawn, even harder than before. There were new perceptions of her father to deal with, a whole new life to plan. There was also pain to be expurgated, the pain of the diary's revelations and her anger at her father for what he'd done. She screamed sometimes as she ran, screamed out her pain and rage. No matter how cold it was she was always soaking at the end, panting, exhausted, her heart thumping wildly, her chest aching, her anger broken, sometimes her eyes streaming tears.

It was in this state that, early one December morning a week after Jared left, she encountered Dr. Bowles. Her landlady was a tall, thin, sensibly dressed middle-aged woman with soft features framed by soft hair, cut short in bangs. Penny was standing just inside the inner door of the brownstone, perspiring and weeping and feeling lost, when Dr. Bowles came down the stairs.

"Oh," said the doctor in a sympathetic voice. "Oh, Miss Chapman, is there anything I can do?" Penny shook her head, trying to smile. "Come, then. Let me help you to your door." She grasped Penny firmly, maternally, and together they walked up the flight.

"Thank you," Penny said, fishing out her key. "I'm so sorry. I didn't mean to trouble you. I'm not usually like this. Oh, dear—" She was stabbing at her lock, couldn't seem to get the key inside.

"There's something very nice," the psychiatrist said, helping her with the door, "something which Camus once wrote: 'Happiness, too, is inevitable.' Think of that when you're sad, and you'll find you'll feel better right away."

"Oh," said Penny, smiling, "that's a lovely quote. Thank you very much."

"Not at all. Now I haven't seen your young man around for a while, so I suppose the two of you have broken up. It's only natural that you should be sad. Nothing's more painful than the ending of a love. But if it's more than that, if it's something more and you want to talk about it, in fact if you ever want to talk about anything at all, remember I'm just upstairs. Call first in case I'm with a patient, but otherwise you're welcome day or night. Now—" she brushed her lips against Penny's cheek, "have a good day. And don't forget Camus." She smiled and then she was gone, leaving Penny suffused with warmth.

* * *

Word of Jared's leaving seemed to have gotten around at B&A. She wasn't sure how, but she assumed Lillian was the informant, and the telephone operators, of course—they knew Jared didn't call her anymore. Roy MacAllister, too, she thought, seemed to be eyeing her differently. Ever since she'd given him that memo he'd gone out of his way to be complimentary. But she knew he was a master of favoritism so didn't pay much attention until he asked if she'd have a drink with him one day after work. She said yes, she'd love to join him for a drink, and then she was amused when he took her to the same bar she'd taken Jared that day he'd appeared in the lobby and refused to accept her rebuff.

It was the same bar, but the conversation was different. No moody young actor this time trying to explain why he'd performed in *Pussy Ranch,* but a mature man exuding confidence and charm, telling her fascinating tales of writers and books. She wasn't "Chapman" anymore; she'd suddenly become "Penny" to him, and from that she sensed that he was interested in her, so even as she listened she thought about what she'd do if he made an advance.

"Look," he said finally, "this is great fun. Let's go on to dinner. I know a place in Soho—no writers, no publishing people. No one will know who we are."

They took a taxi, it was cold, and so they sat close together in the back. She liked the feel of his overcoat, expensive, cashmere. And the restaurant was excellent, not Bohemian, no hanging plants against bare brick walls but everything black and white and Art Deco, and the other patrons looked happy and successful, and no one wore blue jeans, and the food was very good. He ordered a bottle of white Burgundy to go with their sole, was even more charming than he'd been at the bar. His stories were even better, she thought, and it was such a pleasure to sit in a good restaurant and laugh.

She liked him. She didn't think she could trust him, but didn't care, thought he was a magnificent, experienced man. And in her lightheadedness from the wine she knew he was going to ask her to come home. She was receiving all his signals and evidently giving the proper signals back, and she liked that, hadn't done that before, felt very grown-up, very New York and single and free. Yes, she decided, she certainly would go to bed with him if he asked. It would be interesting, would probably be delightful, and why shouldn't she? She didn't have a boyfriend now, she could do anything she liked. Yes, she could sleep with anyone she liked now, and she could keep a diary just like Suzie's, if she felt like it, and grade men on how good they were in bed, and the hell with tears and pain and the family pathology, the hell with living under the shadow of Suzie's death and thinking of herself as a member of a cursed clan.

"Shall I drop you?" he asked as they taxied uptown. "Or would you like to come home with me?"

"Your place," she said with a smile, "so long as it won't change anything at work."

"I can handle it. Can you?"

"No problem," she said.

He kissed her, then told the driver to take them to UN Plaza. His apartment was modern and expensive, a Corbusier chaise longue upholstered in spotted pony skin, couches and chairs covered with soft black leather, the lights dim, wall-to-wall gray industrial carpeting—a powerful man's retreat. It was a little like her father's office, she thought, then regretted making the connection. There it was again, Suzie's hang-up, that feeling she so often had now, that she was inside Suzie's skin.

Mac was so poised, so smooth, she was worried he'd

find her awkward. But she wasn't frightened of him anymore the way she'd been the day he summoned her to his office and bawled her out for being drab. She watched him as he went to a bar, a backlit tortoise-shell étagère, studied him as he poured out two snifters of cognac, checked his body as he handed one to her and then guided her to a couch.

"Why are you smiling?" he asked.

"Just thinking of how you used to frighten me."

"Tell me about it." She did. He was amused, kissed her again, assured her he wasn't scary after all.

"I see that now," she said. "You're just a little lamb."

"You're an interesting girl," he said, looking at her carefully. "I think the papers had you wrong."

" 'The ugly duckling'? If you'd known my sister you might agree with that."

"I doubt it," he said. "I have offbeat tastes."

"Like whips and chains."

"Something like that." He laughed.

"I guess they have your number," she said.

"Who has my number?"

"The girls at the office. They look at your boots and your black leather jackets and they say, well, you know, watch out for Mac, he's into S&M for sure."

"That's great. A little costuming and people take you just the way you want."

"You're not into it, are you, Mac? I don't want to get into anything weird."

"Relax. And don't be such a tease." He unbuttoned her blouse. "Ah, braless—" He touched her breasts, flicked at them. She closed her eyes, felt the vibrations reaching down between her legs.

He took her hand, led her to his bedroom, pulled back the comforter.

"You must be the only person in New York with

white sheets," she said, trying to be casual as she undressed.

"I have black telephones, too." He stood beside her, naked, aroused, then pulled her to him, kissed her on the mouth.

"I used to wonder in edit meetings what you'd look like."

"Well—" he stood back. "Tell me—how *do* I look?"

"Pretty damn great I think." She meant it. He was lean and hard like a much younger man, thinner than Jared, less hairy, more feline.

"And you—you look pretty damn great yourself." They lay down, he put his arm around her, brushed his other hand gently between her legs.

Making it with Mac was completely different than making love with Jared. It was hard for her to define the difference, and she wasn't sure she wanted to. But then, after they finished and she felt satisfied and was falling off to sleep, she thought: *That's what it's all about, this man-woman stuff. Of course he's different. That's why people screw around.*

She slipped out of his bed at six in the morning, careful not to wake him up. She didn't feel up to a shower and breakfast scene, a rush home to change, then the subway ride back to B&A. She much preferred just to slip away, felt elegant riding uptown alone in a taxi at six-fifteen in the morning when it was still dark, thinking to herself: *I'll run and eat and go to work, and maybe tonight I'll ball again with Mac, and that way I'll keep myself sane and busy, and I won't think about bad things, won't drive myself crazy anymore.*

There was something very erotic, she thought as she ran in the Park, something stimulating about running without having bathed after sex. She thought of her and Mac's mingled sweat heating up beneath her run-

ning suit, steaming up in there. She pulled her sweat-
shirt open and sniffed; she could smell the aroma of
sex.

I wonder, she asked herself as she rode to work,
*does Mac think I'm a great lay? Does he think I've got
good tits and a terrific ass? Do I appeal to his "offbeat" tastes?*

She worked well that day, better than she had since
the trip to Maine, and again she thought: *This is the
way—to keep busy all the time, to concentrate each
moment on what I'm doing. Use sex to obliterate pain.
Most important not to brood.*

Mac called her in in the middle of the afternoon.
They talked about some business for a while, then he
said: "It was very chic the way you left this morning.
You're really a terrific kid."

"So," she said, "I'm a kid. My father calls me
'kiddo.' Jared used to call me 'babe,' and my sister
used to call me 'Child.' People always say 'dear' to me
in stores—men and women. Am I all that cuddly? I'd
really like to know."

"You're very cuddly, Penny," he said. "Want to
have dinner tonight?"

They met at a French place this time, a midtown
bistro full of people talking and laughing and eating
well. The wine was even better than the night before,
and again she found him fascinating.

"I'm learning more about publishing by eating with
you," she said, "than in a year working at the house."

He liked her, she could tell. She'd proven herself at
the office, been cool with him at work. She could see
he respected her for that. She liked the idea of being
the cool co-worker who could turn tempestuous in bed.

This time he didn't ask if she wanted to go home.
He simply took her to his apartment, poured out cognacs, then sat beside her and talked. She found his
opinions on people at the office biting and astute.

("Doris Gaff—she's making a big plus out of her meno-
pause"; "Ben Gale—living proof that ass-kissing the
critics pays off in the end.") When she asked about
Lillian Ryan he said: "Personally I find her repulsive,
but there's nothing new about that—some of the most
successful people are. She's getting by now on sheer
pushiness, but she doesn't touch you, Penny, hasn't
your depth or class." Then he smiled. "That's what
you wanted me to say, isn't it? Well, I hope it makes
you feel good. It's true."

They made love as they had the night before, she
following his lead. He was less athletic than Jared, but
more forceful, she thought, his rhythms more subtle,
his movements more efficient—he was a man who used
his body to express his will.

"Ever do anything kinky?" he asked afterwards.

"No. Not really," she said.

"Your boyfriend ever suggest anything?"

"Depends on how you define 'kinky,' I guess."

"Well—like being balled in the rear."

She shook her head.

"You've thought about it, though."

She didn't answer, didn't want to admit she'd ever
considered anything like that. Then he did something
she didn't expect. He spanked her—not hard, just
snapped his hands across each of her buttocks very
quickly. She jerked around.

"Oh, Mac, I don't think I'm into that."

"Relax." He massaged her. "It's part of the trip for
me that your ass be a little pink."

She let him spank her. He did it very lightly. To her
total amazement it made her feel good.

"See—you like it. Tell me," his voice insistent, "tell
me it turns you on."

"It turns me on," she said obediently, and saying
it also made her feel good.

222

"You're a good girl, Penny. A good little girl. Now turn over again."

He took her in long, slow, agonizingly slow strokes. She could feel the waves surging across her body, felt engulfed, blinded by the power of sex and her response. "God!" she screamed. She felt herself climaxing. "God. God!" She gripped onto him. When she came out of it she was bathed in sweat.

"Well," he said, "you do get into it. You're not repressed at all."

"You knew that all along, didn't you, Mac? Tell me how you knew."

"Just a hunch."

That morning she ran five miles in thirty-five minutes, and all the time she kept thinking to herself: *I'm like Suzie, on a father-trip. I like being spanked, punished. What's happening to me? I like it. Why?*

The third night he took her to a Japanese restaurant. They sat on tatami mats, were kidded by the waitresses, drank saki until they were high. Back at his place he asked if it would turn her on to be tied down while he went down on her. When she said she thought it might, he tied her hands to the headboard, allowing her to writhe and thrash as much as she liked while he tormented her with darting probes of his tongue. She loved it, and afterwards she thought: *Now I know what Suzie felt at that orgy in Great Neck.*

They drank their cognacs after sex that night and talked about the psychology of writers. "Basically they want parental love," he said, "but you must give it to them subtly, because they're very sensitive, and if they suspect you think of them as children, they're apt to get annoyed."

He was congenitally manipulative, she realized, a gamesman who would have done well in the movie business or the diamond business or the rag trade—anywhere he'd chosen to play. He was playing a kind of game with her, too, she thought, though she wasn't sure what his objective was. She was worried that their sex might affect their professional relationship. He was offended when she brought that up.

"Really, Penny, I told you—one thing has nothing to do with the other. I'm editor-in-chief and that's a power trip. What we do here is something else. I'm a sophisticated man. I keep my sex life and publishing life apart. Believe what I say, and please don't worry about it."

She liked him more and more, felt aroused by his kinky sexuality and wondered what sort of a man it was who had to dominate and what sort of a woman she was to crave his domination. She decided it all came down to being released. It didn't matter how one got it on.

He spanked her harder the second time while she lay across his lap, struggling, giggling, kicking the air with her legs. He squeezed the back of her neck while he sat back on one of his leather couches and had her service him on her knees. Sometimes when he lay on top of her he set his teeth in her neck. He held her gently but with the unspoken implication that he'd bite her if she tried to twist away.

Breaking his rule about the separation of work and sex, he told her to write him a memo on B&A stationery telling him a fantasy she'd like him to enact. She thought about it all day, didn't know what to write. Be his slave girl; play a prostitute—everything she could think of sounded silly and trite. Finally she wrote that she wanted to be treated like a little girl, as if she were his daughter and they were having incest. She handed the memo to him in a sealed envelope ("that report you wanted, Mac"). He winked at her. The secretary didn't notice. Late that afternoon she received a letter in the interoffice mail. She went to the ladies' room and ripped it open. "OK," he scrawled. "Will do this weekend. Mac."

They spent the entire weekend in his apartment. He bought all sorts of cheeses and delicatessen meats and fresh breads and smoked salmon and wonderful wines. They didn't go out for meals, didn't leave the building at all. He called her "little girl." She called him "dad."

"Oh, daddy," she'd say, "what a great big thing you have down there!"

"All the better to skewer you with," he'd reply, "in your virginal little pussy, my dear!"

They laughed a great deal. He showed her paternal affection. Sometimes he spanked her a little and told her she was bad and would have to stand in the corner until she improved. At other times he caressed her and told her she was the best little girl in the world. When he kissed her good night he implored her to have "sweet dreams."

On Sunday afternoon he broke the spell. "We've gone as far as we should," he said. "It was good for you to live it out."

"I really got into it."

"I saw that you did."

"It was, I don't know—something I've been thinking about a lot."

He walked away from her, went to the bar, and made himself a drink. Sensing he had something important to say she braced herself when he turned around.

"Sex is so complicated, Penny. There're all sorts of fine lines you cross. Perhaps the finest is the one between games and deviations, playing kinky and really getting weird."

"Why are you telling me this, Mac?"

"Because I sense something in you, in myself too— something that makes me think we could cross that line if we go on."

"Are you trying to let me down easy? Is that what this is all about?"

He smiled. "You can put it that way if you like. I'm very fond of you, Penny. I don't want to lead you across any lines. Also I want you to be my assistant, help me with my books. I want things to be tender between us. That might not be possible if we go on."

She was surprised by this sudden termination but delighted by the prospect of the job. And she was grateful to him, too, for sensing her vulnerability and pulling back.

"Thank you, Mac," she said. "You're much sweeter than I would have guessed."

After her week-long affair with Roy MacAllister, Penny felt relieved. The incest fantasy bothered her. She knew she'd been trying to void her horror of Suzie and her father by satirizing their relationship away. It had been interesting, Mac had found a responsive chord in her, but she didn't want to be kinky. She wanted to feel, to explore, and, like Suzie, to *forget*. Mac had been an interlude. She was pleased they'd both behaved with style. Now their professional relationship could prosper, and maybe, every so often, they'd get together and ball for fun. She was surprised, too, at how little she missed Jared, how distant and immature he seemed.

But as Christmas neared, Fifth Avenue turned into a parade of Santas ringing bells, the shops filled with holly and tinsel, the days got shorter and the humming of carols could be heard around the corridors at B&A, she found herself growing increasingly morose. Her father called and asked about her coming up to Greenwich for the holidays. She could barely control her voice as she lied to him and told him she couldn't, that she had signed up for a charter to the Caribbean instead.

"OK, kiddo," he said, "we'll miss you, but I understand. Have a great trip. I don't suppose it helps much but I think you made the right decision about that boy."

Her heart was pounding when she put down the phone. So—he knew. But then, of course, he knew everything. Chapman security kept him informed. In that case, she realized, he'd find out she'd lied about the charter flight. *Well, so what,* she thought. *Let him wonder why I lied.*

One night after work she stopped by Doubleday's Bookshop to browse. Mac had urged her to study the marketing of books, to watch people in bookstores, watch what they picked up and put down and finally bought. "Get the pulse of the marketplace," he'd told her. "Get it into your head so your hunches'll be good about titles and dust jacket designs." Now she was taking his advice, watching all this mad Christmas shopping on December 22, and she suddenly thought: *there's no one in my life I want to buy a present for, no one I care enough about.*

It was shocking, this realization she had no real friends. She left the store, walked over to Rockefeller Center, stood in the cold with masses of tourists, and stared at the big tree of the City of New York. Cold wind swept down among the great buildings; she pulled up the collar of her coat. Tears came into her eyes as she watched the skaters twirl and dance.

She spent Christmas Eve in front of her TV staring at the electronic Yule Log on Channel 11, the log which burnt forever, flames leaping in time to Christmas carols. The pipes in her apartment gurgled. Watching, huddled in a sweater, she felt herself sinking into a depression in which loneliness and helplessness and isolation were all combined. Where could she turn? How long was her misery to go on? Had her father really murdered Suzie? Was he a monster, a maniac?

227

In her desperation she thought of Dr. Bowles upstairs, and how kind the psychiatrist had been that morning several weeks before. Though it was Christmas Eve and the doctor probably wasn't home, she telephoned her anyway. She almost hung up when Dr. Bowles answered, ashamed to be bothering a stranger on a holiday. She was silent, about to put the receiver down, when Dr. Bowles began to speak.

"It's all right. I'll hold on. I know how you feel calling at a time like this. But I know you wouldn't call unless you were really troubled, so I'll just hold on until you feel calm enough to speak."

Such warmth, such sympathy and kindness, without even knowing who was on the line.

"This is Penny Chapman," she said. "The girl in 2-B. I wondered—I was just wondering—I mean I feel so bad now and I wondered—"

"You wondered if it would be all right to come up. Yes, of course it is—I told you that, day or night. You come up right now and we'll see what we can do."

They talked for hours, or rather she talked while Dr. Bowles listened. Penny told her everything about Suzie and the trial and Jared and the diary and how she'd discovered that her father had had an affair with Suzie—and might even have killed her, though she couldn't accept that, found it impossible, far-fetched. Then she told the psychiatrist how Jared had left, and then about Mac and being alone and her feeling that her family was very sick and cursed and how she wondered now whether that sickness had touched her, too.

It was exhilarating to tell all this to a stranger, especially one so radiant with understanding. The woman's eyes never showed shock or disapproval. She listened and responded, brought out the story by helping Penny along, anticipating sometimes by using phrases that precisely described her state-of-mind: "Then you felt just awful"—"That, of course, must have come as a terrible blow."

Dr. Bowles was the best listener Penny had ever met, and there was something cozy and merry about her apartment that spoke of an optimistic view of life— the brightly colored Norwegian rug, the orange and yellow cushions spread about the floor, the plate of Christmas cookies on the table, the flickering candles and the little undecorated tree. There were five or six cats in the room, beautiful ones, Persians, who moved and leaped about with grace. At one point, when Penny stopped her story to admire them, Dr. Bowles said: "Yes, they're beautiful. I think of them as living flowers."

Hours later, when she was finished and exhausted, Dr. Bowles finally spoke. "It's late now, Penny—time for sleep. Go home now and rest. Then, if you like come back tomorrow at noon. I'm having some of my patients in. Oh—I hate that word: 'patients.' My children. That's what they are. We spend our holidays together because we're like a family. Join us, spend Christmas with us. Then in a few days we'll get together and talk some more. And remember Camus: 'Happiness, too, is inevitable.' It *is*, Penny. It *is*."

She could hear the sounds of people as she ascended the stairs on Christmas Day, the sounds of a party, and yet she paused outside the door, feeling shy. What would it be like to spend Christmas with people she didn't know, those strange people she'd seen so often carrying cat boxes up and down the stairs, or out on the street unloading cat supplies from the van?

It was an all-right group, she decided, once she saw them close-up, an even mixture of young men and women who seemed normal and intelligent, if a bit severe and gaunt. But there was something special she noticed about them—an intensity, an almost haughty confidence, a sense of certainty in their eyes. They spoke quietly, seemed self-absorbed, were pleasant to her if a little cool, but then, she realized, they shared the bond of Dr. Bowles, and she was new to that.

Their approach to the doctor was almost worshipful, as if the radiance and compassion of that kindly woman was the force that made them a group. There was something else she noticed and that was they talked a lot about cats. They knew the names of the six Persians in the room, called to them, stroked their backs, and Penny overheard bits of conversation about veterinarians, who was good and who wasn't, the one who'd make housecalls, a girl in Brooklyn, a "cat sitter" you could call if you were leaving town.

She was sitting with some of them eating pecan pie (it seemed as if each guest had brought something: a pie, cookies, a bottle of eggnog, a bowl of punch) when a girl about her own age asked how long she'd been in therapy.

"Actually," said Penny, "I guess I only started last night. I live here in the building—that's how I met Dr. Bowles. I was a little surprised when I first came up here. I'd always thought she had a lot more cats from the smell in the lobby and on the stairs—"

At that the others froze. A little while later the girl excused herself, and a few moments after that Penny saw her talking with Dr. Bowles. They were gazing at her, looking concerned; when they noticed that she was staring back they nodded at her and smiled. The girl returned, was warmer than before, introduced herself as Wendy, said she worked on animated films.

The cat question was disposed of the day after New Year's when Penny officially began her therapy. Dr. Bowles brought it up at once. She said she wanted to explain it right from the start, so that Penny understood very clearly what it was about.

"My patients are protective," she said, "because

there're laws about how many animals can be kept in a private house. If my neighbors discover I have too many cats they can call the Health Department and then inspectors will come around. Some of my patients have been kicked out of their buildings, and a couple of times the Health Department's hauled their little cats away. They murder them outright, or else sell them to laboratories where they're used in experiments, literally tortured to death. Can you imagine? People just don't understand how much love is needed by the harmless creatures of the world. I have many more cats than these six Persians, Penny. Up in the attic I have many more, which is why sometimes you may be able to detect a smell downstairs. I'll take you up there one day and show them to you. But for now I've brought down this pair of kittens. Brother and sister—they're for you. Aren't they just divine?"

She picked up two Siamese blue-points and placed them in Penny's arms. Penny, a little surprised at first, looked at them, their little whiskered faces, their blinking eyes. Suddenly she felt her heart go out to them. She received them as a loving gift.

"They're about ten weeks old now, right in the middle of their kittenhood. They purr so nicely. Go on—place your fingers against their necks. There—that's it. Can you feel them purring now?" Penny could feel them. "They're going to play a considerable role in your therapy, Penny. This old tiger cat, too."

The old tiger, whose name was James, was large and plump and grave. He wasn't very friendly. When Penny reached out to him, he pulled back and began to hiss.

"Don't be afraid of James. He doesn't know you yet. He's going to act as sort of a watch-cat for the kittens. He'll look out for them, and maybe for you as well.

"You like the kittens because they're playful and

frisky, but old James has other lessons to teach, about calm and wisdom, self-containment and inner peace."

Dr. Bowles explained how she used cats in her therapy. People, she said, think only of themselves as they go about plundering and poisoning the earth. They need creatures to love and care for, to distract them from their anxieties. They need examples of simplicity and serenity which only the so-called "lesser creatures" can provide.

"When I started out in practice," she said, "I urged my patients to form strong relationships, find lovers, marry, bear children, raise families. But then I discovered this didn't work. They would continue to act out their neuroses and, in time, the relationships would fail. It was then that I began to think in terms of pets, and this dovetailed with my conviction that the defenseless creatures of the world were being ravaged mercilessly by man. Men, you know, are sadistic beings who slaughter whales and porpoises, kill leopards for furs and alligators for belts, capture the great wild horses who roam freely in the West, capture them and decimate them to make food for dogs whom they enslave. We live in a city where people abandon their pets in Central Park. Imagine! They drop them off there when they're bored with them, as if the creatures were only so much trash! Most die quickly. They have no sense of how to survive. It hurt me so much to see this that I started to rescue cats. I'd find alley cats, throwaway cats, wild cats living in the Park, I'd bring them home, nurse them and feed them, and then, when I had too many, I began to give them to my patients, too. And then I discovered an amazing thing. That by taking responsibility for these innocent little lives my patients became gentler, learned to share and be protective, lost their sense of loneliness and alienation, stopped thinking only of themselves. Over the years this idea of protecting little creatures and helping people deal with their lives has grown together in my mind. It's the basis of my practice. I believe it's my special gift."

The doctor told her how to train her kittens to use a litter box, and suggested some particularly tasty cat foods she thought they might enjoy.

"You'll come to love them, Penny, and caring for them you'll start gaining confidence in yourself. We'll begin to meet now for therapy once a week, and after a while you'll join our group sessions on Friday nights."

She enjoyed her kittens from the start, enjoyed watching them tumble, practice stalking, play games of hunter and prey. But James was something else. For all her efforts to establish a relationship he remained aloof. Sometimes she'd come home from work and find him silhouetted against the window. She'd call to him, he'd turn his face, look at her then turn away. He wouldn't cuddle with her or allow himself to be petted, and whenever she called to him he'd stare at her through strangely flecked slit eyes. He was a silent watchful cat, a "watch-cat" as Dr. Bowles had said, but he seemed more interested in coolly observing her than in teaching patience or the virtues of inner peace. Penny complained to Dr. Bowles that he made her feel uneasy. "A normal first reaction," the psychiatrist said. "I've placed him with other patients and he's done well with them. Give him a chance, Penny. You'll see."

For all the activity in her life now, therapy, caring for her cats, her morning runs, her work with Mac at B&A, she was still haunted by thoughts of Suzie and her father, reduced, when she allowed herself to think of them, to feelings of terror and pain.

There was something so troubling about Suzie's diary, its hard spiteful tone, its underlying cries for help. She looked at it nearly every day, studying the early

233

pages about Suzie's life in New York from the time she quit college until she left for Maine. All that degradation—she'd demanded it, endured it, to make herself forget. And then, when that had failed, she'd designed the "summer project," that mad scheme to woo her father back. It was crazy, of course, yet it had an internal logic. Rational madness, Penny thought, a closed system by which Suzie had almost deliberately sentenced herself to death.

Sometimes I think I'm on the right track, arousing anger, attention at least. Other times I think it's all a bummer, and I'm wearing down my pussy to the bone. Could chalk up the whole summer to experience, the whole year for that matter, and try an austere life come fall—a nunnery somewhere, the kind of place when you spend eight hours on your knees scrubbing germs off hospital floors. Well—WHY NOT? Never did a stitch of work in my whole life. Probably do me good. But would really hate it if people went around saying: "Have you seen the change in Suze? What a turnaround! From whore to saint, and that smile, that glow—remember how sick she used to look when she was being such a cunt last summer in Maine?"—

JAMIE WILLENSEN: perhaps Suzie had confided in him; perhaps he could clarify some things. Several evenings Penny walked by his studio to catch a glimpse, something that would give her an opening, allow her to meet with him and talk. Finally, on impulse, she called him blind one night when she saw the lights in the room above his studio were on. Something inside her, something she couldn't control, turned her voice tough the moment he picked up the phone. "Hi. This is Penny—Suzie's sister. I'm in a booth downstairs. OK if I come up?"

He was stunned, obviously surprised. "I don't know." He sounded cagey. "Just what exactly do you want?"

"Invite me up and find out," she dared him.

"I'm not sure I should. And I'm expecting someone else."

"You should see me, Jamie. It would be in your interest to see me now."

"Sorry," he said. "I don't follow that." He was trying to be cool but she sensed his tension, and the barest trace of a stutter in his voice.

"Suzie left a diary. There're lots of episodes involving you."

"Look," he said, "is this some kind of blackmail? Maybe I ought to get my lawyer over here."

She laughed. "Don't be stupid. I'm rich, a hundred times richer than you'll ever be. I just want to talk. Can't you deal with that?"

236

A brief silence. He was thinking it over. "All right," he said, "ring the bell. I'll buzz you in."

He was waiting for her at the top of the stairs, a slim man about thirty-five years old, she guessed, wearing tight faded jeans and a silk shirt open to expose his chest. His hair was cut short and neat. *The butch look,* she thought as she approached and began to size him up. When she reached the top and they shook hands she saw a network of tiny lines criss-crossing his face. As if someone had thrown a stone at a piece of safety glass, she thought. She refigured him for forty-five, and decadent as hell.

"So, the ugly duckling sister. We meet at last in the flesh."

She noticed his suede couch and unable to help herself, began to laugh. "Ah, the famous couch," she said, "in the flesh, too, so to speak."

He squinted. "What's the big deal about the couch?"

"My former boyfriend doubted you cleaned it up."

"What the hell are you talking about." He set his hands on his hips.

"It was in the diary. Suzie wrote it up. About this friend of yours, Dave I think, who jerked off on it. This is the same piece of furniture, *right?*"

"Christ!" He threw himself into a chair. "Christ— she wrote about *that?*"

"Lots more. Lots of other things."

"Oh, Jesus! I bet she did." He offered her a joint. He seemed a little in awe.

"Were you really fond of Suzie?" she asked, inhaling, not bothering to pass it back.

"Sure. We were chums. Then she deserted me. Quarreled and walked out. She shouldn't have. Wouldn't have gotten herself killed if she'd stayed. But she wanted to go. I told her not to. She told me to screw myself."

"You two were having quite a wild time."

"Depends on what you mean by wild." He paused. "You know, Penny—this isn't really fair. You know all sorts of things about me, but I don't know exactly what."

"Want me to tell you?"

"Yeah. Maybe you should."

"The embarrassing things?"

"Nothing embarrasses me."

"Good. That's really good, because the average guy would be pretty embarrassed I think. OK—well, you took her to an orgy in Scarsdale or someplace and made a lot of split-beaver shots. *Right?*" He nodded. "Still have them?"

"Burned the negatives the moment I heard she was killed."

"You could have made a fortune peddling them, I bet."

"Maybe. But that's not my style."

"Oh? Really? You must be pretty hot shit." She yawned, didn't know why she was acting this way, pretending she was Suzie, acted bored, scornful of his integrity. "Let's see—I guess the thing that should make you squirm the most is the time you both went downtown someplace and bought some kind of leather gizmo to tie around your cock."

He turned away. "What a little cunt she was to write all that stuff down."

"So—you *are* embarrassed. Forget it. No one'll ever know." She patted him on the knee, couldn't believe she was coming on this way. "Now that we're through all that, I'd like to hear if you were just using each other or if you really liked her like you claim."

"Isn't it kind of weird after all these years for you to come around so suddenly and ask?"

"The diary only turned up a couple weeks ago."

"And that made you think of her again?"

"*Right*. There's a lot about you in it, and a lot about

some other guy she was hung up on. An older guy. Know anything about that?"

"Vaguely rings a bell, but she didn't reveal herself all that much. We had a lot of fun together, we balled and we played around, did some pretty wild scenes, did use each other, I guess. But she kept her problems to herself, and that's what I did, too. She was a good-time girl—*sort of.* That was the front she put on anyway. You remind me of her. Not the way you look exactly." He squinted at her, the Great Photographer routine, she thought. "Yeah—you *could* be sisters, though your faces aren't that much alike. No, it's something else. The way you come on. Something in your voice, too. And your mannerisms. Yeah—you bring it all back somehow."

They studied each other for a moment, both of them smiling, he challenging, she meeting his gaze head-on.

"Someone really coming over?" she asked. He nodded. "Guess I ought to be going then."

He didn't stand. "You can stay if you want. It's a guy. If you like each other—well, we could have a three-way if you think you could manage that."

God—it was like stepping right into Suzie's diary.

"Tempt you?"

"Not very much," she said.

He was smirking, trying to goad her into a scene, saying, in effect, "Prove you're really Suzie's match." She yawned again, deliberately, so as to make sure he got the point.

"Three-ways, four-ways—people still do that sort of stuff?"

"Some of us," he said. "And I guess some of us have seen it all."

She nodded, smiled. He smiled back. They made a date to see each other the following night. Walking home she thought: *he's really foul; how much Suzie must have hated herself to have done all those things with him.*

The next day during lunch hour she went to the perfume counter at Bloomingdale's, asked for the sampler bottle of Amazone, dabbed a drop on her wrist. She was about to buy an ounce when she remembered she already had one at home, the bottle that had been stashed along with the wallet and the diary in Suzie's hiding place in Maine. Wait till tonight, she thought, *this'll really blow his mind.*

It did.

"Wow," he said, "you even smell the same."

"But do we screw the same? That's the question. *Right?*"

"Yeah," he admitted. "That would be good to know."

"Tell me how she balled."

He scratched his head. "Difficult to explain."

"You can show me."

"Show me first."

She shrugged. "OK." She started taking off her clothes. He watched, smiling, then undressed himself.

"Well?" she asked him afterwards.

"Not the same. No, I don't think so—not the same."

"How different, then?"

"Can't remember back that far."

"Oh—I'm sure you can, Jamie. Just close your eyes and try to relive those glorious, comradely days."

After ten minutes of very technical questions (Did Suzie sigh? Squirm? Cry out? Pump her pelvis? What was her favorite position? Did she grasp tightly? Scratch? Snarl? Like to kiss?) Jamie became annoyed. "Look—what the hell is this anyway? Am I supposed to be giving Little Sister a sex education course?"

"Too technical for you?" She reached for him, found him limp.

"Yes, as a matter of fact."

"Well, sorry," she said, "but I'm really interested in finding out how my sister liked to screw."

"Isn't that a little on the sicky side?"

Penny shrugged. "Maybe. And maybe not so sicky as someone who's into cock restraints."

He rolled away from her. From the other side of the bed he glared.

"Know something—you are like her. You're just as much a bitch."

"Well—" She smiled and then, suddenly, she knew just what to say. The words just came out of her. She remembered them from that telephone conversation she'd overheard three and a half years ago. She even imitated Suzie's voice. It came out almost exactly the way Suzie had said it to him then: "I'm a bitch, *OK?* If it makes you feel any better just think of me as a bitch. *OK? All right?* Feel better now, Jamie Sweets? And I'll just think of you as a bitch, too. *OK?*"

She got out of his bed, started getting dressed. She could feel the loathing coming off him in waves.

"Cunt," he hissed, "I'll tell you the difference. *She* was a terrific lay. You screw like a corpse."

She blew him a kiss.

"Why did I do it? Why? What's happening to me?"

Dr. Bowles didn't answer. Penny was sitting on a yellow cushion propped against the wall. Dr. Bowles was in her chair, a kitten nestled in her lap. She was nursing it from a bottle.

"Do I really *want* to be like her? That sounds so glib, but that's what it means, doesn't it? Talking to him like that. Forcing him to tell me how she made love. I tried to get Jared to tell me, and when he refused I knew that was the end. But using her perfume! God! I wept when I smelled it in the poolhouse last month. Am I that cold now? I'm scared. I don't know what's going on."

"We'll work it out," said Dr. Bowles. "In time we'll work it out. It's not enough to say you're trying to be like Suzie. The question is why you'd *want* to be."

"It started with the diary."

"You still read it, don't you? Don't you think there's something in there, something you haven't seen?"

"Yes," she said, realizing for the first time the truth of what she was about to say. "There *is* something, something between the lines. The explanation for everything. Even the murder. I think that's in there, too."

"No," said Dr. Bowles, "you unlocked the secret of the diary when you identified the Dark Man. Now you can't deal with it. Oh, you accept it intellectually. You think: 'OK, she and my father had an affair, and then he broke her heart.' But it's too terrible, too frightening, such a forbidden thing, too terrible, too forbidden to deal with. So now you reread the diary and go to people like this photographer, hoping you'll find another explanation, something less painful to bear."

"Maybe—" Penny thought about it. Perhaps Dr. Bowles was right. She'd reread the diary so many times, looking for something—she didn't even know exactly what.

"You're using people, Penny—trying to get them to help you act out your sister's life. It's as if you're trying to set back the clock, go back to that time when you think your lives diverged. Now you want to go back and follow her road, and that's a stressful thing to do. There's a part of you that thinks that if you continue like this you'll end up getting killed."

It was a revelation. She was dazzled by the insight and the astute way Dr. Bowles had brought it out. "Yes," she said, "and that would relieve my guilt about the fact that she was killed and I survived."

"You do feel guilty about that."

"I guess I always have."

242

"Then maybe you should go on. Deep emotions are controlling you. If you yield to them as you're doing now I think in time they'll self-destruct."

Afterwards, when the session was over, they sat, as always, facing one another, talking quietly, not about deep subconscious things, but little things in life, and cats.

"Your kittens are growing now. Isn't it fun to watch them grow?"

"They wrestle all the time."

"Sure," said Dr. Bowles. "They're wild. Cats are never tamed like dogs. Even when they're brought up in an apartment they're driven by a primitive feline need to kill for food." The psychiatrist looked matronly cradling the kitten in her arms, urging it to drink from the baby's bottle. "Touch him, Penny. Feel him purr. You can purr like that, too, once you've worked things out. Tell me—how are you and James getting along? Are things better between you now?"

"I don't think James likes me," she said. "He hisses whenever I come too close."

"Don't ever think he doesn't like you. He just isn't ready for you yet."

"I feel uncomfortable with him. I was wondering if you had another older cat."

Dr. Bowles shook her head. "You must learn to live with James. He's a fine old tiger cat. You must learn to compromise and get along." There was something strict in Dr. Bowles' manner, something of the schoolmarm that was as appealing as her sympathy. "People can't go on lording it over other animals. James is there to remind you you're not alone. All of us, people and animals, trees and forests and lakes and streams— we're all interconnected and must share the earth. You must prove yourself to James, win him over. Then you two will get along just fine."

"Will I get better?" Penny asked solemnly just before she left.

"It is inevitable," the psychiatrist said, patting her on the arm.

She wasn't certain exactly when she knew she was being followed. The notion crept up on her, began as a suspicion then grew into a conviction as she came to recognize her followers. There were several of them—stocky, suited, middle-aged men who worked in alternating shifts and pairs. One would wait in a car outside her townhouse, another in the lobby of B&A. She'd see them standing nearby on the subway or pretending to stare into shops as she walked the streets, four or five of them looking pretty much the same, retired cops, she guessed, now corporate security men. She doubted they were the black-bag crew who'd ransacked her apartment. That would have been a specialty team brought in to do a dirty job. These guys struck her as friendly and unthreatening; in fact their hovering made her feel safe. With them around she was less apt to be pushed in front of a subway or mugged or raped, all the awful things that can happen to a woman in New York.

Once she caught on to them, knew their faces, she began to see them everywhere. And then she felt sorry for them, for they were so incompetent, so easily spotted, engaged in such slovenly work. She didn't want to hurt their feelings by waving or striking up conversations, the sort of taunting games she'd seen played in private eye films by smart aleck detectives trying to enrage lummox police. She felt sorry for them, too, because their job was boring. It wasn't as if she ever did anything except jog and go to work and shop. Her routine was so unvarying she could imagine the staccato rhythm of their reports: "9:57—subject entered office building; 12:29—subject left for lunch; 17:57—

subject took subway to 86th Street; 23:22—subject's lights went off—"

No, she wasn't going to wave at them or humiliate them or show them up. If she did they might be replaced. These men, she felt, could be shaken off any time. All she'd have to do would be to go in one entrance of a building and out the other, and she'd be free until she came home and they caught up with her again. She wondered what they thought of her, whether they admired her or found her sexy, or whether they thought of her as a snotty bitch. Perhaps they respected her for her austerity. Perhaps they felt contempt. But as she thought about that and considered what being followed meant, she realized that they were merely pawns and that it was the opinion of the man they reported to, her father, that she really cared about.

Suddenly then she saw how being followed could be put to use, how her father, out of concern for her safety, had given her a new way to communicate. He'd always been so hard to reach, so cool and distant, self-absorbed, remote. But now, each morning, she could force him to deal with her by doing things which his security men would report. It was a fascinating way of reaching him, forcing him to come to grips with who she was. It struck her, too, that it was almost what Suzie had done in Maine, provoking him, trying to get his attention by deliberate carrying on.

There were all sorts of places in her neighborhood designed to facilitate relationships which would make superb arenas for what she had in mind. There was a lesbian bar where no men were allowed and one had to ring the buzzer to get in, a tough leather bar called "Strut," and an elegant bar for bisexuals with a brass bamboo decor, and then there were the singles' places, the real hard-core singles' bars on First and Second avenues, the sole purposes of which were to provide places for young men and women to make arrangements to screw.

I'm horny, she thought. *What would Suzie do if she were horny? She'd go out and find what she wanted. She'd go to a singles' bar, pick someone up and get laid.*

Her father would know what she'd done. The men who followed her would note it down. Her father would read about it and be shocked. Yes, she would start carrying on as Suzie had and see what he would do. Could she provoke him into rescuing her before her new life turned lethal, give her the love and warmth he'd always withheld? Or would he just look on, remote, removed, a cold and silent man, watching her through the eyes of surrogates?

She chose a place called Aspen, which sounded healthy to her, implied Ivy League types, rosy-cheeked from winter weekends on the slopes. She passed it several times, peered in the windows trying to size up the people inside. They looked all right, so on a Wednesday night the third week of January she cooked herself a hamburger, put on her winter coat, and being certain to pick up her Chapman security man, her "tail," she walked over to Second Avenue to try her luck.

Faces turned as she came through the door. She was prepared for that and relieved. The room was gloomy, false-romantic, she thought. The people had the look of young lawyers and secretaries. She didn't care if they recognized her—she was out in the open now.

Before she even reached the bar she was approached by a guy in a three-piece suit.

"Seen you around someplace, haven't I?" *God,* she thought, *is this really going to be that banal?* "Hey—" he snapped his fingers, "—around the reservoir, right?"

"Right." She nodded. *Jesus Christ,* she thought.

246

His name was Andy. He'd gone to Williams, was an executive trainee at a brokerage house, an early morning jogger, too. "Quit the park for the winter," he said. "Now I run at the Y. You still go out? *Amazing*. You must have a lot of grit."

"Grit. That sounds like the sort of word they use around the hockey rink at St. Paul's."

He grinned, refused to be insulted. "Wouldn't know," he said. "Went to Andover myself."

"How's the Y anyway?" She had an image of a pack of males circling a tenth-of-a-mile wooden track, their feet making a roar.

"It's OK. Warm, at least. Want to discuss running shoes? Adidas versus Nike, that sort of crap?"

She liked him for that. The score was even, they'd each put the other down, they were New Yorkers and the rules were set: no bullshit conversation, no phony-get-acquainted courtship talk.

"You're neat," he said. "OK if I buy you a drink?"

"Neat?" she said. "That's even worse than *grit*."

They took their Bloody Marys to a table. He came to Aspen a lot and was glad to tell her about the other people in the room. "He's with Citicorp. The girls say he's hot stuff. . . . She keeps a record of who she's slept with—gets so smashed she can't remember, and God forbid she should sleep with the same guy more than once."

Penny nodded. *"God forbid."*

"I used to see you running with a guy. You and he still go around?" She shook her head. "Glad to hear it. He didn't look like he shaved too well."

"At least we can't fault you on your grooming," she said. Andy's cheeks were perfectly smooth. His light brown hair was well cut, every hair in place, his clothes perfectly pressed. Even his shoes were shined. "You're not a T-shirt and blue jeans type, except maybe on Saturdays. *Right?"*

"That's me. 'Saturday's Generation.' You'll find me at Bloomingdale's checking out the argyle socks."

She laughed and was already imagining what he'd look like stripped.

"You know," he said, "I bet you could be a lot of fun."

"Is that your way of saying you'd like to try me out?"

"Yeah, you got it."

"OK," she said. "Your place or mine?"

He lived on the corner of Lexington and Eighty-Fourth, and since that was closer they decided to go there. It was a white-brick doorman building with cut-glass lighting fixtures in the lobby, and awful marbled wallpaper in the halls. His apartment was a "studio"— probably cost $700 a month, she thought. The furniture was Door Store and Workbench with maybe some Conran's thrown in. He had an expensive stereo, a color TV, a queen-sized bed, a rubber plant, and a bookcase stocked with texts on economics and a complete Will and Ariel Durant.

It was amazing, she thought, the way you could size people up. The whole setup was so predictable for a trainee stockbroker, an ex-college jock who still worked out. Good upper-middle-class taste. Square and proud of it—just the sort of boy Suzie'd screwed that summer in Maine. Yes, she thought, he'd fit in perfectly at Bar Harbor, but his family went to Nantucket, a fact that came out as they talked.

At one point, when he excused himself to go to the bathroom, she shuffled through the corporate reports neatly arranged on his coffee table. The Chapman International annual report was there. She opened it with trepidation. There was a full-page color photograph of her father on the inside cover. "Dwight Berring," the caption read, "President and Chairman of the Board." She studied his face. His head was backlit, his features subtly modeled. The photographer had caught the squareness of the jaw, the graying sideburns, the commanding yet boyish look. He was attractive, handsome, dominant—for a moment, a split second, she tried to imagine what he'd be like in bed.

She heard the toilet flush. Andy was coming back. She quickly closed the report, stuck it back in the pile.

"Well," said Andy, "shall we undress each other, or shall each person undress himself?"

She glanced at him. "Why doesn't each person make his or her own decision?" she said.

"The undressing part—that's what I call The Big Moment."

"What's so big about it?" she asked.

"Showdown time, when you finally see what you got. I had a girl up here couple of weeks ago who'd had a mastectomy. She didn't mention it, of course, until after the lights were out."

"What did you do?" They were unbuttoning their shirts.

"Told her it didn't matter. Didn't have the heart to tell her to leave."

"But you wished you had, *right?*"

"Sure. A bar encounter is supposed to be a turn-on, not a sensitive I'll-pretend-I'll-don't-notice-you're-missing-your-tit kind of thing."

That made her angry, made her want to talk tough like Suzie and put him down. "I know," she said, "I get turned off, too, when a guy has an undescended testicle. Hey—" she stopped undressing. "You don't, by any chance?"

"Come find out," he said. She reached to his crotch, took hold.

"*Hung,* aren't we?" she asked sarcastically.

"*I* am. I hope *we're* not," he said.

They fucked for an hour with a certain hostility generated by that exchange. She found it totally predictable and not without pleasure, too. They tried three positions. He made her come with his mouth, she got him excited with hers, and then she rode him to a second climax while he lay on his back. Not like Mac with his spankings, or Jamie Willensen with his three-way scenes, and not like Jared either—not so sensuous, so intense, and certainly not loving—just good clean ski-lodge sex. He wasn't a bad lay, she thought, but she didn't tell him that when she left. It was only when she got home, to find James perched on her window seat staring at her with reproach, that she realized the one thing they hadn't done was kiss each other on the mouth.

The next morning, riding the subway, she felt a flush of power. She imagined her father reading the report: "Subject went to singles' bar, left with unidentified male; proceeded to his apartment, spent several hours there, returned home clothes disheveled, satisfied expression on her face—"

Well, she thought, *that ought to give him something to think about.*

She began to drop in at Aspen two or three times a week. Sometimes she only stayed a few minutes. The game was to find a partner and get out. If there wasn't anybody interesting around she'd go home and watch TV. Her kittens amused her, their little cries, their sudden leaps, but she didn't like being cooped up with James. It was as if he *knew* what she was doing, knew all about her degradations, her promiscuity, her shames. When she'd come home he'd be waiting for her, glaring, his back arched, his claws gripping the comforter or the window seat. She saw a connection between the way he hissed and the way her father whispered when he was mad.

Dr. Bowles said she was imagining things, reading hostility into James when, in fact, he was filled with love. But one time when she brought a boy home James stared at them while they were making love. She couldn't concentrate, couldn't come. The boy became irritated, called her "uptight." They quarreled, she ordered him to leave. He said it would be a pleasure, slammed the door. She was so mad afterwards she threw a book at James. He slithered along the wall then hid beneath the bed. Later, in the middle of the night, she awoke to find him hissing just inches from her face.

She decided that if she were going to live like Suzie then she should really live like Suzie—not just assume her mannerisms, talk tough and screw around. No— beyond her compulsive fucking she had to be nasty sometimes, too. She re-read the put-downs in the diary, found them devastating. Her sister could be mean when she summed a lover up:

> *Cox, Ligget, Bigelow, Trowbridge— sounds like an asshole lawfirm. Can't keep these creeps straight anymore. They're all alike in the dark . . .*
> *By the time Carl spilled his beans I was practically asleep (he's majoring in marine biology, talks endlessly of plankton; all I think about is getting PLANKED)—*
> *R. Carter Slade, squickleydrum, squickleydee. Moore gives less. David Frothingham—more ham than froth—*
> *Huge, malodorous, he insisted on extended 69, proved himself deficient both as blower and blowee—*
> *Timmy Hawkins (his was not the cock*

*that launched a thousand ships). Oliver
Steers (his halitosis made my clitoris
wince)—*

*Cindy and Jeremy Caldwell together
last night. Orgytime—hurray! Very
sweaty. Many positions. Then he
shriveled like an untied balloon. While I
was riding him and Cindy was sitting on
his chest fondling my boobs, he
muttered: "What you two girls doing up
there, hey?"—*

*—gone in the morning but left a
message scribbled with lipstick on my
belly. INSATIABLE CUNT with an arrow
pointing down. Thought this showed a
certain amount of perspicacity and was
thus sad to learn he left for Martha's
Vineyard today, no doubt to further
conquests, to fulfill less insatiable
needs—*

Yes, Suzie's put-downs were snide, but there was
the pathos of self-hatred underneath. Penny wondered
if her father found a similar pathos when he read his
surveillance reports on her. Did they suggest to him
that she thought of herself as worthless? Did he think
how he might rescue her from her debasing adventures
in singles' bars? She tried to imagine his face as he
read them, could only conjure the coldness of his stare.

On the men who followed her she began to notice
a look of concern. Had they received new orders?
Were they worried about her safety? They were probably, she knew, worried more about their jobs. She

decided to give them something new to worry about by giving them the slip.

It was easy. She did it one Thursday evening in the maze of designers' rooms at Bloomingdale's, pretending she was pondering buying a chair, then losing her man between a rattan bedroom and a French provincial entrance hall. Pleased to be free of a tail for the first time in weeks, she went to a double feature, then prowled an all-night bookstore. When she returned home after two A.M., the man she'd lost stood nervously before her brownstone. She pretended not to notice him when she went inside, but couldn't help but observe his relief.

She waited but there was no reaction from her father, no solicitous call, no invitation to play squash or lunch. She felt angry, unloved. What was the matter with him anyhow? Was he forcing her, the way he'd forced Suzie, to new provocations, new, more desperate acts?

The next night she went back to Aspen. Andy's type, she decided, was about the best available in the bar. She went home with a couple of others who approximated his style, junior investment bankers or advertising account executives from upper-middle-class families who'd gone to the better schools. She thought of these guys as "honest brokers"—they were clean, had good bodies, were polite and more or less competent in bed. To go home with one of them was to enter into an unspoken contract: "I'll get you off two or three times, and you'll do the same for me."

She went home with others from Aspen, not so clean, not so polite. Once she went home with a medical student who lived in truly grubby graduate-student style (tattered fifth-hand furniture; dirty laundry heaped in the corner; sink filled with filthy dishes; ragged posters Scotch-taped to the walls). He was all nerves, ejaculated prematurely, apologized, then tried to tell her the story of his life. There was a browbeating mother, an anal-compulsive father, a brother who beat him up. "Oh, shit," she said after half an hour, "you're just one big Portnoy's Complaint." Driving back to her apartment she beat out her frustation on the back seat of the taxi while the driver eyed her anxiously in the mirror.

She fell into the habit of checking certain things as soon as she got inside a lover's home. The furniture, of course, the books if there were any (too often, she found, there weren't), the pictures on the walls (she saw everything from a signed Picasso litho to a boy's chart depicting "Weapons of World War II"). But the place that revealed most was the medicine cabinet. Here, she felt, the subconscious was truly expressed. If an apartment was clean, but the cabinet full of old toothpaste stains, she could almost predict the sort of sloppy screw she was going to get.

Everyone, it seemed, took some kind of drugs—she found more Valium bottles than she cared to count. The fewer prescription medicines, the more normal and straight the sex; the more bottles, the more bizarre. Pep pills—watch out! Baby blue toothbrushes indicated immaturity. And there were certain things that decidedly turned her off, like designer signature colognes, artificial tanners and shower curtains fringed with mold.

One lover named Chuck, an ambitious dentist with an apartment full of barbells, had stacks of back issues of *Screw* and *Smut* and *Raunch* and *Suck* piled up under his bed. He pulled them out as soon as they hit the sack, and they laughed together as they read the personal ads. They ended up going to a hard-core porn flick on Eighth Avenue, then rushed back to his apartment for a final screw. Wouldn't it have been incredible, she asked herself, thinking the evening over, safe at home in bed under the stern scrutiny of James— wouldn't it have been incredible if they'd happened to catch one of Jared's old pictures, maybe even his famous *Pussy Ranch?*

It was the middle of February now, the coldest time of year. As soon as she awoke she called the weather bureau. If the wind chill factor brought the temperature below zero she didn't bother to go out and jog. On those days she felt awful, so on the days when it wasn't so cold she ran with a vengeance, leaving a trail, like an old-fashioned train, of puffs of freezing breath in the winter air. Running was the same as going to Aspen, a way to get out, bury herself in intense sensations, forget her misery, her pain. But sometimes she thought she was trying too hard, running so hard her chest ached, screwing so hard she made her vagina sore.

She tried, too, to bury herself in work, writing memos to MacAllister so brilliant her intelligence would shine through like a diamond. Her remarks at edit meetings became piercing, sharp. Several times she noticed colleagues staring at her, whether hurt or dazzled she couldn't tell. She knew she could go to the top in publishing. Mac had told her that, and now other editors began to ask her opinion on their proposals, too. Lillian Ryan, realizing she was being left behind, tried again to become her confidante. Penny ignored her and asked Mac for a cubicle of her own. He assigned her to an office with a window. Lillian was trumped again.

After her night with Chuck-the-dentist, Penny stayed away from Aspen for a week. She was fed up with young men, their bodies, their mannerisms, most of all their superficial poise. She longed for a mature and powerful lover, stern and tender, someone like Mac, she thought. But she knew that, alas, such as he were not to be found in singles' bars.

Then one night she couldn't bear staying home. Her kittens, James, her TV got the better of her, and she found herself going back. As she re-entered Aspen she was filled with hostility. She hated her life, hated herself, hated this need she felt to try and break through her father's cold facade. It was as if she were now *possessed* by Suzie, as if Suzie's drives and cravings had taken hold. She wasn't sure anymore she wanted to live like Suzie, but she felt driven by a force beyond her will.

Contrary to Dr. Bowles' prescription she found that the more she yielded to her compulsions the more she felt compelled. Dr. Bowles listened to the tales of her sexual adventures with a beatific smile. When Penny complained that she didn't seem concerned, the psychiatrist's response was mild.

"Of course I'm concerned, Penny. I think you're very sick. But you're in therapy now and that demands some rigor. The process is not to make you feel better. What we're trying to do is get you *cured*."

"But I don't feel I'm being cured. I feel I'm being *devoured*."

"Devoured by Suzie? Haunted by her? Could that idea and your extraordinary sex-life and this need you feel to get your father to pay attention—could all that just be a cover-up, a screen?"

"I don't know. What could I be covering up?"

"Perhaps you're distracting yourself from your real problem."

"I wish I knew what that was."

"Don't worry about it, Penny. In time it will be revealed. Meanwhile, I want you to start attending Group."

"Group," which began at eleven on Friday nights and often lasted until two or three A.M., left her feeling exhilarated, if a little unsettled by the other patients' obsessions with their cats. Each of them owned a herd of the animals and they spoke constantly of the troubles they had with them: sickness, plagues, the economic

burdens of feeding them, the amount of time this took.
And they expressed great anxiety, too, about the con-
stant threat of the Health Department which hung over
all their heads.

They had a means of dealing with that—distress
calls, "Maydays." Each patient was on duty at a certain time. If a raid by the health authorities was im-
minent then the patient in trouble would call the patient
on duty, who would in turn track down as many other
patients as he could. Patients who received the Mayday
signal were obliged to rush to the site, rescue the
threatened cats, carry them back to their apartments
and house them there until the crisis passed. It made
sense though it occurred to Penny that people living
under such a threat were living in states of extreme
anxiety, and that this was counter to Dr. Bowles' idea
that caring for cats was a gentling thing. She wanted
to point this out but was hesitant to assert herself. She
was new, after all, and the others seemed so *sure*.

They were gentle with her, concerned about her
welfare, full of questions about her relationship with
her kittens, and particularly curious as to how she was
getting on with James. They all seemed to know the
old tiger cat, and a few, she gathered, had even lived
with him. When she complained that James refused to
cuddle and often stared at her and hissed, they smiled
their all-knowing smiles and assured her he'd come
around. "How well you two get along," said Wendy,
"can be a barometer of your progress. When Dr. B's
therapy starts taking hold, then you and James will
start being friends."

"He frightens me. He seems so hostile sometimes."

"That's your projection," said Bob.

"I feel he's judging me. Watching and judging."

"Perhaps he is." They all smiled and nodded their
heads.

The men in the group seemed weak to her. They had

drooping mustaches and slumped shoulders, and they didn't sit very straight. The women seemed stronger but astringent, asexual, dried up. Their legs bore scratches, and their clothes and hair were rank sometimes with the odor of their pets. Both men and women were intelligent, all mildly successful in their work. But there was an aura of marginality about them (though no more, she thought, than about the people she'd met in bars), a sense she had that they were nice neurotic people, undriven and totally entranced with Dr. Bowles.

This wasn't so difficult for her to understand for she was entranced herself. The psychiatrist was so radiant with sympathy, so full of kindness, so calm and self-possessed, she acted as a perfect advertisement for her claims. Her theory was appealing, too, a cosmology, an over-arching concept of man's place in the universe in which all of nature, particularly the lesser animals exemplified by cats, had lessons to convey.

Sometimes, ascending the stairs to Dr. Bowles' apartment, Penny would feel attracted by the stench. It came from the attic, Dr. Bowles' catroom, which she'd heard about but had never seen. The smell was like a pheromone that drew her up. If only, she thought, she could drop her defenses, give up her vanities, and yield, then perhaps she could come to love old James and learn the lessons he had to teach.

There was a Mayday the last week of February. Penny was at an editorial meeting when a secretary came in and handed Mac a note. He raised his eyebrows—Ms. Chapman, it seemed, had an emergency call. Penny excused herself and took the call in her office. The patient on duty told her to hurry. The cats belonging to John, Dr. Bowles' oldest patient, were under attack. His neighbors had complained about the odor and a Health Department van was on its way.

Penny, doing just as she'd been told, taxied home

from work. She grabbed the two cat boxes she'd been issued, took another taxi to an address in Chelsea, and met the others there. It was an old brick tenement. Wendy was organizing things at the curb. Everyone was working together, rushing up the four flights to John's apartment, stashing cats into carrying cases (three cats or six kittens to a box), then dashing back down to the street where Wendy was dispatching cabs.

Penny felt her heart speed up as she charged the stairs. John's Puerto Rican neighbors were standing on the landings cursing in Spanish at the rescuers. A woman with a shrill voice yelled "Cat Freak!" as she swept by. She barely squeezed by two descending patients, their rescue boxes filled.

When she reached John's apartment she was out of breath. The stench hit her even before she crossed the threshold, a nauseating odor of cat urine and male cat spray so foul, so sickening she feared she might throw up. John was in a state, flailing around his little apartment, grabbing for cats, missing, then grabbing again, finally catching one, cuddling it, telling it not to be afraid, then forcing it into a box. Though it was a cold February day, his shirt was wet with sweat. He told Penny he was giving her six females, then rattled off their names so fast she could barely take them in. "They like Puss 'n Boots brands," he yelled after her. "Chicken parts and tuna bits are best. They've all been vaccinated of course. I hope they get along with James—"

His voice trailed off as she descended. She ran into three more patients on the stairs. They were worried, on the edge of panic. The Health Department van had just pulled up, and now John's neighbors were yelling to the officials while Wendy tried to distract them until the Mayday was complete.

Penny was confronted by a chaotic sight as she stepped out onto the street. Wendy was gesticulating at a pair of men in uniforms, calling them "sadists" and "murderers," while the Puerto Ricans, leaning out of windows, were urging them to be quick. The woman who'd called her "cat freak" pointed at her as she came out. Penny turned, walked swiftly away, her arms sore in their sockets from lugging the carrying cases filled with cats.

In the taxi riding home she found it difficult to blame John's neighbors. The smell that emanated from his apartment was horrible. Nobody should have to live with that. Yet, she thought, there was something lovely about the way they'd rescued the cats. She felt part of something bigger than herself, a group that cared more for little defenseless lives than the Health Code and the law. She even felt smug at the thought that she was a rescuer, a protector of animals normally brutalized by man. She'd subordinated herself, snatched away threatened creatures from the brink. For a few minutes she'd forgotten her troubles, so petty, she realized, in terms of creatures' lives and deaths.

Now she had six new cats to serve in addition to her own. Suddenly there were cats leaping all over her bed and crying in the night. Her apartment was getting messy, the litter box in her bathroom was overflowing, there was shrieking and fighting, and she couldn't remember all the new ones' names. It was like having all these strangers in her home, having to play hostess to them, feed them, clean up after them, and all the time she felt James watching her, studying her, daring her to meet his stare. She felt dominated by the animals, felt that they were running her life. She complained to Dr. Bowles and told her she couldn't handle them. The doctor assured her that she could.

"There're too many," Penny said. "They're taking up too much time."

"What would you do if you didn't have to care for

them? Go out to singles' places, bring home strange men?"

"Not necessarily that," she said, "but I need quiet to read, peace and calm to think."

"People think too much, worry too much about their problems. Better to do constructive work, take responsibility for little lives."

"Can't someone else take some of them at least?" Surely, she thought, Dr. Bowles would agree to that.

"I'm afraid not, Penny. Everyone else has more. Some of our friends take responsibility for forty or fifty lives. You'll just have to wait until John finds a new place to live."

"I don't know," said Penny, "don't know if I can wait that long."

Dr. Bowles' face turned stern, her tone a little cross. It was the first time Penny had seen her annoyed. "I'm disappointed in you. I wonder if my therapy has taken hold. Maybe you should worry a little less about your personal life and a little more about why you can't deal with cats."

Penny thought about it, decided she could deal with them. It was James she couldn't deal with—he wasn't loving, wasn't sweet, made her nervous, seemed to gloat over her frustration, made her hate her apartment, hate staying in. The others, John's females, and her two little blue-points, touched her, but James just gazed at her, cold and arrogant.

Cindy really impossible these days. I'd make her a fucking slave if I wanted a slave, but since I don't I'm stuck with her on another level. "You're really making an ass out of yourself," I told her today. "You're really acting like a jerk." She stared at me like I'd just told her she had incurable cancer of the tits. "All right," I said, "take out the garbage. And you'd better drive down to the village and pick me up a couple boxes of Tampax. I feel my period coming on." Well—that ought to keep her off me a couple of days at least, unless, of course, she's a vampire (ugh!) on top of everything else. (All I need now—right?)*

WHERE COULD she go? Where could she find relief? She was bored with Aspen now, the mad scramble to find a partner and get out. The Chapman security men were still following her, especially attentive, she noticed, since the night she'd given them the slip. She could toy with them, she supposed, continue to try and use them to provoke her father. But she'd pretty much given up on that—it seemed like a lost cause to her now. Still she couldn't stay in, had to get out, get away from James. Desperate one night, she thought of Cynthia French. She called her at the hot line number and was amused to hear her Daisy Buchanan voice: "Hi! Lesbian hot line. Cindy speaking. What can I do for you?"

She was about to identify herself when Cynthia put her on hold. She'd just meant to see if Cynthia were free, if she could meet her someplace later for a drink, but something about the way she'd answered reminded her of the Cynthia portions of the diary, and then, when Cynthia came back on, she found herself assuming Suzie's mocking tone.

"Gee," she said, "I got a real problem."

"That's what we're here for. Fire away!"

"Well, it's kind of complicated *really*—"

"Don't be shy."

"It's kind of strange."

"I have a feeling, whoever you are, that you're trying to put me on."

"No. It's true. I really am growing a penis."

"Who is this?"

"Hi, Cin! Who do you think it is?"

"Child?"

"Uh-huh."

"For a minute there—*Jes-sus.*"

"Thought maybe I was someone else?"

Cynthia paused. "Thought you were mad at me," she said.

"Why should I be mad?"

"Well, for talking to those security guys, I guess."

"Forget it. I told you that."

"I'm really sorry about that, Child."

"Believe me, it's OK."

"You sound just like her, you know."

263

"I know. Listen—I'd like to see you. Let's get together. I've never been to the Sahara. I was wondering—would you take me there?"

"You really want to go?" ·

"Sure. Why not? I'm trying to open myself up to different things."

They made a date for Saturday, because Cynthia was on the "hot line" for the next three nights. After Penny hung up she asked herself what she was doing. Was she putting Cynthia on? Trying to be her "Suze"?

The Sahara was dark and atmospheric, full of slinky models in beautiful clothes as well as women dressed as men. Penny had dressed in a tight blouse and jeans, then had splashed herself with Amazone. Cynthia wore an army surplus jumpsuit and paratrooper boots. She obviously felt secure at the Sahara, nodding to people, exchanging whispers and pats. "They all want to know who you are," she said.

"I'm surprised they don't recognize me."

"Well, it's kind of dark, you know."

They went upstairs to the disco and began to dance. Penny could feel the "vibes," the smell of women on the make, perfumes mixing, female perspiration. She didn't feel repelled. The music took over, sweat broke out on her forehead, and for an hour she became lost in the mood. People came up to dance with her and ask questions: "How are you?" "What's your name?" "What do you do?" Finally Cynthia squeezed her arm. "Want to come home?" she whispered. Penny nodded and they left.

It was bitter cold out on the street. Cynthia hugged her for warmth. In the taxi going downtown Cynthia kissed her on the mouth. Penny paid off the taxi at Bank Street. Cynthia unlocked the door, led her to the bedroom, lit up a joint, inhaled, passed it, urged her to take deep drags. While Penny inhaled, Cynthia reached to her, slowly unbuttoned her blouse.

264

She lay back then, watching Cynthia take off her top, the joint hanging Bogart-style from her lips. They lay together for a while, smoking, getting high. Their legs entwined. They strained against each other. Then they started kissing and stroking each other's breasts.

"You're hot," said Cynthia. "I can feel it coming off you." She unbuckled Penny's belt, unzipped her fly, pulled off her jeans, then reached in with her hand. "Hot. Are you *ever*, Child. Oh—you're *really* hot."

Penny lay back, letting Cynthia do what she wanted. Again she felt as if she'd walked into the pages of the diary. She thought of those nights when Cynthia had come into New York from Sarah Lawrence and Suzie had let her "do me" while she lay back thinking about her own attempts at oblivion. Then she heard herself gasping, crying out. She was excited, coming. Cynthia smiled.

"You're really into it," she said. "You're not like Suze, not a tease at all."

They were sharing a second joint when Penny heard a key turning in the lock. She looked around for her jeans. "Stay cool," Cynthia said. "That's just Fiona coming in." Cynthia went into the living room. Penny could hear whispering, then Cynthia came back. "Hey, meet my roommate." Penny looked up, saw a stunning black girl leaning in the doorway, smiling wryly at the scene.

"Hi," Penny said.

"So you're little sister, huh?"

Penny shrugged. Cynthia smiled. Fiona stood there examining her, her hands set on her hips. "Well, well, well—what a sweet duet." The girl laughed. "How 'bout I join the fun?"

"Here, take a drag." Cynthia handed Penny another joint. "That OK with you?" she asked.

Well, she thought, *why not?*

"Good girl." Cynthia patted her cheek. Then the

three of them were together, snuggling, kissing, making out. Mostly Penny watched. She didn't feel she had to "do" anything. She was Suzie now—she felt as if she were.

"Her sis was my first lover," Cynthia was saying. They were lying around at odd angles to each other, exhausted, close to sleep.

"Yeah," said Fiona. "I've heard a lot about *that*."

"Ought to be getting home," Penny said, beginning to feel embarrassed, not wanting to intrude upon the delicate relations of these roommates. Cynthia went downstairs with her, stood with her while she waited for a cab. "Ever find that diary?" she asked just as a taxi pulled up. Penny shook her head. "Guess it's just as well. No good could come of it." She made a kissing motion with her mouth, then gently closed the taxi door.

Back at home Penny found her apartment smelling of cats, filled with the acrid odor of their urine. *Sometimes I hate the damn things,* she thought, as she flushed the litter down the toilet, scrubbed out the box, refilled it, and set out the bowls of water and of food.

James was staring at her. He *knew* what she'd been doing. "Wasn't so bad," she whispered to him. "Lot better than some of the slobs I've had." James blinked, arched his back. *A sign of recognition,* she thought. She reached out to pet him, but he hissed and then recoiled. "Screw you, James," she said. "Screw you and go to hell."

She wondered what the Chapman security men thought as they followed her to the burial grounds. She spotted two of them in a Chevrolet crossing the George Washington Bridge, tried to imagine their report: "11:04—subject and two young women carrying aluminum suitcases, subject's landlady, and two young men carrying shovels drove black van toward New Jersey, destination unknown—''

The dead cats were in the suitcases; each had been wrapped carefully in silver foil, labeled and stored in Dr. Bowles' enormous freezer until enough had accumulated to justify a trip. At first it felt strange accompanying a load of dead cats to the country, but after a while the sincerity and friendliness of her companions pushed the macabre aspect of their mission out of her mind. To the Chapman men following the van, she thought, they probably seemed a convivial group out on a weekend outing, perhaps a nature walk.

The burial grounds were in a state park. It took them nearly an hour to hike their way in. It was a cold winter's day; the chill burned her ears. When they finally reached the site Wendy showed her little piles of stones which marked the other graves. The two boys, Tom and Doug, set to work digging a hole in the nearly frozen ground. Penny helped Wendy weed around the older markers, then searched out stones to mark the new remains. When the hole was finally dug, the suitcases were opened and the sausage-shaped silver packages were placed in a row on the ground. Tom and Doug stood in the hole while Penny and Wendy passed the bodies down. The boys arranged them neatly at the bottom of the grave, then they all stood with bowed heads while Dr. Bowles read the names:

'' 'Peanuts,' female, three years old, dead of unknown causes; 'Lucy Blue,' female, daughter of 'Big Sylvia,' stillborn; 'Mike,' much beloved king-cat of Richard, sire of numerous kittens, dead at seven years—'' Sometimes Dr. Bowles paused in her reading to recount a little incident about one of the cats. Penny was surprised the psychiatrist could keep them straight— she seemed to know them as well as she knew her patients. The compassion of this woman never ceased to astound her—she was always available to listen to one's troubles, usually cuddling a kitten, or nursing one while she talked. She often gave Penny special tidbits which she thought her kittens might enjoy, and catfood cookies she made up specially for James.

When the reading of the list was completed the five of them stood in silence for a time. Then they each tossed a little bit of earth upon the foil-wrapped carcasses, and then the boys filled up the hole. Penny erected the marking stones, having studied the pattern at the other graves. It was late afternoon and extremely cold when they were finished. Dr. Bowles put her arm around her, embraced her as they hiked back to the van.

"I saw you shared our anguish," she said. "I'm glad you helped us bury our fallen little friends."

"Look what I got," said Lillian on Monday morning. She came into Penny's office waving a telegram. "A *classic* author's missive. Jesus, what a nerve! I saved this guy's book, edited out all the artsy-fartsy stuff, got it down so maybe somebody would want to read the thing. Now he tells me he wants all his *precious* prose restored. Threatens to withdraw it if we don't print every word." Lillian was one of those editors who seemed to have a special loathing for writers, hating them for their vanity, their complaints, their demands for expensive lunches, their requests for gratis copies of other B&A books. ("They think because we're their publishers we're a free bookshop or something. Yuck!") Penny nodded as Lillian ranted on, but she knew the author was right, that Lillian had harmed his book, didn't know the difference between functional writing and graceful prose.

She spent the day brooding over her miseries, felt herself becoming unhinged. The glow she'd had after the cat burial trip was superseded now by anxiety. Some madness was driving her, but she didn't know toward what. MacAllister, noticing her lack of concentration, spoke brusquely to her for the first time since their affair. When she looked up at him to apologize he asked her what was wrong. "You've got tears in your eyes."

"It's nothing, Mac. Just the weather, I guess."

He looked at her, nodded. "Yeah—the Februaries." He told her to go home early so she wouldn't have to face the rush hour. She stayed until five-thirty anyway. The elevator felt claustrophobic when she rode it down. The men who always followed her were waiting in the lobby. Noises were too loud. The city shrieked. The subway seemed to scream.

That night she sat in front of her TV and watched the awful news: more on a mass cult suicide and a madman in Chicago who was torching winos on skidrow. The whole country, except for the eastern seaboard, was blanketed in snow. A professor of meteorology came on, said the weather patterns were changing, that within a hundred years the earth would enter a new ice age which would drive populations to the tropics and cause unprecedented famines, social dislocations, political upheavals and strife.

So—the whole world was going crazy. What else is new, she thought. She couldn't bear being cooped up, being stared at by James, knowing that Chapman security men were waiting downstairs for her in their cars. She wanted to go out, but there was no place to go. Aspen was out of the question; Cynthia lived too far downtown, and anyway she wasn't in the mood for that. She thought and thought: whom could she call? There wasn't anybody—she had no lover, no friends. For the first time in many weeks she thought of Jared, wished he were back, wished he were there to hold her in his arms. Finally, tired of self-pity, she pulled out her copy of Suzie's diary, flipped through it, read passages, wondered as she had so many times just what it really meant.

There was something too cruel about the way Suzie mocked her lovers, their ineptitude, their incompetence in bed. Penny wondered whether all this overstatement had a purpose, whether these mockeries had been written with a particular reader in mind. Her father? Could Suzie have been addressing the diary to him? There was something about its tone that made her feel it had been written for her father's eyes. It was the same feeling she'd had about Suzie's actions—the too-deliberate overheated way she'd carried on those final weeks. Could the diary, too, she wondered, have been part of Suzie's plan to make her father jealous, try and win him back?

She pulled out the old worn wallet, the one with the photos and the keys she and Jared had found in Maine. She spread the photos out on her bed, studied the shot of her father in his bathing suit. He was poised to dive into the pool, his body extended, muscled, sleek. She hated him for being so attractive. No wonder Suzie had let him drive her to despair.

She lay back on the bed, the photo in her hand. Then she became lost in a reverie. Memories started pouring in: her father lifting her when she was a child, putting her on his shoulders, walking with her on the beach. That time they'd all gone to Switzerland, ascended the mountain in the cable car, then met the young Swiss photographer with the Leica, and the four of them had sat for him as a perfect American family posing on a mountain top. She'd loved her father. He used to come to her room to kiss her good night. He brought her her first two-wheel bicycle, put it out on the back terrace of the Greenwich house, then took her hand, led her to it, and there it stood, the best bicycle in the world, with a big red ribbon tied around the handlebars and an oversized card: "Happy Birthday, Kiddo. Love from Dad."

Yes, she thought—she *could* imagine Suzie making love to him, she could imagine that his body would be fine to touch. How had it started? Perhaps he'd come into her room to say good night, had stroked her cheek, kissed her lips. Perhaps Suzie'd complained she was sore from tennis and asked him for a massage, then had raised her top so he could knead her back.

Penny closed her eyes, tried to imagine the scene. Suzie had known intuitively how to arouse a man, and there was her father, lusting after her, ready to take advantage the moment he saw an opening, as he'd always done in business and in life. He would have been affectionate. That was his attraction—that for all his aura of power and control he could be fatherly and sweet. Yes, she could imagine it all, could imagine Suzie's pleasure, her aroused sexuality, as the massage turned into love-making, the kneading fingers beginning lightly to caress. Suzie'd have known what was happening, but she'd have let him go on. There was that tantalizing mystery about any new lover—what would he do? Where would he touch her next?

Yes, she could imagine it, could imagine him turning her, his mouth suddenly crushing hers, then his body pushing her down against the bed. He would reach for her, slowly, gently stroke her breasts, then take one of her hands and press it upon the swelling hardness between his legs. He'd let it rest there, let her feel his desire. After that she would be his. She'd lay back, let him take over, let him do with her what he wished. He'd lie on top of her, his strong body heavy on hers, his beautiful arms, the arms she'd always admired when they played squash, wrapping her, pinioning her, then his cock, so big, so long, suddenly revealed— she'd feel it prodding, would move and twitch to help it find its way, would gasp as suddenly it slipped inside,

271

would feel it filling her, would push against him, begin to sigh and moan.

Afterward, it took her some time to realize what she had done—she had let Suzie take her over. She had indulged in an incest fantasy inconceivable a few minutes before.

*Think things are coming to a head now,
though hard to say for sure. Now
suddenly I got a sideshow on my hands:
Child mooning around over her actor;
him creaming in his jeans over me.
Forget that! First things first! There's a
new element, something I didn't suspect,
something dangerous, maybe wild and
out of control. Feel it coming—the crack-
up. A shitstorm maybe. Well—isn't that
what I want? We all dig our graves in the
end—*

LATER SHE would look back and think that
the next ten days were the craziest of her life.

The day after she imagined Suzie making love with
her father she left work early, used the freight elevator
to give her tail the slip, then took the IRT to Fifty-
First Street, walked a block to Park Avenue, and stood
in the frigid air. Her ears were covered by her ski cap.
Her winter coat was huddled around her neck. Arctic
winds ripped down between the buildings, freezing the
moisture on her cheeks.

She stood across the street from Chapman International watching the workers storm out at five. Her father's limousine was parked in front. She could see his chauffeur inside. She had no idea when her father left work, whether he stayed at his desk until late. She wanted to see him without his seeing her, so she waited a full hour in the doorway of a bank until the sky was dark and the rush-hour mobs were gone. Just before six the chauffeur opened the back door of the limousine. She caught a glimpse of her father stepping in, a quick look at him through the window as the car sped uptown, toward the FDR Drive, she assumed, and the highways that led to Connecticut and home.

The next night she waited for him again, arriving later, losing her tail in the subway, hoping her father would still keep to his routine. She was in place at a quarter to six, this time on the same side of Park Avenue as the Chapman Building, positioned so she could see him better when he strode out the door at six. He was punctual, his walk firm. She saw him nod to the driver, then settle back in the cushioned seat. As the car pulled out he was staring straight ahead.

The third night she asked herself what sort of madness it was to hang around outside his office, to catch these fleeting glimpses as he came striding out. This time she leaned against the Chapman Building just beside the revolving door, and again he was punctual, walking within three of four feet of where she stood. She felt her heart quicken as he came by, so close she could have reached out and caught his sleeve. She stood there a long time after the Cadillac sped away.

There was something elating about the strangeness of it all, giving her shadows the slip, spying on her father as she waited for him the fourth night in a row. It was an elation she recognized from the past, the thrill of the voyeur, the spy. She'd watched Suzie, suffered but still had watched. Now, lingering in the shadows of the Chapman Building, feeling it was important that she see her father from as many angles as she could, she experienced that same infusion of power and of pain that had filled her in her rocking chair those summer nights.

Six o'clock came and went. She saw the chauffeur become restless, check his watch. Her father came out finally, the chauffeur came around to open the door, her father spoke with him, the chauffeur nodded, got back in the car and sped away.

He was at the next intersection before she decided to follow him. Perhaps he was going to the theater, meeting a mistress at a bar, going shopping, would take the train home later on. He was wearing a black overcoat and his head was bare. It was easy to keep him in sight. He had no idea she was behind, never turned, never looked. They moved up Park Avenue half a block apart.

At Fifty-Seventh Street he paused, waiting for the light. He turned west, walked over to Madison, turned north again, continued uptown. There were fewer pedestrians now—she decided to drop further back in case he turned. He stopped in front of a wine store, examined the window display, went inside. He reappeared five minutes later carrying a paper bag.

On the next block he entered a take-out shop. She knew the place, an emporium of over-priced cheeses, cold cuts, quiches Lorraines. She crossed the street, stood in a darkened doorway, could see him clearly through the plate glass as he pointed to this and that. The counterman assembled his purchases. There was something familiar about the way he paid. He'd always handled money like a bank teller, peeling off bills between his forefinger and his thumb.

She followed him up to Sixty-Sixth, saw him turn, walk toward Central Park. He entered a narrow building between a big Fifth Avenue apartment house and a private club. She waited a few minutes, then walked up to have a look. Suddenly she drew a sharp breath. She knew the building. It was where Suzie used to live.

Did he own it? Was he the landlord? Or had he just kept up Suzie's lease? She crossed the street, craned her head, found the ninth floor, saw the lights were on. She crossed back, entered the lobby. Beside the buzzers there were names. She looked carefully, found Suzie's buzzer—beside it there was an empty slot. Why had he kept the place? What was he doing up there? He'd brought food and wine. Perhaps he was with someone, waiting for someone to arrive. She left quickly in case his guest should come and recognize her. It was too cold to stand outside and wait. She walked home feeling strange and torn.

There was something so spooky about him going up there, keeping the place as his pied-à-terre. He could afford much better, but then she realized the building had no doorman: he could come and go without being seen.

That night, hoping to find some measure of sanity, she looked forward to attending Group. She felt so lonely, so rotten—maybe listening to the others, hearing their troubles, would help her forget her own. But the session wasn't pleasant. Dr. Bowles had them draw caricatures of each other, then passed them around. Later, trying to sleep, Penny found herself dwelling on troubling things: Suzie and her father and what they'd done, and how she might fit into that.

She'd been lucky, she realized; she had obtained important information. She'd only wanted to see him, study him close-up, but now he'd led her to his lair. If she could just get into that apartment, have a look around. Could she bribe the super? She wondered how much that would cost. She could pretend she was her father's secretary, say she'd been sent to get some papers he'd left behind. No—she knew that was im-

possible, that she could never tip the super enough.
He'd take her money then tell her father. Like Tucker,
he was in her father's pay.

Then, early in the morning, she had an idea. Those
keys in Suzie's wallet—could they be the keys to her
old apartment in New York? There was a chance they
were, though her father had most likely changed the
lock. Still there was one way to find out: go over there
and see. She was excited, jumped out of bed, got
dressed then sat down. She mustn't be stupid, mustn't
go over to the building and try to get in if there was
a chance her father was still inside. Also, she knew,
she had to be careful about her followers, whom she'd
shaken off four afternoons in a row. They mustn't think
she'd shaken them off deliberately or they might double or triple up. They'd be afraid of being fired if they
reported she was giving them the slip.

She decided to throw them a bone and bore them
a little, too. Though it was Saturday she spent the day
at the office catching up on work. She wrote some
memos to Mac on projects he was considering, rec-
ommended against a book on Vietnam, suggested he
buy a fast-food industry exposé. That afternoon, on
her way home, she walked nonchalantly by Suzie's
building. She looked, checked the ninth floor for lights.
The apartment was dark.

Sunday morning she called Greenwich. Mrs. McIver
answered the phone. Penny asked how her mother was
doing, and by the way, was her father at home.

"He's out playing squash," Mrs. McIver said.

"Here, in the city?"

"No. At his club out here. I'll tell him you called."

"Never mind," said Penny. "I'll call him tomorrow
myself."

She dressed as nondescriptly as she could. In case
people saw her in the building she didn't want them
to remember how she looked. She was dizzy with an-

ticipation as she pocketed Suzie's keys, walked to Fifth Avenue, lost her followers in the Metropolitan Museum, then rushed down Madison to Sixty-Sixth.

She rang the buzzer in the lobby just in case. No answer, so she tried the keys. The silver one opened the inner lobby door; she couldn't believe her luck. She rode the elevator to the ninth floor, got out carefully, looked up and down the hall. There were only two apartments, one in back and Suzie's which faced the street.

She held her breath as she tried the second key, knew it was going to fit even before she turned it in the lock. She opened the door cautiously, stepped inside, quickly pulled it shut.

From the first moment she was shocked. It was as if the years had never passed. The apartment—no more than a bedroom with bath and kitchenette—was just as she remembered it, as if it had been in Suzie's time. The huge king-sized bed was open, unmade, the blankets crumpled, the pillows askew. The pictures were the same, rock album posters and some blowups of Suzie taken by Jamie Willensen, tacked up on the walls. Suzie's books were on the shelves, her cosmetics on the dresser, her old address book beside the phone. Penny opened the closet, recognized the clothes, dresses and pants suits and an old raincoat from Saks.

Pervading everything was the aroma of Amazone, the scent she always associated with Suzie, the perfume she now used herself. *This is madness,* she thought; *he maintains her apartment like a shrine.* She couldn't believe it, couldn't believe he kept the place like this, brought up delicacies and wines and picnicked here, splashed drops of her perfume around, spent nights in her bed. Her head reeled, ideas clashed. Thoughts threw off sparks, exploded like fireworks. She lurched around the apartment, felt faint, lost her balance. She was stunned, baffled, dazed by what she found. She sat down to regain composure, stop the bubbles of craziness rising to her brain.

What did he do here? Think of her, dream of her, worship her, pretend she was with him in the bed? He seemed more human doing that, making fetishes out of her clothes, sleeping with them, pretending she was there, than as the cold and ruthless businessman devouring companies, whispering orders, ruling his empire from a telephone.

Her father was a pervert. As she gasped at that notion, turned it over, thought it through, she was pleased for it revealed he had a weakness, was flesh and blood and passionate underneath. The apartment spoke to her of a man with a vivid personality, a strange man with a dark underside who harbored fantasies and lived them out. Suddenly her perception of him was upside down. She'd discovered a man she'd never known.

She examined the apartment carefully, opened all the drawers, checked everything. He kept an electric razor and deodorant in the bathroom cabinet, side by side with Suzie's razor and a cycle of her birth-control pills. In the dresser she found sets of his underwear and socks, beside her panty hose and underthings. There were matchbook covers from fancy restaurants she'd gone to, a box filled with pennies, her costume jewelry, expired charge cards for department stores. Some of these items were so intimate she could hardly bear to touch them. Reading the diary had been hard enough, her eyes roving the loops of Suzie's script, the orderly handwriting that contained so many feelings, so much hurt. But this was more painful for she was confronted by Suzie's essence: strands of her hair caught in a comb, a jar of cold cream that bore the imprint of her fingers, a lipstick worn down by pressure from her lips.

She found the letter in the kitchenette, in a drawer

filled with steel silverware. Small patches of it were smudged, a letter or two washed out. Had Suzie wept as she wrote it? Did her father weep as he reread it? Or were these smudges the marks of their intermingled tears which they had separately shed?

Dear Powerful One what are you doing to me? What are you doing? Remember that time you came up to Bronxville, picked me up behind the dorm in your rented car, and we drove to White Plains and checked into that tacky motel with the porn films on closed circuit TV and drank bourbon from a bottle like I was a whore and you were a traveling salesman with sample cases in the trunk? We watched TV and listened to the couple screwing in the next room, and then we made it rough and tough like the ball breakers that we are, and I asked you why you weren't tender with me afterwards and you said maybe we'd played out our string and maybe the time had come to "cut the deck." Oh, Daddy-O! Didn't sleep that night, watched you instead, the sheets around your waist, your head straight up, watched your lovely hirsute chest rise and fall and your beautiful eyes flicker and wondered what you dreamed and if you dreamed of me. OK. It was all my fault. It was me who started it. OK, I take the rap. You said you'd be in for it if we were ever found, and you were scared and nervous and had to get away, enough was enough and we couldn't keep this up—we'd be ruined if we did. You said you were worried most of all for me, afraid I'd end up with scrambled brains. But I always thought you were talking about yourself, 'cause you were the weaker one I always thought, you were the romantic one, and I was just out for kicks. Me—Ms. Kickypants. Ms. Hotbitch, she of the hungry-thirsty dripping twat, yes, ME, your hard-assed daughter, she of the too too solid flesh, your sexaroo little sweetheart, flesh of your flesh, cunt of your cock—she's the one who's got her brains all scrambled, she's the one who's gotten bashed.

Daddy-O, daddy-o—I have read deeply in the annals of incest. Yes, I have. Child's given me some hints in this regard. Helped me to work up a reading list for a paper I claimed I had to do. Very helpful Child was. Ever hear of a novel Edith Wharton planned to write? Beatrice Palmato it was called. Child dug some excerpts out. The seduction scene between the father and Beatrice is much too much. Listen if you can to this: "—she flung herself upon his swelling member, and began to caress it insinuatingly with her tongue—" Sound familiar? Yes! Except it was old Daddy-O Palmato *who started the whole thing off! And* Tender Is the Night, *old Scotty's* Tender Is the Night. *Daddy-O Devereux tells Dr. Dohmler what he did: "We were just like lovers—and then all at once we were lovers—and ten minutes after it happened I could have shot myself—except I guess I'm such a goddamned degenerate I didn't have the nerve to do it." Nicole forgave him: "Never mind, never mind, Daddy. It doesn't matter. Never mind." But then we learn there were "plenty of consequences" and Doc Dohmler looks at Daddy-O Devereux and thinks: "Peasant!" Delicious— right? Except it wasn't like that with us was it Powerful One? Yes, I've read widely in the literary annals and it's never written the way it was. It's always the baddy daddy-o who does the wicked deed, never the poor little badly used daughter—never NEVER does she take him on. It's always poor old baddy-daddy. Poor old lusty guy. You'd think some of these writer fellas would get it straight for once. You'd think at least one of them would have the imagination to see it like it was. Well, they don't know anything, don't know whereof they speak. But WE know, don't we DADDY-O? We know who turned the trick.*

You were such a sucker for a piece of fresh young pussy, such an easy mark. All

I had to do was set my sights and in a fortnight you were mine. Course I had your paternal affection going for me, had that and the tits you gave me, the figure, the bod, all that out of your lovely genes. Remember how we used to kid around? Remember that time on your boat when we got undressed and sunbathed nude and I said "I bet I can give you a hard-on, ball breaker," and you bet me a grand I couldn't and then I did? We laughed about it. It was just a joke. You gave me a thousand dollar bill, the one you kept in the salt shaker just in case, and then when you came back up on deck I was lying there with the money clenched between my legs. How could you resist? How could you? You couldn't. No! You were my mark. I hustled you good. So glorious it was, such a perfect match.

We always thought the same way, saw things the same, knew the world was divided between those who do the breaking and those whose balls get broke. Two hunter-warriors—that was us—a pair of killers with a passion for fucking finally come together to lick each other and to eat—CUT THE DECK! Time to CUT THE DECK! Bastard! Coward! You think it's so simple. You think you can just screw for six months, have your fling, then cut the deck. What the hell is wrong with you? Are *you fucking made of stone? What about me? What happens to me? Where do I go now? Twenty-one, a burnt-out case, launched on life, the long ride down? Jesus. I'm crying now, Jesus—I'm crying tears. Me, Ms. Cry-Never, Ms. Drippy-Twat, Ms. Brass-Pussy, Ms. all-screwed-up-inside. Whew! Just wiped my eyes. Got to stop the flow. Don't want to be a pest, you know. Don't want to be boring. (God forbid that anybody be a pest and/or a bore. Right?) Don't want to recriminate. Don't want to play it like I think it's all your fault or something when I know perfectly well it's mine. But that's the problem, see— that's the catch, that's the part that ain't so great. Brought this whole mess down upon myself. You were innocent, victim of my game.*

Sometimes after you left me, after we'd played and you had to go, I'd lie there and think to myself: "This is real cool—balling pop." Thought it was a gas you see. Thought it was just a fun little deviation. Good way, too, of course to get back at mom—put a little fire to the old disciplinarian, not that she ever knew what was happening though I sometimes thought maybe she did. Anyway, what to do now Daddy-O? Head in the oven? Noose around the neck? Take a dive from one of the city's lovely bridges? Take a couple bottles worth of pills, pen a little note and end it all in sleep?

That would show you, wouldn't it? That would show you what can happen when one party to a deal decides it's time to cut the deck. Give you something to think about wouldn't it? Rack you with guilt—wouldn't it? Make you miserable. Really make you PAY.

Yeah—thought of that. Won't pretend I didn't. Seriously too. Thought it through. But where does that leave Suzie? Leaves Suzie dead and that's no good for me. Big Deal—I teach you a lesson but I'm not around anymore to lick my chops. You always taught me to play to win. This way, taking the count, I can only lose.

So—what to do? That's why I'm writing. Want to make you an offer, one I hope you won't refuse. Deal's this: OK, cut the deck. Cut it, move on, find someone new to play. I'll do the same. Everyone needs a new cock to ride, a new pussy to sheathe his sword. But still, every so often, let's get together and ball. We can control it. We can keep it cool. Use each other to buzz-off on, relieve the old tensions, rub away a little excess lust. I know I flung myself at you, know I was naughty, know I was bad. So punish me then for Christ's sake,

*but PLEASE PLEASE PLEASE don't cut
the deck for keeps.*

*Can't go on like this. Really can't. Try
to catch your eye but always you turn
away. Only man in the world whose eye
I can't catch. Only guy who looks me in
the eye, doesn't see me at all. I model,
squirm, smile, grin, make sucking motions
with my mouth, whisper "cheese." But
can't catch you, can't catch the lens.*

*Do you love me or do you not? Why do
I care? Who are we anyway? Just bodies,
animals I guess, hungry for flesh, thirsty
for sweat and come. Got to save ourselves. Got to save what we got, what we
had. Salvage something. OK? All right?
Can't write anymore. Tears pouring out
again. Can't go on. Don't want to make
myself sound crazy, raunchy-sleazy-cheap.
Suzie's in trouble, Dad. Hurting. Help me.
Please. Punish me with kisses. Please,
PLEASE. OK?*

She read the letter standing in the kitchenette, her
palms down on the counter, the pages spread on the
Formica between Suzie's toaster and the plastic rack
where the dishes dried. So many things became clear
as she read it, things from the diary she'd never really
understood. Her fantasy of him massaging her, then
turning the massage into sex, was wrong. She saw that
now and was stunned, stunned too by Suzie's agony
and pain. Had she really done it just for kicks? Had
it really just started as a lark, then turned into this

devouring love, this obsessive love that ruled her life? What would have happened if the intruder hadn't come? Would Suzie have won him back, gotten his agreement to her "deal"? She'd won him now. He kept this shrine to her, came here at night, slept in her bed, the same huge bed that Cynthia had described, upon which she and Suzie and the basketball player from the Midwest had had their orgy, upon which Cynthia had made it with Suzie the first momentous time. No—he hadn't killed her, couldn't have—Jared was wrong. She'd known that from the start. Her father had made a cult of Suzie; she'd finally won him back in death. The suicide that she'd contemplated and then rejected because it was a loser's game—being murdered by that insane intruder had had the same effect.

Penny moved out of the kitchenette, stood in the main room, looked around again. She was more confused, more distraught than ever, deranged by her discoveries, full of terror and pity and a deep longing she could not explain. She looked at the bed. He'd slept there. She stared down at it, aroused, wondering whether there would be some trace of him, some faint odor of him upon the sheets, some trace of that body which Suzie had so fiercely loved.

Slowly, carefully she lay down on the crumpled sheets, then centered herself and sniffed. She stood up suddenly, worried—worried about herself. Something was happening. A force was moving over her, a force she'd felt since she'd begun to follow him, a power that appealed to a part of her she feared. She backed away, retreated to the windows, turned and stared again at the bed. It seemed to beckon to her. She could almost imagine him naked upon it, calling to her, summoning her to come to be stroked and kissed.

She turned so she wouldn't have to look at it, moved over to the dressing table, sat down and studied herself in the mirror. She reached for the atomizer, sprayed some Amazone on her neck. Then she opened Suzie's lipstick, the worn-down one she'd been afraid to touch before. She brought it to her face and with trembling hand applied it to her lips.

She looked at herself again. Then she reached for Suzie's hairbrush and ran it several times through her hair. She gazed at it—her hairs caught in the bristles, merged with Suzie's now. *She could be like her.* She knew she could. Jamie Willensen had seen it in her manner. Cynthia had heard it in her voice. *Would he see it, hear it?* Could she turn him on the way she'd done with them? Yes, she thought, it was possible. If she really tried she could.

She stared at the bed again, feeling the pull of it. She wanted to resist, felt flushed and breathless as she tried. It was pulling her, pulling at that part of her she knew was sick, that Suzie part that had been emerging all these months. It was strong, so strong—she felt dizzy again for a moment, and torn.

There had been some faint trace of him upon the sheets; she thought she'd caught the scent of his soap when she'd lain down there before. She went into the bathroom to check, sniffed at the bar in the recess of the sink. Yes, it was the English soap he liked, the soap with the smoky leathery smell she'd given him on his birthday so many times. So, this is what he smells like, she thought—this is what comes off of him when he's hot and making love.

She couldn't fight it anymore, felt it pulling her, too strong, too strong. She flung herself wildly upon the bed, closed her eyes and writhed there on the sheets. She thought of Suzie and her father, the two of them clinging, fucking, biting, licking each other, copulating like dogs, and then she saw herself with him doing all that, too. She pulled down her jeans and her panties, pulled them down to her knees. It felt good to be bound by them there—it was as if she were being forced, were tied. Then she reached down, touched herself, began to press and stroke and knead. She didn't care now whether she was sick or not. She only wanted to come, there in the very bed where he had slept.

Afterwards she was disgusted with herself, and then, quite suddenly, angry, infuriated with him. How could he have this power over her, to make her follow him, dream of him, imagine him holding her in his arms? First Suzie; now her. Was she doomed, then, to replicate her sister's agony, drown in a sea of perverted sex? She loathed him now for this power he had, wanted him to suffer as he'd made Suzie suffer, as he was making her suffer now, making her lose her mind. *Send him a message,* she thought. *Teach him a lesson. Freak the bastard out.*

She went into the kitchen, searched the drawers, and found what she was looking for, a thick-bladed carving knife. She tested it against her thumb. It was sharp enough. He had violated her apartment, sent his black-bag crew to break in, break her dishes, throw her books on the floor, slash the cushion of her window seat. Now she'd do the same to him—she'd desecrate his sacred shrine.

She took the knife, ripped it across the sheets, cutting at them wildly, slashing back and forth. She cut and slashed until they were ribbons, then she plunged the knife into pillows, gouged out the feathers, flung them about the room. She'd teach him. She'd scare him. She'd make him suffer now. And he'd never suspect. He'd wonder who'd done it, and how they'd gotten in.

She went to the dresser, pulled out his shirts, punctured them again and again. She shredded his underwear, his socks, kicked his electric razor across the room, but somehow, for all her efforts, she felt she hadn't done enough.

No—it wasn't just that she hated him; she hated

Suzie too. For all the men she'd had, how easy it had been for her to catch them, for stealing away Jared, for seducing her father—most of all for that. Her anger was fed now by raging jealousy. She attacked Suzie's clothes, her pants suits, her raincoat from Saks, then the blowups on the wall. Slash! Slash! It was like her mother throwing the Christmas stocking in the furnace. She'd destroy all traces of that little slut. She'd cut and slash until Suzie was really dead.

When she was finished, panting and exhausted, she let the knife slip to the floor. Trembling from her labors she examined the apartment—in three or four minutes of rage she'd reduced her father's shrine to trash. The mess pleased her, especially the ripped-up bed. She felt released from her demons. She let herself out, quietly locked the door, rode the elevator down. No one had seen her coming or going. She wobbled slightly on the street, still nursing a bit of pain.

Early Monday evening she was at her post across the street from Chapman. She watched the limousine, saw him come out at six, get in the car, speed away uptown. She came again on Tuesday, and again he drove away. But on Wednesday, he dismissed the car and started to walk uptown.

She followed him, excitement rising, as he stopped at the wine store again, and at the food take-out place. She could feel her pulse quicken as he turned on Sixty-Sixth and walked up the block. She stood just around the corner on Fifth Avenue, against the wall of a synagogue where she could watch the apartment house, could see Suzie's windows, and could see him, too, when he came storming out. She waited there trembling. Suddenly she felt a little leap—the lights had gone on upstairs. She tried hard to imagine his reaction, his shock and then his fear. The sheets and clothes all cut, the dishes and glasses smashed—he'd take that in, know this was no ordinary break-in, feel hostility and danger, would know that someone powerful enough to obtain a key was issuing him a threat. Perhaps he'd be so frightened he'd drop his package. The wine bottle would break when it hit the floor. She watched, throbbing with satisfaction. Then the lights went out.

She stood very still, flat against the synagogue, as still as she'd ever waited in her rocking chair, gripping the arms, not allowing the rockers to move, to squeak. She willed herself to become part of the building, to be unseen when he emerged.

He came out fast, stepped into the street, waved frantically for a cab just emerging from the park. She stepped out, feeling a need to see his face, and caught a glimpse of him looking distraught as he jumped into the back seat and the cab roared away. She leaned back panting against the synagogue; she could feel sweat on her forehead though she'd barely moved and the temperature was forty degrees. She'd done it, terrified him. He'd never go back to the apartment again. She felt ecstatic. It was good to make him quake, make him feel afraid.

She waited for him on Thursday night; she had to see his face again. She was worried about the Chapman men, too—they'd become frantic; it was getting harder and harder to shake them off. She considered letting them follow her, follow her as she followed her father. "Subject tracking father"—that would shake him up. But she didn't want him to know she was the one who had desecrated his shrine. Not yet.

When her father came out he dismissed his car, then started to walk. He headed downtown this time, the opposite direction from the apartment, down Park Avenue between buildings made of steel and glass. She followed, but then he crossed Forty-Seventh just as the light changed, forcing her to dodge between a pair of cabs then jog half a block to catch up. He turned onto Vanderbilt, passed the Yale Club, turned again, passed Brooks Brothers, then crossed Fifth Avenue, turned south, walked to Forty-Second, walked west beside the Public Library, then along small and dangerous Bryant Park.

The crowds were thicker as he crossed Times Square. There were camera-watch-binocular discount stores, and restaurants offering steak dinners for $3.99. Banners announced close-out prices on "odds and ends." Old men stared aimlessly from cavernous cafeterias grotesquely lit by fluorescent lights.

At the corner of Eighth and Forty-Second, in the midst of utter sleaziness, he paused as if deciding what to do. There were sex shops all around, hookers and male hustlers speaking over telephones in doorless booths. He turned uptown on Eighth, walked several blocks, then went into a porno cinema. She waited a few minutes until she was sure he was seated, then bought herself a ticket from a whiskered old lady cashier.

The lobby was dark, the theater small, smelling of stale smoke. She stood at the rear looking over the heads of the men inside, inspecting them row by row while hearing moaning and sucking noises coming from the screen. There weren't many customers. She spotted him right away. She moved down the opposite passageway, took a seat apart two rows behind and a dozen seats to the side, then watched him, his face immobile, cold and hard, his familiar squared-off jaw illuminated by light reflected off the screen.

The movie was horrible, tawdry, badly made, the print scratched, the soundtrack, barely audible, consisting of sighs and moans, whispers of "suck me" and "fuck me" enunciated by despicable men. She couldn't follow the story. It seemed to be about two roommates who had a variety of adventures with ghastly looking males. Mostly she watched her father, studied his iron jaw, the immobility of his face. She searched his profile for some response—a moan, heavy breathing, some indication that he was involved or moved, but all she could find was the same hard grimace she had known all her life, that cold mask she'd dreamt about, that mask that Suzie, at the end, had so desperately tried to crack.

Finally, after forty minutes or an hour, she saw him gather up his coat. He stood and began to leave. When he reached the back of the theater she followed him out. She reached the street just as he turned the next corner and headed east on Forty-Fifth.

She rushed after him, nearly running down an old wino who growled at her as she brushed by. "Hey! Hey you. *You,*" a black pimp said. She walked faster to get away. She reached the corner just in time to see her father enter a doorway a third of the way down the block. "Hey!" the pimp said. "*Hey!* Stop a minute. I want to talk to *you.*" She walked faster, saw her father had entered a hotel, one of the innumerable fleabags clustered around Times Square where whores kept rooms and lonely old people lived on welfare checks—the sort of place Jared had stayed his first few weeks in New York.

She passed, glancing in. She could see him chatting with the clerk. He was employing the same bantering manner she'd seen him use so many times with waiters, golf caddies, chauffeurs. The pimp was still following, calling. She ran up to Broadway, lost him in the crowds, then circled the block and passed the hotel just in time to see her father mount the stairs behind the desk.

She stopped, wondered what to do. Should she follow? There was a risk of running into him, and she couldn't just barge in and interrogate the clerk. What was he doing? Were there whores upstairs? Did he act out his fantasies with them? She didn't know what was driving her except a tight breathlessness, a need. She didn't care if he saw her now. She didn't care about anything. He was a monster, a pervert—she was going to find him out.

She brushed past the clerk, mounted the stairs, found herself in a passageway leading toward a door. There was a sign on the wall, neatly lettered, directing her toward "Martha's Massage." She entered. A girl sat behind a desk, cute and cheap looking, a girl about her age. A black man, huge and muscular whom she figured for a bouncer, looked her over as she approached.

"Sorry, honey," said the girl, even before she could open her mouth. "No openings here, but try Freida's up the block. I hear she's taking girls."

That night she dreamt wild vivid dreams. She was a whore at "Martha's Massage." There was a parlor illuminated by bare bulbs hanging from the ceiling. She stood in line with other girls while her father walked back and forth. He chose her. She led him down a narrow corridor with open cubicles on either side. She led him into her cubicle. He made love to her without a word. She received no pleasure from it—he averted his face and she averted hers. Afterwards he pulled out a roll of money, peeled off some twenty-dollar bills, pressed them into her palm. After he left she stared at the sheet in the doorway, trembling from his exit, swaying back and forth.

She woke up suddenly to find five of her cats sitting on the bed. "Get away, damn you, lousy cats," she said, waving her hands at them, trying to brush them onto the floor. They peered at her, then leapt off one by one. She lay back and willed herself to sleep. Then she had cat dreams.

Dr. Bowles stared at her with slit cat's eyes. She

had whiskers and sharpened teeth. Then Penny was running down a side-street off Times Square pursued by a pack of cats, scampering, meowing, closing in, reaching out with their claws to tear her flesh.

When she woke this time James was sitting on her chest. He was so near she had to squint to see him. His breath was hot upon her face.

She pulled herself back and met his eyes. He *knew*— she could feel that—knew all about her incest fantasies, knew she was willful, worst of all that she hated him. Dr. Bowles had said animals could sense such things. The psychiatrist had warned her that James would read her mind. Yes, she was sure of it: James knew she despised him. He was sensing her hatred even now as he stretched and arched and hissed.

Suddenly she was terrified. He was like an incubus. "Get off me," she shrieked. "Get off! Get off!"

James peered at her, then crouched as if he were going to leap. She was afraid, raised her hand to shield her face. Then she felt a fierce pain. He'd grabbed her wrist. His jaws were open, his teeth sunk deep into her skin. She screamed. He wouldn't let go. She shook her hand, tried to pull her wrist free, but the more she pulled the harder and deeper he bit. She screamed again, thinking she might faint from the pain. Looking around frantically for something to hit him with, she grabbed the alarm clock beside her bed with her free hand and brought it down hard against his skull.

This time it was James' turn to scream. His eyes rolled back in his head. Then his jaws loosened, and she pried his mouth away. She hit him five or six more times, then stumbled to the bathroom, turned on the faucet, and let water wash over her gushing wounds. The pain was still bad—the searing had given way to a deeper throbbing hurt. Blood poured from little holes. There was blood all over the sink, on the tile floor, on her sheets and comforter, too. James lay on the bed where she'd hit him, twisted, still. She went to the closet, brought out her broom, poked him with the handle. He didn't move. Her hand was getting numb now. She knew she needed medical care. She dressed, stumbled out to the street, and searched frantically for a cab.

They fixed up her wrist in the emergency room at Lenox Hill. The intern told her she was lucky, that James had had her in a "killer bite" and she could have been badly hurt. The cat could have severed her tendons, cut the veins in her wrist. He gave her a tetanus shot, sprinkled sulfa on the wound, bandaged her up, then asked her for a date. She returned to her apartment, cleaned up as best she could, then threw James' carcass and the bloody sheets and towels into a garbage bag and deposited them on the street.

In the morning it began to snow. She marched to Eighty-Sixth, deposited her token in the turnstile, watched the subway screech toward her out of the tunnel, thought how easy it would be to throw herself before it on the tracks.

On the way up to the editorial floor at B&A she thought of staying in the elevator, continuing to the roof, jumping to the street from there. She could imagine the headlines: Ugly Duckling Sister Leaps; Follows Slain Debutante Even Unto Death. But she wouldn't do it, couldn't, knew she didn't have the nerve.

Somehow she got through the day. She tried to do some line-editing but couldn't concentrate. Little noises bothered her, the sounds of traffic outside, typewriters and telephones in adjoining offices, voices muffled by the walls. She went to the women's room, found the corridor ominous. She was startled when she flushed the toilet—the rush of water was like a roar. She spent most of the afternoon staring out her window, watching snowflakes fall, huge and wet. The city seemed merciless. There were men down there who followed her, men she had to evade and trick. There was her father who went to porno cinemas, who kept a shrine to Suzie—a shrine she'd destroyed. There was a cat who'd tried to kill her, a cat she'd bludgeoned to death. Forces were conspiring to squeeze her toward a corner. She tried to resist them but was too weak. The forces were inexorable, the corner dark, full of shadows, perils, lusts. She was backing into it and the pressure was unrelieved.

By the time she got home the snowfall had turned into a storm. There were four inches on the streets. People slipped on the subway stairs.

She knew she had to talk to Dr. Bowles and tell her what she'd done to James. She was a little fearful as she rang the bell, but the psychiatrist greeted her with a smile. "I was making a pot of chocolate. Sit down, you're just in time."

While Dr. Bowles puttered in the kitchen, Penny met the eyes of her Persian cats. *They know,* she thought. *They all know what I did.* When Dr. Bowles came back with a pitcher and mugs Penny told her about her dreams.

"Oedipus complex!" The psychiatrist smiled. "That's just nonsense from your fancy schools. It's so easy to pin everything on that, such an easy way to screen the truth." Penny looked down. "I know you didn't come here to pass the time. Something's bothering you. Tell me what it is."

Penny nodded, described her fight with James. She looked up only when she finished, to find Dr. Bowles staring at her, anger and incomprehension on her face.

"You killed him! A defenseless cat! I can't believe it! I can't believe you did!"

Penny tried to explain about the "killer bite," how she'd had no choice, but the more she talked the more furious grew Dr. Bowles until her face was twitching, her head bobbing up and down.

"You brought it on yourself. What an idiot you are! You might have petted him, whispered to him. How could you strike him? How could you beat upon his head?" The psychiatrist stood up, began to stride the room. She was so furious, so enraged, Penny felt afraid. "No patient of mine has ever harmed a cat. And now you've murdered one. You—" She pointed her finger at Penny. "You're a sadist. That's what you are."

"Please!" Penny began to sob. "I was so scared, confused, following my father, and then those dreams. The pain was awful. I thought he'd chew off my wrist." She held up her bandaged hand. "The doctor said—"

"I'm your *doctor*," the psychiatrist snapped. "When all this happened, you should have come to me."

"I know. I'm sorry. Please forgive me, Dr. Bowles. Cats just don't work for me. I can't stand them, I really can't. I've come to tell you that. I hate them. I want to give them up."

The psychiatrist stared at her a moment, nodded curtly then sat down. "Your fear of cats is your real sickness. That's what you've been covering up."

It was then that the notion that Dr. Bowles was mad first flitted through her brain. She rejected the idea at once. Dr. Bowles was her psychiatrist, the person who'd been helping her for weeks. She was trained, accredited, kind. Her patients worshipped her. She rescued little animals, found them homes. She quoted Albert Camus.

"—cats are the key experience in therapy, the way you break the chain of shackles around your soul. Cats release you from your sickness. Cats—"

Cats, cats, cats. Every other word was *cats.* Whenever she wanted to discuss her troubles, Dr. Bowles always steered the conversation to cats. Suddenly she understood the madness of it all, how she'd been recruited into a cult. Maydays. Burial rituals. An eccentric cosmology with a dominant leader. Cats as a cure for every ailment of man. Dr. Bowles preferred cats to people. She was a crackpot. She was off the wall. Penny knew she had to get away from this woman, break with her right away. As her mind began to focus on that a revelation struck, a terrible, terrifying thought.

"You set me up with James, didn't you?" she blurted. "You knew he was bad. That's why you asked about him all the time."

Dr. Bowles threw back her head, concentrated her eyes. "Don't get hostile with me, Penny. Don't project your hostility on *me*."

"It's true, isn't it? He attacked people before."

"James was a little neurotic, yes. I put him with you because I thought you'd help. Unfortunately it never occurred to me that you'd bash in his little skull."

Penny ignored this attempt to make her feel like a murderer. "What do you mean 'thought you'd help'? You kept saying he'd help *me*."

"Did I? Yes. But it wasn't necessary for you to know certain things. You'd have been frightened, and that wouldn't have done either of you any good. The point was that James had to learn to deal with people. He had trouble with some of the others. I thought you might gentle him. I hoped you two would get along."

"What kind of trouble?" She was angry now.

"Oh, he bit a couple of them, but not with any 'killer bite.' I don't believe that—not at all."

"He tried to sever my wrist."

"I think you made that up."

"You were just using me. Using me to treat a psycho *cat!*"

"This is part of your sickness, Penny—this way you twist everything around."

"It's your sickness." She stood up. "I'm finished

with it. And I'm finished with you now, too." She glared at the psychiatrist.

Dr. Bowles glared back. "You're sick," she said. "You can't walk out on me. You know all about us. You could harm me now."

"That's ridiculous." Penny turned, started toward the door. Then she stopped—she heard a peculiar sound. It was a little cry, more like a chirp, the sort of high-pitched chirp a little animal might make. She turned back toward Dr. Bowles. The psychiatrist, who had been slumped in her chair, was poised now, as if she were about to spring.

"Beware," she hissed. "We have a saying. Anybody who walks out on us—that person is Fair Game."

"You're crazy. You're threatening me."

Dr. Bowles' eyes flashed with hate. "We are who we are," she whispered cryptically, "and nobody does us in."

It stormed all night and the next day, too, a blizzard they called it on the news. Penny spent the entire day inside, listening to the grinding gears of the bulldozers, the scraping of shovels as people worked to free their cars.

She was afraid.

She heard them assembling near the end of the afternoon, trudging up the stairs, whispering as they passed her bolted door. Dr. Bowles must have summoned them, called an emergency meeting despite the snow, a special kind of Mayday to discuss how Penny could be dangerous and whether they should designate her "fair game." They were fanatics—she knew that; single-minded and obsessed. They were smug and sure, in thrall to the psychiatrist. They were the cat people, she was their enemy, and now she was afraid.

She huddled on her window seat staring at TV and ate dinner while she watched the evening news. Inflation was up. The oil ministers announced another rise in the price of crude. There was fighting in Central America. Boat people were adrift at sea. A commentator said the world's problems were "intractable." Mobs ruled the streets of Teheran.

What were they saying about her? That she'd betray them, call up the health department, reveal the locations of their precious caches of cats? That she hated little creatures, was cruel and sadistic, had to be dealt with before she did them in? Would they try and talk to her first, win her back, persuade her she was wrong? Or would they pass sentence on her, seize her, lock her up with a dozen vicious cats like James, leave her alone to be clawed and chewed?

The wind roared outside. Snow still fell upon the streets. She could hear the sound of exerting ignitions, buses and taxicabs rattling their chains on the avenues. She tried to engross herself in a TV drama, and was just getting interested when the telephone rang.

"We'd like you to come up and talk things over," said Dr. Bowles, her voice sweet as always, as if the confrontation of the previous evening hadn't taken place. "We're all waiting for you. Why don't you come? We've got cookies here, and punch."

"I'm finished with you. I told you that."

"Now just a moment, my pet."

"That's my decision. It's irrevocable." She hung up, proud of her steely tone.

A few minutes later the telephone rang again. This time the doctor didn't bother to conceal her rage. "We've been discussing what to do about you."

"Discuss me all you like."

"You better come up here."

"I'm not coming. Don't bother me again."

As she hung up for the second time she felt her pulse begin to race. She expected another call, resolved not to answer the phone, but then, suddenly, her doorbell rang and she jumped up from her window seat.

They'd sent someone to try and lure her out. She moved toward the door, stood as still and silent as she could. The bell rang again, a long time, harsh, insistent, and in the silence that followed she heard whispering in the hall.

What if the whole group was out there? What if they tried to break in, take her upstairs by force?

"We know you're in there, Penny. Time to come out now, come upstairs and face the group." It was John, the one whose Mayday call she'd answered, whose cats were gazing at her now, their eyes still and flat.

"Come on, Penny. You're holding everybody up." It was Wendy, her voice hard, more impatient than John's.

She didn't answer. Her heart was thundering. She backed up quietly into her bedroom, then slowly, carefully lay back upon her bed. She wrapped her arms about herself and began to pant and shake.

Click.

She knew the sound. They were opening up her locks. She remembered now: Dr. Bowles had a set of keys, had insisted on having them in case of fire. One more lock to go, and then the iron-rod floor lock—she had a few seconds, she calculated, before they got to that.

She jumped up, rushed to the door, threw open the locks herself. She burst into the hall, shoved Wendy against the opposite wall, pushed John aside, started down the stairs. But there were two of them down there blocking her way, the young men who'd dug the graves. She turned, adrenaline pumping, ran back up, shoved John again, then realized she was trapped. She was heading straight for Dr. Bowles' apartment. Several cat people flattened themselves against the walls to let her pass. She caught a glimpse of Dr. Bowles, a beatific smile on her face, as she passed her doorway and charged up the attic stairs.

She knew the catroom was there, of course, knew Dr. Bowles kept a multitude of cats in the attic of the house, knew the smell that filled the stairwell couldn't come from the half dozen Persians in the apartment, but nothing quite prepared her for what lay behind the steel door when she flung it open and rushed inside.

There was a small hallway stacked to the ceiling with boxes and sacks, cat litter and canned cat food she'd seen delivered so many times at night. And there was a huge freezer, for storing dead cats, she assumed, but she didn't look too closely at that for she was aware, as she ran down this little hall, of a strong odor, stronger than anything she'd ever smelled in the house before, and also of a noise. It was not loud, anything that pierced her ears; it was more like a background sound—meowing and scratching and the tread of tiny feet.

This smell, these sounds, came from behind another door. She unhooked the latch, pushed it open, and then she saw the cats—three hundred, maybe four hundred cats, a chaos of live creatures, some in pens, others in cages, most scampering about loose, wrestling, standing still, defecating and urinating in troughs of litter, some scratching at posts nailed to the walls, others nursing kittens or engaged in sex. Siamese and Persians, tigers and mongrels—they ran about, a mass of moving fur, in air so foul with the stench of urine and male spray that Penny thought she'd retch.

"She's in the catroom!" It was Dr. Bowles shouting from down the stairs. "Get her out of there before she harms our friends. Bring her down to me."

There was no way out, Penny saw, except the way she'd come in. For a moment she felt defeated, grabbed a broom from the corner, decided to try and fight them

303

off with that. But then an idea struck. She started thrashing the broom about. "Whoosh! Whoosh! Scat! Scat!" she cried, making sweeping motions toward the door. Some of the cats just stared at her perplexed, but others started out. "That's it! Scat! Scat!" she shouted again. Twenty or so cats began moving down the stairs.

"My God! The cats! She's letting them out!" It was someone from the group.

Penny beat her broom against them, forced out more and more.

"Catch the cats!"

"Block the cats!" There was frantic screaming from below. And then it was as if the cats suddenly realized that their chance for escape had come. There was a mass stampede of animals toward the stairs, Penny behind them, urging them on with the broom, yelling "Scat! Scat!" following them down.

"Never mind her," shouted Dr. Bowles. "Save the cats! Save the cats!"

Penny rushed down among them, this cascade of slithering bodies, as they evaded the outstretched arms of the cat people, pouring down the flights and landings. The cat people were screaming with frustration as the cats slid around them, crawled beneath their legs, jumped out of their flailing arms. When Penny reached the lobby and opened the door, a hundred scurrying cats plunged out into the snow.

She ran as hard as she could, high-stepping through a drift. The plows had cleared a car's width passage through Eightieth Street. She ran over to Madison Avenue, then downtown a block to a phone booth at the corner of Seventy-Ninth. She looked back. No one had followed her, but she could hear their cries. She imagined them running about, stumbling in the snow, trying to catch the cats.

She was about to dial 911, the emergency number for the police. But then she paused—there was someone else who would help her, someone else she could call.

V

Whatever made me think this summer project was going to be so wonderful, that all I had to do was get out of that carnival of a studio and then the sweet air would blow away my cobwebs, and the glittering sunlight would cauterize my wounds? What an asshole I've been! Now everything is getting WEIRD. Project's out of control. Tension's incredible. Anything can happen now. ANYTHING—

THE EAST River shimmered in the dusk, fifteen floors below, and as Penny gazed down upon it, she thought for the first time in months of her old walk-up on Eightieth Street, how far away it was, the miserable life she'd led there—how far away and long ago.

She finished her drink but continued to stand at the window, watching the shadows deepen, the river turn black like oil. She pondered the evening ahead. *Our first anniversary,* she thought. Then she smiled: *Tonight I'll tell him it was me.*

She drew a bath, the water as hot as she could stand, then submerged herself. As she soaked she thought of Jared. He'd phoned that afternoon. She'd refused to take his call.

The first time he phoned, collect from Taos, she was curious what he'd say. He told her he was working as a dishwasher in a restaurant there, was thinking of moving down to Santa Fe. Then he called her "babe." He sounded so slummy and immature that she winced at the memory of having lived with him. But she was polite, and when he asked her questions, she was crisp and firm with her replies. No—she didn't want him back. Yes—she was with someone else now. Yes—she was happy. She wished him luck in life.

He wrote her a few times after that, but she didn't bother to reply. There wasn't anything to say to him anymore—he was part of a past which now was dead. Still it made her a little sad to think of him in his apron standing by a pay phone in New Mexico while her secretary said she wasn't in. She wondered whether he'd hitchhike to New York and try to see her. She hoped he wouldn't. It would be a waste of time.

She stepped out of the tub, dried herself, started getting dressed. She put on simple things, tight designer jeans, a silk blouse. No bra. She selected an antique turquoise necklace everyone admired, then brushed out her hair. It was longer now, layer cut, soft and coppery and full. She loved the way it glowed, the way it bounced and caught the light. It was as good now as Suzie's hair—even better, she thought. It was one thing to copy her sister, another to find her own way and excel.

She dabbed on some Amazone, inhaled the strong, erotic aroma, and checked herself in the mirror. Her gray eyes shined with passion. She looked sexy, in full bloom. She glanced at her watch. It was time to go. She stepped into the hall.

While she waited for the elevator she chatted with her security man. He wasn't one of those Chapman oafs; he was ex-Secret Service, accustomed to guarding presidents and kings. She never was afraid anymore, never took the subway, never walked alone. She went to work by limousine. When she ran he trailed behind.

The elevator man smiled. "Up or down?" he asked. She pointed up as he closed the door. He waited at the penthouse while she let herself inside.

She looked around the apartment. His briefcase was on the entry table, his raincoat thrown across a chair. The dining table was set. Dinner was waiting. Cold poached salmon and a salad. A bottle of white Burgundy and fresh raspberries for dessert.

She could hear him in the bedroom whistling to himself, knew he was getting dressed. She smiled, sat down, thought back over the last few months, how wonderful he'd been that wild night she'd called, how helpful and understanding, how he'd straightened things out so fast. The way he'd taken care of Dr. Bowles, for instance—sent a couple of his men around to see her and have a little talk. Just a few words about her license and malpractice litigation. The psychiatrist had crumbled right away.

He'd set her up in the apartment a few floors below his own. They'd started seeing a lot of each other then, lunches and dinners but not like the ones they'd had before. These meetings were different—outwardly serene, emotional underneath. They reappraised each other, parried and thrust. She could tell he was discovering things about her he'd never noticed before.

She realized what was happening before he did, knew she was reaching him by the way he responded when she threw back her head. Her gestures, her laugh, her tone—she seemed to do everything right. And they were *her* gestures, *her* tone, like Suzie's perhaps, but her own, still her own.

Suzie had used Jamie Willensen and Cynthia and her college jocks to divert herself, exorcise the memory of her unhappy love affair. But her own parade of lovers, her own experiences with Jared and Mac, Jamie, Cynthia and the boys in Aspen were a recapitulation in reverse. So she hadn't really been imitating Suzie—not really imitating her at all. She'd been doing the opposite—Suzie had been heading down toward death while she'd been heading for the sky.

"Kiddo?" He called her from the bedroom. "Want to put some music on?"

She went over to the stereo, looked through his records, chose a Cole Porter album she knew he liked.

"That's nice."

"Dinner looks great."

"Be out in a minute. Can really use some chow."

She filled their wine glasses, then wandered over to the window. It was dark, the river looked romantic and mysterious. There'd been an early evening rain, and now she could see soft reflections of headlights as cars streaked along the FDR.

"Hi," he said. She turned around. He stood there grinning at her, so handsome, so marvelously groomed and dressed.

They sat down and began to eat, and he told her about his day. It was like that now most nights of the week. They dined together and talked. He rarely went to Greenwich anymore. On nights when he was busy or out of town, she got in bed and read manuscripts. One weekend they flew out to Vegas and he handed her ten grand to throw away. She won some money and he was proud. "Riverboat gambler," he called her. "Godfather," she whispered back.

"Whatever happened to Suzie's old apartment?"

she asked when he was finished recounting the day's events.

He glanced at her, a careful glance. "You knew about that?" he asked.

"Oh, sure. I followed you there." His eyes were wide open now. "Yeah, it was me who slashed it up." She met his eyes straight on.

He looked at her stunned for a moment, then he shook his head. "Wow—kiddo. What a move that was! Scared the beegeezus out of me. Thought one of my enemies did it, maybe someone downtown on the Street." He grinned. "Closed the place down right after that. Laid on all this security we've got. You really spooked me pretty good." He raised his glass to toast her. "Didn't figure you for a move like that. Guess I underrated you, kiddo. Sure won't do that again."

After dinner they sat listening to music, and then, when she couldn't control herself any longer, when the desire built up inside of her so much she couldn't stand it anymore, she looked at him very hard in a special way that was her signal, and then whispered "Powerful One" softly, sensuously under her breath.

She'd said that the night when she'd first made it happen. It had all come so naturally to her, the way she'd comported herself, the moves she'd made, the things she'd said, that she'd marveled afterwards at her facility—it was as if she'd *known* just what to do.

Now they made love, wonderfully, and afterward, when they were playing around the way they liked to do, kissing and stroking, she started kidding him with the mocking tone he liked.

"You're going to kill me now, aren't you, Daddy-O?" she teased. "You do that to your women, don't you? Kill them after making love."

He laughed, stroked her thigh. "Still think I killed her, kiddo? Still believe all that?"

313

" 'Course I don't, silly. But I bet you know who did."

He smiled, nipped her ear. "You, too, kiddo. You know as well as I."

"Do I?"

"Sure you do."

"Jared?"

He laughed again. "No, not that loser, for Christ's sake. He never had the balls."

"Who was it then?"

"You saw the intruder."

"Come on. Tell me." She tickled his ribs. He squirmed. "It wasn't any old intruder, was it? Tell me who it was."

"Guess," he said. "Think real hard. Use that old noggin of yours." He kissed the back of her neck.

"How about—*Cynthia!*"

"Not poor old Cynthia." He began to chew her ear.

"Tucker?"

He rolled his eyes. "Now that's really dumb," he said.

She slid her tongue across his lips. "I give up. Can't think of anybody else."

"Think. Think, dammit. I spent enough moolah on that education of yours."

"There isn't anybody."

"Oh, yes there is." He laughed, brought his head down, kissed her on the mouth five times hard. This was a little ritual they had. Usually she'd say: "Punish me with kisses," and he'd do it, kiss her hard like that—*bang, bang, bang, bang, bang.*

"Figured it out yet?"

She reached down, took hold of him. He was so big, so thick, so magnificent down there, so powerful and delicious. Just to touch it made her go weak inside.

"Well?—"

"I'm just dumb, I guess."

"You want to know, don't you?"

She nodded. "Of course I do."

"Won't make much difference now. It was a crime of passion, you see. Jealousy, envy—all that sort of stuff."

"Really?" She was dying of curiosity. *A crime of passion.* He made it sound romantic.

"It's so obvious you'll kick yourself. The motive's so crystal clear. She knew what was going on and hated it, used to berate me about it all the time. That's why I called it off, but I never told Suzie that. Yeah, she told me she'd do something if I didn't put a stop to it, and if I didn't stop all her wild screwing around, too. Didn't believe her. Should have. Said Suzie was evil and had to be destroyed. She's cuckoo mad, you know. Going to have to put her away one of these days, I guess."

"You're saying—mother? Is that who you mean?"

He looked at her, nodded. "That's the ticket. You got it now, kiddo."

Sure, it made sense when she thought about it. There were even some clues in the diary, she guessed, though she couldn't concentrate too well just then. The Powerful One was touching her in a special place, in a way that always made her lose her mind. *Mother—well of course—*

Then Penny began to scream—mostly in ecstasy but a little in horror, too.

178